NEW WORLD SHIFTERS

TAMSIN BAKER

THE OMEGA SHIFT

NEW WORLD SHIFTERS BOOK 1

CHAPTER 1
CADEN.

I couldn't feel my toes, but at least that wasn't a permanent thing...I didn't think. The all-encompassing cold sapped my will to move and check. The first rays of the sun stroked my cheek, but even that didn't give me a reason to get up. This new world sucked. In every way.

Bad enough that we had to fend off attacks from the vampires and the other animal shifters in this new world. But as an Omega wolf, the weakest and smallest of my kind, how was I going to survive with my own pack killing each other for sport?

"Get up, you lazy bag of shit."

My eyes popped open and my heart hammered against my ribs in fright. That grizzly voice haunted my nightmares and most of my day time hours. My tired legs moved so fast my head spun like a top as I jumped from my make shift bed on the dirty floor.

"Yes, Alpha," I croaked out.

Bear wasn't an Alpha, nowhere near it. The men that had ruled us before the fighting began, they'd helped us, protected us...they were true Alphas. Real leaders.

The cruel bastard only ruled our pack because he was older and stronger than the other Betas left standing. But Bear, the pseudo Alpha, liked to hear those words from my lips, and I wasn't going to deny him. I didn't deny him anything. I had the sore arse and black eyes to prove it. I didn't fight back. Ever. It kept me alive.

"Go with the Betas and collect food. The women have nothing to cook." Bear's snarl was as ugly as a muddy toad, but I kept the cringe from my face as he leaned close and the scent of his dank breath wafted up my nose.

"Yes, Alpha."

I scurried off through our disheveled camp. An old, fenced off section of what was once Seattle. Composed of not quite ten whole houses, and about a hundred people living in conditions not fit for the wild cats that roamed the streets.

I jumped over playing children and tried to ignore the crying, hungry babies the best I could. The stench of the open toilets burned my nose hairs as I ran by. No matter how long I lived in this world, that wasn't a smell I ever got used to.

No one had enough to eat. We lived like scavengers. Eating what we could find. Not growing anything. It wasn't a sustainable, nor healthy way to live, and our community was going to die. Soon, if we weren't careful.

Yet, the men who were meant to keep us alive, the stupid Alphas, didn't give a shit.

I sidled up next to the hunting party that congregated by the front gate and cleared my throat. "Uh...hi, Tommy. Bear sent me over to help."

Tommy, one of the half decent Betas, nodded. His cheek bones were so angular they gave him a hard look that didn't suit his sweeter personality. "All right. Let's go."

I tucked in behind Jerry, another Beta, and as a group of four, we walked to the front wall. Our closed in community had only one gate at the front of the tin panels that surrounded the houses. Barbed wire twirled over the walls and a shudder coursed over my body as the memories flashed inside my mind. I'd been tangled up in them more than once when I'd displeased the Alphas in some way. I was never quite sure what I'd done wrong, but I definitely had the scars to prove it.

Tommy held his hand up and flicked his wrist, giving the signal to move out. Together, we moved through the front gate that opened up and walked into the dangerous world around us.

My breath caught in my throat as my gaze darted left and right. I hadn't stepped out of the compound in months. Not since the last attack.

Overgrown greenery flourished in front of my eyes, and even though the beauty of our new world made me want to relax, I reminded myself that it was all a façade. Evil lurked out here, in amongst the roses and ivy. The vampires were sleeping, away from the powerful rays of sunshine, but there would be other shifters about. I kept a lookout for any signs of danger, and once I was pretty sure there was nothing but the tranquil overgrowth, I moved forward.

"This way," Tommy called out as the other Betas and he crouched low and wove around the trees growing wildly through what was once a beautiful, thriving city.

The broken, crumbling sky scrapers, highlighted against the crystal blue sky, caught my gaze and I looked up. Sadness filled me up like a rising cold tide, making my skin crawl and my gut ache. I could still remember what this city looked like before the mass genocide.

And Seattle had been beautiful.

A decade ago, a powerful, clever, obviously sadistic paranormal created a virus that targeted human cells. Some people said he was a vampire, others believed him to be a half cast beast. But no matter what he actually was or had been, he'd done something that changed the surface of the planet.

He'd released a virus into the air that, within a few years, killed off every human on the planet. Only the paranormals remained, and every different faction fought for supremacy.

The vampires fought against the werewolves, who fought against all the other animal shifters. And within each race, we fought against each other. For land and power that equated to nothing in the long run.

This new world was chaos.

Tommy stopped and pointed, whispering to us, "There. Look."

A group of brown, large hares sat nibbling on the overgrown grass. *Perfect.* My stomach growled and saliva pooled in my mouth as I imagined sinking my teeth into a single piece of the delicious meat. Warm, nutritious flesh. It had been so long since I'd eaten any fresh protein. I swallowed hard, amazed to see the creatures out in the open like this.

The Betas slipped away from me in formation, silently surrounding the group of hares in a circle. Tommy held up his hand to signal we were to wait, and I held my breath in anticipation. His hand came down sharply and we all charged.

I raced forward, arms extended and teeth bared, my heart banging away in my chest.

The hares bolted.

My hand shot out and I grabbed for the fat, brown bodies that ran past me. Two slipped by my hand.

Damn!

I jumped and rolled, frantically grabbing at a little hare that had gotten confused amongst the fray. My hand found the soft fur and I managed to snare him. My fingers clenching down hard on the single ear I held, then I pulled the body into mine.

It wriggled and kicked out, bucking for its life.

And it was. Literally.

My fingers managed to grab it by the back legs and held on tight. My ass would be black and blue if I came back with nothing tonight.

Tommy broke the neck of two hares that he held. The snap of the bones made me flinch and cling tighter to my own little hare. My teeth clamped together and a strange coldness crept over my neck.

I'd heard that noise too many times in my life.

Too many battles, too many deaths.

I looked away as Tommy grabbed my own soft hare and killed it for me.

The other Betas had at least one each too. Which was good. At least some people would eat tonight. Time would tell if I was one of them.

"We're going to go out further and see if there's anything bigger to hunt down. Caden, take these back." Tommy grabbed all of the hares from the Betas and walked over to me, tossing me five dead bodies.

I struggled with the weight for a moment, pulling them all up into a warm, soft pile of still floppy bodies.

"Are you sure?" I asked him. That would ensure my favor when I returned to the camp. Did Tommy realize that?

He gave me a half smile that indicated that he knew he was helping me. Would he ask for anything in return? "Yeah. Go. Let Bear know we'll be back in a few hours, hopefully with a bigger kill."

I nodded, intensely grateful for the reprieve. How to repay such a thing? Bear didn't like me bonding with other pack members. He was nasty possessive like that. But I could wake Tommy up one night and say thank you with a head job, or something if he asked me to. It wouldn't be too bad with a gentle guy.

Tommy nodded once and headed off in the opposite direction of the compound, not asking for anything in return. Warmth filtered through my core as I was shown the first bit of kindness I'd experienced in too long.

I watched the Betas disappear into the brush and let the warmth of the sunshine flitter across my skin. I had to go back to the place I called home, but the reluctance to return to my pack was a tangible thing, pulling at me with cold, insistent hands.

I could run away and hope someone else took me in.

I shook my head and went back to the only thought that ever gave me hope.

Better the devil you know, and it can't get much worse. Surely.

Eventually, the fear of being found outside the boundaries of the pack's walls tickled up my spine and got my legs moving in the direction of the compound. Despite the threat of being found by another shifter and probably killed on sight, I wandered back to my *home* as slowly as I could manage, enjoying the freedom of the space around me, the air.

Bear wouldn't know that I'd been dawdling, and the naughtiness of what I was getting away with tickled me. A smile lifted my lips for the first time in ages.

Finally, the silver barriers that kept our pack safe, *supposedly*, came into view. An uncomfortable tightness found my belly and gripped hard. I sighed heavily, a wave of sadness flowing over me. I was sick of living like this. Hand to mouth, no food, no control over my own life.

But what choice did I have?

I glanced down at the dead hares in my arms, their heavy weight making the muscles in my thin limbs ache. The saliva in my mouth began to accumulate again. Would they notice if I ate one myself? Would Tommy say something if I did?

Probably. It isn't worth it.

As an Omega, I would be lucky to get any of the meat off these bodies, but I was alive, and should be grateful. Unlike so many of the Omegas before me. As the weakest and smallest, we were the first to die in the pack wars.

So many people had died. Children, women, even the Alphas had been torn apart. No one was safe in this world. Not even my parents, nor my grandmother. My nana had died in my arms when I'd been thirteen years old, and with her dying breath she'd made me promise to fight, to stay alive. No matter what I had to do.

And I swore it. I hated to think of what my nana would say if she knew what I'd done to stay alive, but I'd kept my promise. Through some luck, and a whole lot of sacrifice.

I stared up at the bright blue sky, the beauty of the day annoying my soul. The world taunted us now. It still flourished, while we were panicked and starving.

The world had been so much better when the humans ruled. There was order, and industry, and food.

Who was in charge now? No-one. And it sucked.

The doors opened for me with grinding, metallic sounds, and the guards stared at my arms as I clutched the hares to my chest. The men began to crowd me, all of them as hungry as I was.

Self-preservation made me rush towards Bear's house. The grey roof was sliding off the foundation, and most of the windows were cracked, but it was still the best building by far. At least it had four walls to keep out most of the elements. I lived in a lean to against a wall. Nothing kept out the cold on those wintery nights except a hot body.

The door opened as I approached and his hungry gaze bore into me.

"Is that all you got?"

His expression transformed into an angry scowl and I tried hard not to cringe. What else did I have to do to please this man?

"Tommy told me to bring these back for you. The other Betas are travelling out a little further to catch something bigger. Where would you like me to put these, Alpha?"

He licked his lips, his nostrils flaring like a wild horse. "Take them to the women in section three. They're cooking tonight. And after that, come back here. I'm in the mood for your arse."

This time my cringe was impossible to hide, and I heard the growl that rolled from his throat. I bowed my head and turned towards section three, hoping my move hadn't angered him too much. He'd punish me further if he thought I showed any sort of disrespect. Not that he needed an excuse to be abusive towards me.

I took the hares to the skinny women in section three, who looked at the animals with the same hunger I knew was mirrored in my own eyes. The oldest woman, who was a head chef in the days before the virus, nodded and ran a finger along one of the stiffening bodies. "Tell Bear we'll have this ready in an hour."

"I will."

I dawdled on my way back, walking the longest route to the main house. So many dirty men and women slumped around the streets and sat upon the porches of the ruined houses.

No occupation. No drive. What had happened to our proud pack? Our powerful shifters that once upon a time thrived?

Bear stood in his doorway, his jeans already unbuttoned, his shirt open to reveal his disgustingly big belly. My stomach turned at his gluttony. Our community may have no food, but alcohol was still abundant. Some of the older Betas made the foul stuff from food scraps and old potatoes.

"Get in here," he yelled.

My legs trembled but I forced myself up the stairs, calming the rising panic in my gut. I'd done this a hundred times before, and this would be no different.

He grabbed me by the back of the neck and pushed me inside.

"Where do you want me, Alpha?" I asked, hoping to minimize the damage by going along with whatever he wanted.

"On your knees."

I dropped to the floor and watched his hairy hands unzip his fly and flop out his already thickening cock. Bile rose in my throat and I swallowed hard, forcing the screaming in my head to calm.

Now is not the time to freak out, I can do that afterwards. When the disdain and guilt will overwhelm me.

My mind begins to wander to my past life when food was plentiful and clean clothes was a daily occurrence. *Damn I miss my parents.*

Bear stepped up right in front of my face and the scent of his dirty crotch shoots up my nostrils, forcing my warm memories into the dim recesses of my mind. The need to gag overwhelms me and he grabs my hair, hard, making sure I won't move away. He doesn't need to be so rough and a touch of anger whirls inside me.

I relax my jaw and wait patiently so he doesn't hurt me too bad, parting my lips in readiness for the rough treatment they would receive.

It should be easy now. Common place. But every time he does this to me, I hate him a little bit more.

His hot flesh is shoved against my lips and I open for him, wishing for a lightning storm to hit...right about, now!

"Alpha! Come quick! Alpha!"

The shouts from outside came barreling through the windows and Bear pulls away from me, the fresh air bringing coolness to my face. Bear staggers to the window, reddened cock still in hand.

My shoulders droop in relief. Saved by the Beta it seemed.

"Oh fuck! Get up." Bear shuffled past me, grabbing for his jeans that are around his ankles. He eventually hauled them up to his waist and ran straight out the front door.

I pushed myself up from the floor boards and turned around to follow, slightly dizzy with happiness and hunger. I wasn't quite sure which was more prominent, but considering hunger was a daily occurrence and happiness wasn't, I'd put my money, if I had any, on me actually being happy for once.

I wandered outside and froze. There was something very wrong. People were screaming in terror.

"They're coming! They're coming!"

Women grabbed the children around them and ran down the streets towards the back of the compound.

"What on Earth?"

I stared at the people by the fence, trying to decipher what was going on, and what the panic was about. I'd lived through too many raids already, and although my heart rate picked up in worry, part of me was already deciding which corner to hide in quite calmly.

This was a common occurrence in our world. But as the tension around me shifted away the calm inside of me, I knew something was different. Bear looked scared.

Someone moved out of the way of the circle and that's when I saw Tommy, his guts spilling out of his body and blood plastered all over his face. I ran towards him, jumping down off Bear's balcony and racing forward. I put my arm beneath Tommy's shoulder, helping him over to the steps of Bear's home so that he could sit down.

"You need the doctor," I said, my stomach turning queasy at the look of what bulged beneath Tommy's hands. He was trying to hold his stomach in, and yet veins and organs bulged, purple and grey between his fingers.

"They're coming. They're coming." He collapsed on his side.

Then the roaring began. Howling and growling. The hairs on my neck lifted and pulsed with awareness. Another wolf pack was here.

As an Omega wolf, I couldn't shift. I provided no help in this fight, nor any. But the need to do something pounded into me and for once, I wasn't running to hide.

I put a hand on Tommy's face, hoping to God, or whoever still watched over this forsaken earth, that he would live. "I'll get someone for you."

Bear, the other Alphas, and the Betas all ripped at their clothes, falling to their hands and knees as they shifted into a range of snarling black and brown wolves. The gates were open and the fighting would begin all too soon. I turned and ran as fast as my legs would move to section three, where the women and children hid and the only doctor we had still, lived.

"I need help. Tommy's been hurt."

Most of the women ignored me, but Maree stepped forward. She'd been a surgeon back in the day, and still did most of our doctoring.

"What's wrong with him?" she asked.

"His belly has been all cut open and his..." I swallowed. "His organs are spilling out. I don't know what to do for him. You have to come."

She cringed and shook her head. "He's dead."

Horror struck me in the gut like a sucker punch, forcing the air from my lungs and my body to shudder in pain. "No. You have to come and help."

"No, Omega. I will protect those that live, here. You go and do something." She glared at me with all the heat and hatred I've dealt with my whole life. Me, an Omega. Useless in every way.

I backed away from her fire and turned around to face the fray. Hopelessness washed over me as the snarls and sounds of the fight reached my ears. There was only one thing to do and that was to hide until it was all over. I crept around the central house that five family's shared, the violent noises of battle assaulting my ear drums. Tearing flesh, screams, and savage growling.

Whether we were losing or winning, I did not know. But I was pretty certain, that when this was done, we'd all have a new man to call *Alpha*.

CHAPTER 2

MAX.

The last of the wolves fell with a sickening crack, and as we all transformed back, I watched the blood of the last shifter drip between the teeth of one of my Betas.

"That it?" Jon asked, indicating the dozens of dead bodies littering the disgusting camp.

When we'd found the Betas wandering the woods for food, we'd assumed they were a threat. But maybe we should have left them alone? What had these men been doing to their people? God only knew.

The wolves were half starved. They'd barely been able to put up a fight. Guilt coursed through me several times as I'd taken them down. Except for the few over weights of the group. I had to assume they had taken on an Alpha role to hoard any food they found. No guilt ate at me for those kills.

If this pile of men were what the strongest of the pack looked like, I could only imagine how emaciated the women and children would be. So the question really was, should we bother taking them back with us?

I looked around at the strange mix of disgust and hope on my men's faces and knew we had to take them back. We were low on female mates after the last vampire attack, and my men needed something to fight for.

"Round up the women. Be careful. Don't hurt them. I mean it, Barry."

The Beta inclined his head as I glared at him. Barry had a mean temper and a chip on his shoulder—not a good combination. But I kept him around for his keen hunting skills.

I let my wolves venture into the small compound as I walked around the dead of this rival pack. I sniffed them, prodded their backs, and checked for the rise and fall of their chests. Each one was bloodied, and not breathing.

Good. As it should be.

This was a war, and it was now time for us to take home the spoils.

The men began walking back and my heart sunk. With them were a ragged looking bunch of strays. Their tattered clothes hung from their thin limbs, the scent of open sewerage made my chuck reflex bounce.

I swallowed hard and cleared my throat.

Best to get this over with quickly.

"I'm Max, Alpha of the Olano Pack, half a day's walk from here. We have killed your men. If you want to survive, you will join our pack and make yourselves useful."

We were low on women, and these, though not overly attractive, were obviously toughened by our new world. And that was the only important thing nowadays.

"I..." The words froze in my mouth as my gaze was drawn to the only adult male still standing in the compound. I double checked for signs of femininity as my gaze rushes over him.

No boobs. Stringy muscles. Soft face.

My fangs bite into my bottom lip as my heart began to pound. The first stirrings of lust I'd felt in months throbbed in my loins as my blood heated like it's on the boil.

"Boy. Who are you?" I bark at him, my voice unusually gravely.

He flinched and hit the deck, hands on the dirt palms down, head bent in total submission.

Silence.

I could hear the few birds in the trees twittering nearby. Nobody even took a breath. I couldn't pull my gaze away from him despite the fact I knew my Betas would be sharing confused glances amongst themselves.

Was this man...an Omega? They'd been rare when life had been normal, back fifteen years ago. But now...they were extinct, or so I'd thought.

"Please don't hurt him. He can't shift like you," one of the young girls piped up, stepping closer to him and laying a hand on his back.

I can see white striations on the flesh of his back exposed above the tank top line and bile rises in my throat. I turn away and spit it out onto the blood-covered ground.

This place was worse than we even thought. I scowl down at the dead men on the ground, glad they're gone. Who would treat anyone like that? Let alone an Omega wolf that my father had always said was to be revered, protected.

"Rise Omega. You all have half an hour to gather your things. Bring only what you can carry. We leave soon."

The women grab their children and turn away to do as I ask. A few of the older women step forward, their faces lined far beyond their years I'm certain.

"We will not make the journey," one of the declares.

They don't look like they will, either.

My first response is to ignore them, forget their plight. After a decade of trying to save everyone I meet, being betrayed by so many, I am much tougher now. But I have made provision for such an eventuality.

"Then why should we take you with us?" I ask, sneering down at the woman.

Surely there is a reason the wolves of this brutal kept these women around. They wouldn't feed them otherwise.

"I was a doctor. A surgeon," the woman at the front replies. She wouldn't be more than fifty years old, now that I take a better look at her. But these past years had aged her dramatically.

I try not to show how excited I am by that news.

"We could use one of those. What of these two?" I gesture to the women beside her.

"I was a chef," the women with a black eye said.

Good. More cooks were always needed in our pack. Especially ones that knew what to do with the modest supplies we had.

"I'm a midwife," the other one answered. She was even older than the other two, but anyone who could deliver babies safely into this world, would have a highly esteemed place in my pack.

Most of the other women were too young to have collectible, needed traits. They wouldn't have been able to study before the virus destroyed everything. But the older women were definite keepers. No wonder the pack had kept them around.

"We have a cart of sorts for you," I explained. Something I had hidden and would have used for the children if they had no worthy elderly. "My men will pull you. But we can't fit all of you in the cart. Only two at a time. You will have to walk some of the way."

And that would ensure they had the strength to live through the change of packs. Wolf shifters were loyal and territorial creatures, which is why we had never before tried an assimilation like this.

But desperate times, and all that...

The women exchange a glance and nod. "We will make it."

The surgeon's hands tighten into fists and I can see the strength behind the thin skin.

They need a good feed and some rest, and they should turn out fine.

Our pack needed strong women, and healers would be even better.

"Thank you." The surgeon extended both hands and I offered

her mine. She clasped it for a moment, her clear blue gaze locking with my own. There was relief there, and hope. Something I recognized, for it still thrived within me.

The women headed off also and I turned to search for the Omega, but he was gone.

"Is that really an Omega wolf?" Turner, one of my Betas, asked as he stepped closer to me.

A growl rolled through my vocal chords and my teeth came down in a snap.

Turner fell back, his head hung low and to the side.

"What's wrong?" Barry asked, looking between us.

Anger rolled through my veins, and the need to stamp my authority all over the Omega became my number one priority.

"No one is to touch him. Do you understand? Punishment is death."

I'd never threatened such a thing on my pack, but as I glare at them one at a time, they bow their heads in acquiescence. My chest releases for a moment and I focus on breathing.

What is this shit?

When I was younger, I'd heard of the fated mates prophecies that our parents had lived by. But this new world didn't allow for any of that. You grabbed what you could, when you could. Who you could. But there was something magical at work here and I would need to work hard if I was going to overcome it.

"Get the cart with the food. Store the meat under the cart in the compartments. I'll distribute what we have evenly. Then we start moving."

We'd been out hunting and gathering food when we'd come across the other party of Beta wolves. Luckily, we'd brought the cart for supplies.

It would have been my preference *not* to kill all the male wolves of this pack, but I'd learned the hard way, that shifters in this new world could not be trusted. No matter if they swore allegiance or not.

And in the end we'd no choice. The other wolves had attacked, and then for our own safety, and that of our own pack, we followed the wounded Beta back to his compound. Then it had been decided that we needed to wipe them out. My Betas had suggested it, and I'd let them sway me.

The women born of us wolves were non-shifters, and so they relied on us for strength, shelter, and food. That bred loyalty, and so I would try to blend our pack with what remained of this one.

The women began to come back, their bodies laden with clothes and children.

I called out to them. "We have food for you all. Form a line here. Take a small portion, and we will be on our way."

The women formed an instant line and shuffled forward, taking the fruit we had gathered and what was left of the flat bread we had brought with us for our day. I noticed that with a smile, as Jon pushed the food towards the women. That bread was for my wolves, and yet seeing the frailty of these people, it was obvious my men would stay hungry until we returned home.

My mouth watered as I remembered the bread of the old days.

How I use to take for granted my daily coffee, picked up at a café near work. My beef sandwiches my mother made for lunch. Back when I was a police officer, and an Alpha's son.

The Omega shuffled behind the last woman, his body now covered in, what appeared to be *all* of his clothes.

He'd layered up like someone heading for the snow, and his face looked cleaner now. Perhaps he stopped to wash? He averted his eyes and kept his head down as though he knew I was watching him, and my hand raised of its own volition to touch him. Comfort him. Tell him everything is okay.

He cowers like a wounded animal, his body folding into its self. I drop my hand back and anger boils in my blood once again. What did those men do to him?

I have to assume that this Omega is my intended mate. There is no other explanation for the hunger I feel when he is near. The need to protect him, kill anyone who comes close to him.

That has to be it.

Having a male mate was not too surprising to me. Had I assumed I would mate with a woman? Certainly. Not due to natural taste, but due to necessity. There were no Omegas left, or so I'd been told. And I wanted children. But the heat in my body that this dirty Omega arouses by far surpasses anything I've ever felt with anyone else.

The Omega takes some food, as much as I would give a child, then holds it close to his chest like it's a prize.

My throat aches with emotions I cannot express and I turn to the entrance to this...home. "Let's go."

I make a rousing motion with my hands and the women move quickly, clinging together and moving in a formation that shows their ability to work together is strong. Lucky for them. They'll last a lot longer in this world if they do.

I stay close to the tail of the party, looking out for anything moving in the bushes. We hadn't come across anything except those few Betas in our travels, but it would be dark once again soon enough and the vamps would rise.

I thought back on our day, one of a planned hunting trip, and shook my head at how it had turned out. The hungry Betas had attacked first and that's when I'd decided to go on the offensive. We couldn't have savage packs in our area when we needed our strength to fight the stray vampires and lone shifters that came our way. I'd lost half my pack a few months back when a trio of vampires attacked in the night. That wasn't happening again.

The young women would help. We needed to grow bigger and stronger once again, and that meant more wolves needed to be born.

I glanced ahead to where the Omega carried a child on his back. He barely looked strong enough to stand up himself, and yet he appeared to carry the child with ease. There had to be steel beneath the surface.

No one survived in this world without a whole lot of guts, and some luck.

"Keep moving. Got a long way to go," I shouted, moving up to where one of the older women was getting out of the cart. I hold out a hand and she stares at it for a moment, before taking it, and stepping down. I help the wheezing woman who has been walking next to the cart up, and then circle back around the group, listening for any movement.

The women give me puzzled looks and I ignore them. Chivalry is dead, I know. But a helping hand costs me nothing, and may just win me the loyalty of women that could help my pack.

We make our way through the overgrown world, following the same route as we took to get there. We cut quite a path through the growth on our first trip over and we arrive back much faster than I anticipate.

Our fortress of metal rises up to meet us, cut into the side of the mountain.

The position means that no one can sneak up behind us, and we have over twenty well-maintained homes. Not to mention hand-built walls twenty-foot-tall with UV lights attached to the tops.

Not even the leopard shifter we met a few years ago could jump over the new walls.

"Open the gates," I call out and we slow down as the locks clunk and grind as they open the huge front doors.

The women and children are panting from exertion, but not one of them make a sound of complaint.

"Let's go," my men shout as they herd everyone inside.

The women's group gets even tighter, if that's possible, the Omega at its center, now holding a baby in his arms as well as the child on his back. The gates slam behind us and the men that guard the entrance to our pack's village nod once as they slide the massive dead bolts in place.

This area was originally a retirement community. Which means it's a group of closely knitted together units, and has community hall facilities, and even medical rooms. Completely self contained, even with vegetable gardens. Soon after the humans were wiped out, my pack took it over, scavenged what building stuff we could find, and built a fortress around it. It has been ten years since the world went to hell and we haven't moved.

Our survival depended on it.

"Follow me to the hall."

The women shuffled together like a strange ball shaped group into the center of our town, their children crying and shrieking in terror, as the pack came out to greet them.

They were shushed by their mothers quickly and Jon yelled out, "Keep moving."

My Betas opened the doors of the hall and as a group, the women surged inside.

The doors closed behind us and I gestured to the trembling group.

"Sit. Please."

We had tables and chairs, and by the way the women were standing about gaping, most of them hadn't seen anything civilized for a very long time. They didn't do as I asked, but after assessing the cleanliness of the situation, I thought it was probably best not to ask them to do that again.

"All right. First things first. You need showers, clothes, and houses assigned. We have two free units at the moment. Can you arrange yourselves into two even groups?"

The surgeon stepped forward, lifting her chin and showing strength, though I saw the tears shimmering in her aged eyes. "Yes. Of course we can... Thank you, Alpha. Thank you so very much. If we'd known your community was here, we would have left our pack years ago."

A smile tugged at my lips as my gaze was once again drawn to the Omega, now looking at me with an open gaze. I can finally see his big blue eyes and my heart stutters in my chest.

He nods once and seems to mouth the word, "Thank you."

Warmth spreads through my body and I turn away to stop the inevitable blush I feel rising from the Omega's approval. "Well, I'll get Turner here to show you into the units. And I'll send some of the women over with clothes. After you shower."

"You have running water?" one of them asked.

We had several plumbers and electricians in our pack thanks to my father's preferences for manual laborers, and they'd worked out a system that worked very well for all of us. "Yes. It's minimal, and it's cold, but the water's fresh. You'll be able to wash properly."

I turned to move away and a soft, male voice calls out, "What do you want from us in return?"

I stopped and made myself count to three before answering. I turned back around slowly and looked him straight in the eye. Everyone seemed to be holding their breath as they waited for my answer. Even the babies were quiet. Considering where they'd come from, I was pretty sure they'd do almost anything to stay. "We are short on women and I will be encouraging you all to mate with my wolves, to keep the pack strong."

The women inhaled a deep breath as a whole and though some of them closed their eyes and held their children tight to their chests, they also nodded with determination.

"Will we have a choice?" the surgeon asked me.

I frowned at her sarcastic tone.

"Of course. I do not abide force in my pack. If you have any trouble with my men, you come see me. But for your own sakes, I encourage you to bond with the group. And if any of you others have talents, step forward. We have to work together if we're going to stay alive. Disobedience, sabotage? Will not be tolerated. You will be out on your arse so fast you won't know what hit you. I'll leave you to the vampires that roam this area."

The women shrieked a little and two stepped forward.

"I was a nurse."

"I'm a teacher."

I liked the speed in which they responded. They would do well here.

"Your pack maintained a good standard, didn't they? Any more doctors?" I asked, half jokingly. What would be the odds of that?

My own pack didn't have anyone with a university education.

"Our original Alpha made sure whoever wanted to go to college did. He was a good man," the surgeon said, swallowing hard as her eyes glistened with tears. "My mate. He was killed in the first year. During the raids."

My heart went out to her. Another Alpha Mate. My mother would find her to be of comfort, though little made her smile anymore. "I'm sorry for your loss. My father was killed in that first year too. It was crazy. And cruel."

When the virus first swept our world, the humans died practically where they stood. It took only a few months for the whole world to be infected.

The paranormals had been left standing. All of them. The shifters, the vamps, even the wolf packs began to fight for survival. For food. For power.

We had the whole world, and yet that didn't seem to be enough. It was ironic, in a bitter and twisted sort of way.

We had all the land, all the food. But with no humans to run anything, the whole world fell apart. And quickly.

The water. The electricity. Schools.

I'd tried my best to keep the world turning in the confines of our bunker, but with the constant threat of danger, it was a hard life. But it was what it was.

"Good. Now, Turner, take the women."

My gut clenched as I went to step away once more. Could I trust my men with the Omega?

I hesitated.

He would be prey to anyone, and there was something so incredibly broken about him... I couldn't shake the feeling that leaving him here alone was a very bad idea.

And my gut had kept me alive through ten years of being a cop in Seattle. So I trusted it.

I twisted back. "Omega, come with me."

CHAPTER 3
CADEN.

"**M**e?" I repeat, embarrassed by the squeak that came out of my mouth. But the last thing I expected the big Alpha to do, was address me.

"Yes, you. Come with me."

I look towards Anna, who's always helped me. She was like a big sister, and her kids were the most adorable things ever.

"Go," she whispers, taking the baby from my arms. Her eyes are intent and speaking, and I know what she means. If he wants me, then I should go. For all our sakes.

I stumble forward and move towards the Alpha. He is the strongest man I have seen in a decade and my legs turn to a weird jelly the closer I step. His muscled arms are like those old magazines, where men graced the front covers in little more than their underwear.

"Yesss, S-s-sir?" I stammer, my belly tightening and quaking. With the food I'd received, or nerves, I didn't know.

He crooked his finger. "Follow me."

His tones sounded sexy, deep, and dark. A shiver of arousal

coursed through my body, a foreign but not unwanted feeling. Anything that would help me get through this was good.

I bite my lip and follow behind him as he walks back into the afternoon sun. I'd felt true desire once or twice in my life. I was twelve when the world fell apart, and I'd only just started to come into my hormones. Then everyone was dying, and I was starving. Trading my body for some shelter and comfort from our Alphas.

There had been one boy that I'd shared a glance or two with. I remember those tingly, happy feelings. He'd died pretty soon after that.

But this...

My gaze travelled down the Alpha's back, clinging to the tight roundness of his arse. I'd never known a true desire like this. If he was taking me home to fuck me, I didn't mind. If he was really going to look after us, as the Alphas of old had done. Then I'd even do it willingly.

"Here's my place."

He indicated to a small house at the front of the compound. It was one of the smallest by the looks of it.

I lifted a hand to shade my eyes from the sun and squinted at the white front door.

"You don't live in the biggest home?" I asked, confused.

Bear, and all the other Alphas before him, had always taken the best and the biggest of everything.

This new Alpha, *Max* I think he said his name was, was obviously very different.

"No. I like living alone, so the families have the other, larger houses."

He opened the unlocked front door and walked inside. I followed, the cleanliness of the room making me nervous. I wrapped my arms around myself, willing my skin cells to cling to my clothes.

I was so dirty, and he had furniture. *Real* furniture.

"Oh my god." The words left my mouth, though I didn't know why I spoke.

The past decade had been so surreal, in a tragic, nightmare sort of way. Now...I felt like I was in a dream. And this time, I didn't want to wake up.

I ached to reach out and touch the clean, fabric couch that stood out like a single red rose amongst the thorns. But my gut clenched and fear overwhelmed me at the unknown. The knowledge that I would be punished if I made the wrong move.

I must have made a noise, because Max was soon in front of me holding my arms and staring into my eyes with those big blue orbs of his. "Are you okay?"

"Ah. I...just..."

Heat prickled along my arms, a moan rising in my throat as my balls began to throb with longing. The attraction I had to this Alpha was such a new thing for me. And it didn't help that my body was starved for affection. It had been so long since I'd had an orgasm. Months even.

Max brought me in closer to his body and wrapped his arms around me, squeezing tight as he stared down at me. His heart pounded against my chest like a repetitive punch. The tangy scent of his arousal rising and surrounding us like a cloud of heat.

"I want you." He groaned against my lips and I lifted my mouth so that he could kiss me if he wanted to.

"You can have me," I say and close my eyes to accept whatever he wants to give me.

A loud groan rolls through the room and he pulls away. The coldness of his absence hit me like a snow storm. I shudder and wrap my arms around myself once again.

"Let's get you showered."

Shame washes over me like a hot rain. I hadn't even thought about how much of a turn off to him my dirtiness would be. At home...in the old compound...we were all the same level of disgusting.

He takes my hand and pulls me into a small room. The bathroom. I look around the room, memories of my parents' home flooding into my mind. Of clean tiles, and shower screens. Hot water and steam.

"I'll help you. Strip off and step in."

I jumped to do his bidding, pulling off my clothes as fast as possible. I'd raided Bear's closet when I left so, I wore a jacket, a hoodie and my tank top.

I dropped them all to the ground, on the clean tiled floor. It had a nice, flower type of pattern that was strangely calming.

"Fuck." The word shot out from his mouth and made my heart pound.

"What's wrong?" I ask, slinking back against the shower wall. Max stared at me, his eyes wide.

"You're so..." His eyes ran over me like they'd never seen a person before. The horror in their depths making me want to crawl into a ball and die.

I shrank down against the tiles, my hands shaking even as they clung to my knees. He looked away.

"Do you know how the shower works, Omega?"

His voice is back to being gravelly and strange, and I don't know what to make of it.

I nod, but then remember I shouldn't rely on subtle gestures. "Yes. The taps."

"Good. I'm going to get you some food. Don't leave the house. Towels are here."

He tapped some folded towels with his fingers. I haven't seen towels like that in years. "Make sure you wash your hair. We have someone who makes soap. Here."

He hands me an oddly rounded block with a flower type scent.

I drop my arms down and reach for it, staring at it in awe. "Wow. It's almost like the world didn't end here."

The soft chuckle makes me look up, his face relaxed and happy. I could see the kindness in him now. The softness.

"Yeah. We try to keep it that way. I'll bring some clothes back for you too."

Max left the bathroom and I let my body relax, my shoulders crawling down from the place near my ears where they sit when I'm tense. There is something strangely un-settling about that Alpha.

And not in the normal way either.

I'm used to being terrified by these Alphas. Always have been.

But I'm not scared, I'm...excited. Aroused. Wanting to please him in a way that's less for my own safety and more for my own need. Perhaps I'm finally coming into my Omega heat that my parents once talked about?

There used to be a monthly type of flux that all Omega's would go into. We were revered for our sex drive, wanted by all Alpha's... until the virus. Then we became a liability. A weakness in this new world that required only the best fighters. The scavengers.

We couldn't shift, couldn't fight, could barely hunt.

And then the Omega's started to die.

I was lucky enough, or young enough, or pretty enough, to always make it through. Every attack.

I shook my head and turned towards the shower, loving the thrill that ran through my body and up my spine as I flicked on the chrome taps. A jolt sounded and water began to come out of the shower head.

Tears gathered in my eyes, stingingly sweet in my lashes. I jumped beneath it, tilting my head back and letting it gather in my mouth, swallowing and gulping at the cleanest water I'd drunk in forever. Since the bottled water had run out and I was thirteen.

There should have been enough food and water for us shifters to live on for decades. But the vampires, who didn't need food, set fire to most of the city early in the wars, and soon there was nothing left.

Nothing but the fight for survival.

I drank and drank, loving the old, familiar taste. This water didn't smell dank, nor make my stomach curdle. Instead, it ran down my throat, parching a thirst that had been around forever.

It was a crime to drop my head, but I had to. My stomach was hurting from the cold, and Max had told me to get clean. I let the water pour over my body and goose bumps formed on my skin. The water was so cold, but it didn't put me off. It was incredibly amazing to feel it racing over my body. I gasped as a shiver ran over my spine, the coldness sinking into my bones.

Clean.

I wet the soap and scrubbed it along my arms, watching the soap blacken and the water run grey. How many years of dust could one person contain? Did I really want to know?

I scrubbed and scrubbed, my arms, my legs, my cock. I continued to shake with cold, but the freezing was pushed away with the happiness bubbling inside me. I could see my skin, smell roses around me.

Surely that was worth the cold. I even washed my hair the best I could, as Max had instructed

It was matted and knotted. Perhaps someone would cut it for me?

Then I realized how much fresh water I was wasting and rushed through the rinse, turning off the water as soon as possible.

"Brrrr." I shuddered, grabbing for the towel, feeling the softness of the material between my fingertips. A moan escaped my throat as I hugged it to my body.

I held it up to my nose and that same floral scent wafted up to meet me.

"Who *are* these people?" I asked the room. Had I fallen into the twilight zone? Or perhaps I was dead and had reached heaven, though that was unlikely considering all the things I'd done in my life.

A smile lifted my lips and the feeling was as foreign to me as the flowery towels. If I'd known this morning that I would be entering a whole other world, where people looked after one another and houses would resemble those of the old world, I would have tried to prepare myself better.

I wrapped the towel around my body and tried to stop shivering.

"Omega!" Max called and I realize I haven't even introduced myself yet. Not that any other Alpha had cared what my name was before, but for some weird reason I wanted to tell him.

I tiptoed into the main room where I assumed Max was.

"Yes. Alpha."

He stared at me, his eyes wide and his mouth slightly open. "Damn you're beautiful."

Heat flourished in my face while desire twirled in my gut. I dropped my gaze, unsure of what to make of any of this. "Thank you, Alpha."

"It's Max."

I nodded and waited, staring at the clean patterned floor that reminded me so much of my grandmother's kitchen. She'd been lovely. A true leader in our pack. Taking care of the sick and weak. She'd died soon after my parents.

"And your name?" he asked, and my stomach flipped over. I'd known he'd ask.

"Caden," I answered, the word rolling off my tongue in a strange way. I hadn't said my own name in years.

"Pardon? Speak up."

I lifted my head a little and cleared my throat with a cough. "It's um...Caden."

The intensity of his look was far too much to handle and I dropped my gaze again, and my towel. It slipped from around my waist and I froze.

A growl rolled through the Alpha before me. One of anger and frustration. I knew those sounds well.

"Put these on and come eat. You're like a walking skeleton. You all are."

Clothes dropped at my feet and I bent to pick them up. A clean, soft T-shirt, an old, well-worn hoodie.

I slipped both of them on, my skin loving the feel of the soft fabrics against it.

The pants were next.

"They have some holes in them, but they're warm," he explained.

And they were. Black, fleece-like material that was heavy against my thighs. I pulled the draw string tight, hoping to keep them up around my waist.

"Thank you so much."

"Come. Sit."

I shuffled forward and fell into the chair he held out for me at the table.

It was so surreal to be sitting at a table again. An image of the dirty kitchen and floor we had to sit on back at the compound flew through my mind as a comparison, and I shuddered, wrapping my arms around myself as a bowl of some sort of stew was placed in front of me. Steam floated up from the brown chunks.

"Thank you." I picked up the spoon that lay beside it, my fingers struggling to grip the foreign object.

Tension hung thick in the air, though Max didn't speak. Fear of upsetting or disappointing him shadowed my every move.

I dipped the spoon into the bowl, and brought some of the liquid to my lips. I had no idea what it was, but I'd eat anything they asked me to if they kept me safe and clothed.

The flavor exploded through my mouth. So clean, so strong. I swallowed it down greedily, then took a bigger spoonful. The next piece had a tender chunk in it and some white stuff that was soft. I moaned and ate, and some sort of flat bread was pushed at me.

"Dip this in the meat and eat it. It needs softening, but it's not bad once you get used to it."

I almost spat the stew out on the table in shock. Surely this wasn't real meat? Then I did as he told me to, dipping the whiteish bread into the stew as I stared down at the gift given to me.

"This is meat?" I asked, looking up at him.

Max sat down into the chair opposite me. "Of course."

Hot tears welled in my eyes and I let them fall as I continued to eat, savoring every last morsel while my stomach noisily consumed the food before me. I wiped at the tears and Max didn't call attention to them, thankfully.

"Now, you'll sleep in my room."

"Of course, Alpha."

A tiny tremor of fear ran through me at the payment that would be needed for this world. It was stupid, really. I'd been treated better already by this pack than any other in my life. But the unknown was cause for worry.

Though, what could he ask of me that I hadn't done before? I'd promised my grandmother I would do anything to survive, and I would.

Max stared at me as though he wanted something from me. Perhaps he wanted me to thank him now?

"Can I...service you now, Alpha?"

"S-service me?" Max's voice cracked as he repeated my question.

I nodded, stood up, and walked around the table. He was staring at me with huge blue eyes and for the first time ever, I truly wanted what was about to happen between me and the big man in front of me.

"Would you like me naked? Or not..."

When he didn't specify I went down onto my knees and reached for his cock where it hid behind faded, patched up jeans. I laid my hand on the bulge and slid my fingers in to get the zipper.

Max stayed my hand "Wait. Why are you doing this, Caden?"

"Because I should."

I reached for him again, a new fear gripping me. If he didn't want me, where would that leave me? Out in the cold? Or open to any other man who wanted me? One that I didn't want.

He stood up and relief filled me.

I ripped the zipper down and opened his jeans, his cock already thickening. When I moved the fabric aside, it thrust forward against my waiting lips. I sucked him straight into my mouth and the groan that sounded from Max had my own cock twitching. Odd. But nice.

I focused on the head, sucking hard where I knew he'd be sensitive and wrapping a hand around the thick shaft. He was so clean and smooth.

His hand slid into my hair, so much gentler than anyone who'd come before him. Then he was tugging me back and lifting my chin up roughly so that I was looking into his eyes.

"Why are you doing this?"

I didn't understand his question. Not one little bit. In this world of barter and trade, I was doing my bit, the way I'd been taught. "I..." Pain prickled under my scalp but I didn't flinch. I'd had a lot worse treatment before.

"Tell me," he demanded again.

I reached for the only explanation I could think of, though it seemed obvious to me. "Because you saved us. Me. The food, the clothes. I'm trying to pay you back...although I know it's nothing compared to your gifts. I will do anything you need me to, Alpha." The words spilled from my lips and the pressure on my head disappeared.

Max stepped back, tucking his swollen cock into his jeans and zipping himself back up with efficiency that was frightening.

I threw myself to the ground, arms out stretched, head bowed. "Please don't throw me out. If I did something wrong, tell me. I'll fix it. I learn quickly."

What would he do to me? He was so much healthier and stronger than any of the Alpha's I'd known before. How bad could he make me hurt?

"Caden. Stop. Sit up now."

I jumped back as fast as I could, sitting back on my haunches. A lump formed in my throat that made it hard to breathe, and my heart was pounding in my chest so loud it sounded like it was inside my ears.

He squatted down so that we were eye to eye, and for the first time I noticed several scars across his eyebrows, chin, and nose. "Listen closely, Omega. I will never expect sexual favors in return for looking after you. We are a family, a pack. If you want to help, protect the children, keep the home tidy, help with meal prep. But don't you ever go down on your knees for me again unless you want to. I won't accept it, ever."

I stared him, horrified to see the flaring of his nostrils, the clenching of his fists. He was going to hit me. I hit the deck and covered my head with my hands. "Please don't hurt me. I'll do anything you want. I promise. Anything."

A heavy vibrating silence filled the room, like the calm before the storm. I curled up in a ball, tucking my legs against all my vital organs, and hoped he wouldn't hit anything that wouldn't heal quickly.

The sound of the door slamming ricocheted around the room and I popped my head up from between my arms.

He'd left.

Why?

Relief flowed through me, but so did the confusion. He hadn't hit me. But he hadn't taken any payment for what he'd given me either. No one did that, not in this world. That had been drilled into me every day for a decade.

Everything had a cost. Breathing had a cost. And as an Omega, the only thing I had to offer was my arse, or my mouth. Or both. I'd been told that more times than I could count. Well, it had been beaten into me really. Back when I'd struggled against it. Not wanting to submit to any man who wanted me.

But that had changed, and I'd grown stronger.

My parents would be disgusted to know how I'd managed to live through these years, but I *had* survived. And as I looked around this clean, small Alpha home, it occurred to me that maybe it was for this reason.

To get here. To live long enough to actually find a home.

I pushed myself to my feet and forced my robotic body to move. The bowl I'd eaten from needed to be cleaned, I was sure. But how did they do it?

I looked around the room and saw the sink, and a vision of my grandmother doing the dishes came into my mind. I picked up the bowl, lifted it to my mouth, and licked the juice from the ceramic surface. A moan rolled through me and I cleaned it of all final drops of taste. Then I put it in the sink and stepped back, having no idea what I should do next.

Max's voice came back to me and I knew I had to find another way to re-pay his kindness.

I was young and willing, I would find my place within the pack.

I took a deep breath and opened the front door, intent on finding someone who would give me a job to do. Then perhaps, life would finally make sense.

CHAPTER 4

MAX.

For fuck's sake! My balls are so bloody blue, I'm gonna have to deal with this myself.

Anger rolled through my blood with the speed of an old steam train. What the fuck had that been back at the house? One minute I was feeding him, trying to look after him. The next he's on his knees sucking my cock like his life depended on it.

It'd been the last thing I'd expected. And if I'd known, I would have stopped him straight away, but damn...what a mouth! Fuck me! It'd been like all my Christmas's had come at once to have the beautiful boy sucking me.

I'd thought of course, that it had been because he wanted me as much as I wanted him. That he too felt the connection between us. The heat and attraction like I've never known before. The one I was warned about. The Alpha attraction to a true Omega.

But I'd been wrong. Caden wanted to pay me back for helping him. For rescuing him from that hell hole. Shit! I'd have rescued a dog from that place.

"Max..." One of my Betas walked towards me to ask me something.

37

I held up my hand. "Give me five minutes, Terry. Need the can."

I strode into the hall and headed straight for the toilet, intent on relieving the strain in my body. I shook my head as I recalled what happened next. He'd thought I was going to hit him! For fucks sake. I just rescued him from men who did that, why would I want to perpetuate the cycle?

Of all the stupid things...

I ripped open my jeans and pulled out my aching cock, gone soft now from the horror of what had happened, but throbbing with a need that I hadn't felt in years. I wouldn't be able to function today if I had to deal with this surge of angry testosterone.

A groan of frustration left me. Such a waste of sperm too. There were so many new females that I was sure would breed good, strong children.

I thought about it for a moment, then shuddered at the thought of going to one of them in this state. True disgust turned my stomach. Acid coated the inside of my mouth.

I shook my head.

Damn Omega's got me towing the line already, and he doesn't even know it yet.

I pushed my anger as far away from me as I could. There's no room for it here and now. Instead, I retreat to the safety of my mind. I closed my eyes, wrapped my hand around my cock, and put myself back in the house. The beautiful little Omega is on his knees, sucking me. Licking the head of my cock. His big eyes staring up at me with need.

Then I changed the image into how it should have gone before I realized the driving force behind his proposition. I would have bent him over the kitchen table. Licked his arse until he was screaming with need. Rammed my cock up inside him until he was coming for me. White, tangy squirts of Caden's seed all over the table.

Heat coursed up my spine as the images did what I wanted them to. My cock exploded in my hand and I had to swallow the groan that rose in my throat as the pulses of pleasure drained away all my anger.

My eyes slid shut and I let the bliss flow over me as the stress floated away. I slumped against the wall and sighed.

That felt so much better. All the tension in my arms and neck were gone and there was even a nice jelly type feeling to my legs that I knew would only last for a few moments, but it was a great relief after the last ten minutes of anger and stress.

I flushed the toilet and tucked my cock away for another day.

I had no idea what I was going to do with the Omega now that his survival training had come to the front. Obviously, I couldn't let him loose in the pack. He'd do anything for anyone willing to feed him. And probably anything for anyone who won't.

I scrubbed my hand through my hair and stared at the ground in frustration. Was that normal for an Omega? To prostitute himself for shelter? I didn't think so, but then again, I had no idea. I'd never met one. My mother was probably the best person to ask.

I headed out into the sunshine and took a big breath of clean air. My head was clear and my body sated. I knew it wouldn't last long, with that gorgeous Omega living in my house, so I took an extra moment to enjoy it while it lasts.

"Max. You free?" Terry finds me once again.

I nod and move over to him. "What's up?"

"Your mother was calling for help and asked for you."

Perfect, because I had a few questions for her too. "Thanks. Where is she?"

"With all the new recruits in the empty houses," Terry answered with a rueful expression.

My mother had been an Alpha Mate for thirty years, and she still ran the pack like she was at the head. I didn't mind of course. There was already too much for me to do in this crazy world, without having to worry about who was being fed and how much.

Once I've mated the Omega, hopefully he'll step up into the Alpha Mate role.

I growled at the errant thought. Obviously, my wolf had already made up its mind about who was my mate. And I'd always believed I had a choice in the matter. Ha!

"That would be right, Sam. Thanks."

Even at her age and her failing health, my mother was still helping others, making sure the pack ran as well as possible. I walked over to the two, once empty houses to see people bustling about, clean children dressed and playing on the floor. It gave me a sense of calm to see people happy and relaxed. It was how it was meant to be.

"Oh good, Max. Come in."

I heard my mother's voice and stepped into the small lounge room of the house she was in. I looked around. It needed a bit of maintenance, some fixing and painting. But already, women were in every corner cleaning the walls and scrubbing the floors.

This was a good move. Bringing them here.

"Yes, Mother?"

"I need your help moving these beds around. Can you come?" She gestured to me to follow her into one of the bedrooms.

"Of course." I moved through the lounge and Caden popped out of the bathroom, a wriggling, naked child in his arms.

"Settle down, Kane," Caden scolded with a smile, and gave the newly washed child to a woman who took him away.

I moved closer, unable to stop the need to touch the beautiful Omega. Stroke his startling blond hair. As my hand left my side to reach out for him, Caden's nostrils flared and his eyes widened dramatically as he took in my scent.

"But why?" he asked, the disappointment and sadness in his face so strong it kicked me right in the guts.

"What do you mean?"

Then he ran, out of the room and outside before I could stop him. I frowned after him, not understanding his reaction at all. Was my rejection of him earlier really bad enough to affect him in such a way? I'd thought he'd be more resilient after his past.

"What was that about?" my mother asked.

"Not sure. He's very skittish," I said. My eyes followed him as he ran past the windows until he vanished.

I turned back to my mother, who's eyebrows were high on her forehead and raised in question. "What?" I asked her.

"What do you mean, what? Have you claimed the Omega already? You smell like sex."

Oh damn! That's what he sensed. Caden probably thought I'd left him to go fuck some other guy, or girl.

"No. I just... Never mind." I was not having this conversation with my mother. "Show me what you need me to do."

She pointed, and I pushed and lifted until the furniture was arranged how the women wanted. It was quite clever really. The beds were now pressed together so that they could sleep as a group, and the children could be bundled together, warm and safe.

Now that they'd all been showered, I could see some potential for all of them. The women were painfully thin, but they were strong, and some of them had rather beautiful features. My men would be seducing them before long.

My mother sidled up next to me. "Max, I'll walk you back. I need to ask you something."

I nodded, accepted the timid thanks from the women in the house and walked outside.

"So, tell me about the Omega, son."

"What about him?" There were so many ways I could answer that question.

"You've claimed him?"

I wanted to roll my eyes at that one. Why would she assume that? "I told you, I haven't."

My mother frowned. "But I was told that you've taken him as your own. Is he living with you?"

So word had gotten around already?

"Well, yes. But I haven't mated with him, or anything. I have no actual claim on him."

Her smile was goading as she crossed her arms over her chest and stared at me. "Really? So, any other man in this place could take him from you, is that the deal?"

Red flashed through my mind and a feral growl ripped through my throat. No words came out as I fought with my wolf's need to emerge.

My mother laughed at me. "Yeah, I thought as much. He is a true Omega, a rare find in this world. A perfect mate for an Alpha, Max because when you bond with him you will be unstoppable."

I nodded, swallowing hard as I forced my wolf to recede. He was not impressed at the idea of anyone else claiming Caden, and my muscles twitched with the need to fight even as we spoke.

"Be careful with him though, Max. He's seen a side of this world that you and I have not."

I cringed, remembering the flashes of his damaged body that I'd already witnessed. "You've seen the scars then?"

"Not as much the physical ones, although I'm sure he has them. The emotional whipping he's taken has shaped him, and I think you're going to find that you need patience more than anything else if you're going to pull out the best from him."

"I'll try, Mother, but there's something else I wanted to ask you. I assumed you've met Omega's before?"

Her mouth twitched a little. "I did, a long time ago when we use to associate more with the Alpha's of other packs. The Omega's were always the Alpha Mates, and protected above all. Why?"

"Because he tried to...prostitute himself to me. And I just didn't get why he'd do such a thing. Doesn't he know how rare and sought after he is?"

She shook her head sadly. "Oh now, I doubt it. From what I've heard, his parents died when he was young and the pack that has looked after him has just taken advantage of him. But I hope you sorted him out?"

"I tried. I certainly didn't take him up on the offer. Sickened me actually. But you think I need to explain more to him?

"Probably a good idea."

"Thanks, Mother."

"You're a good Alpha, Max, your father would be very proud. Now, let's get back to our jobs. I'll make sure everyone is fed, and then it's time to bed."

I nodded and looked up as the skies were darkening. "The vamps will be prowling soon. I'll go switch on the lights."

We had no power for anything else. We used wood to burn for cooking and heating. Electricity and lights were a thing of the past. Except for the Ultra Violet lamps we had. One of the electrician Betas, who'd been killed last year, had worked out how to hook the solar power cells we'd found up to the lamps. They had saved us more than once from the vampires.

"See ya later." I left the presence of my powerful mother and went to the front of the pack's walls, flicking on the switch that would illuminate our outer limits with UV light through the night.

On the way back, I went in search of the Omega who was my mate, though I wasn't telling anyone that yet. If I did, Caden would feel like he had absolutely no choice in the matter. He would do what everyone was telling him he must do, and I didn't want that.

Quite the opposite. I wanted him to choose me.

I froze in place, anger vibrating along my spine as my eyes soaked in the vision before me.

Caden was leaning up against one of the houses, flirting with one of my Betas. Jasper. There was no mistaking the tilt of his head, the open body language. The smile on Caden's lips and the come hither look in his eyes.

Stupid pup.

I stormed forward and grabbed Caden by his thin neck. His shoulders bunched up beneath my hands, a tangible fear rolling off him. "Back off," I barked at Jasper and the Beta fell over himself to get away.

"Come with me," I growled into the Omega's ear, pulling Caden along the road with me, his fragile spine within my grasp.

I kicked open the door and pushed the impudent Omega inside.

He fell to the floor, crawled around, and lay down in the most submissive position possible. Head to the floor. Arms outstretched. I was surprised he didn't just lay on his back and open his legs.

"What the hell were you doing, Omega?"

"I'm sorry, Alpha. I'm sorry." He covered his head with his arms and this time I wasn't letting his fear overwhelm me. We would have this discussion no matter what.

"Stop that. I will not hit you. No matter what you say or do. Stand up and have a conversation with me, Caden."

At first nothing happened, but then he tilted his blond head so that I could see the tips of his blue eyes. Then he slowly raised up so that he was still kneeling but his spine was almost straight.

I wanted to grab him by the head and yank him up to his feet, but I held onto my patience with my fingernails. These first moments between us would determine what sort of life I would have with him, and I needed them to build a good, strong bond. I didn't want him scared of me. Hell, I wanted a real partner in this life. Not someone who was terrified to speak to me.

"Caden, seriously. I swear on the life of my mother, who if you have met her, would know, is a vital part of my pack, that I will never, ever hit you. Do you understand?"

Shadows danced in Caden's eyes and he reeked of fear. When he finally nodded, I sighed with relief. He still wasn't standing up, so I took a few steps back. Now when I looked down on where he knelt on the floor, I wasn't towering over him as much.

Anger still burned in my gut and my legs ached with restlessness. I couldn't sit down. "Great. Now tell me, what the hell were you doing trying to seduce Jasper?"

Caden's face fell and he looked away, down at the tiles. "I wasn't."

Heat rose in my gut and I pushed it down. Back when I was a cop, I dealt with every type of person. The prostitutes and drug dealers, the ultra-rich narcissists. I could see how influenced Caden was by his up-bringing. He was used to lying and cheating to getting through each day. But that stopped now. I had to convince him that his world had changed.

"Now...for that lying, I would usually punish someone harshly. But for you, being new to my pack, I will give you one more time to answer me with honesty."

Caden's thin shoulders trembled and it only hardened my resolve. He would learn how to be a part of this pack, or it would kill us both. I would not have a liar, or an unfaithful mate. And Caden didn't seem to know what that entailed.

"I...was looking for someone else to look after me."

That surprised me with enough force to knock the wind out of my sails. I grabbed one of the dining table chairs and dragged it over, falling into it so that we were almost at eye level now. "Why would you do that when I'd already told you that you would sleep here with me?"

Caden bit his lip in a way that had me swallowing my moan of arousal. He was too damn hot for his own good my beautiful boy.

"Because...because you left me...and had sex with someone else." He whispered those last words and it was only my accelerated shifter hearing that made it possible for me to know what he said.

"No, I didn't. Oh fuck." I ran a hand through my hair. Damn it. I should have known that an Omega would be insanely sensitive to such things. After all, his main function in life was to keep the Alpha happy. And that of course, included the sexual roles. "I just went and jacked off for a minute. To clear my head."

Caden's gaze rose again, his blue eyes now gazing into mine. "I don't know what you mean."

"I mean, I..." Fuck, was he kidding? "I just sorted myself out. You know, gave my cock a few tugs and made myself blow." Damn it was embarrassing to say it aloud, but in this way, it seemed Caden was very young. "Don't you do that? How old are you?"

The old cop in me came forward and the horror rose. What if he was some underage minor that I'd taken in? Oh fuck...no.

"Twenty-three."

"Oh, thank God for that." I took a breath of pure relief. He may look sixteen, but he wasn't. And that was all that mattered. "Looks like we need to set some rules, and then educate you on the pleasures of your body, gorgeous boy."

Caden's head came up properly finally so that I could look at him. "I... don't understand."

It was also time to lay my cards on the table it seemed. No point asking him for his full loyalty when he didn't know what the payment would be at the end.

"I want you to be my mate. Be by my side. I'll look after you, and you are not to be with anyone else. Don't approach any of the other wolves. My shifter won't cope with you touching another male."

"All...right. What else?" Caden's eyes shone brighter and he sat up straighter.

What else did I want? "You need to be an important part of the pack. Help the women, stick close to my mother. Protect the children to the best of your ability."

As an Omega he couldn't shift, but there was a lot more that he could do.

"I can do that, Alpha."

"Swear it."

"I promise, Max." His words were soft, but there was a clear honesty in his eyes that made me want to trust him.

Should I bind Caden to me now? Bite him and claim him as my own so that he would be loyal? My wolf didn't move inside me at the mental suggestion, sensing more time was needed to further our relationship.

Caden cocked his head to the side as he stared at me. "But you didn't want me this morning. You chose to take care of yourself, rather than let me take care of you."

Well, that was a misunderstanding that we could immediately fix.

"That isn't exactly correct. I did want you to touch me, but not out of obligation, Caden. I never want you to touch me because you feel that you have to. I'm not like those other bastards you lived with before. Don't ever have sex with me because you feel like you're earning your way or paying for your food. You never have to do it, and I won't accept it."

Caden's brow furrowed as though confused. "So...how..."

Seriously? What sort of life had this kid had, that the only way to repay a favor was with sex?

"You re-pay the pack's kindness by putting back into the pack. Tend the gardens, help with the children. I've already told you there are so many other ways."

"But I've always had to—"

A growl rolled through me. I didn't want to know what he'd done in the past. "I know. I can tell. But it will not be that way between us. If you don't want me, then you won't ever have to put up with me. I can look after myself. And it won't ever mean that you get kicked out, or aren't fed. You can always say no to me. Now and in the future. Be it as my mate, or not. You always have a choice. I promise. I'll look after you even if you choose not to be my partner."

I waited, holding my breath as emotions flitted across Caden's face. It would kill me to have a mate that rejected me physically. Sex and touch was such huge part of being a healthy man, and a wolf. But if I had to wait, or find a way around Caden's dislike of me, I would.

"But I do want you. It's very strange. My stomach's tight, and I'm...aroused around you, I think. It's been so long since I felt safe, it's hard to distinguish between all the different feelings."

That made more sense than the idea that he didn't want me at all, when I was dying to put my hands on him. He did look like one confused young man.

"Then, we'll start something, and if I see you looking scared, or you feel pressured in any way, we stop."

He nodded rapidly. "Okay."

"Swear you'll tell me if you want to stop. Anytime."

Caden rose to his feet with graceful fluidity and took a step closer to me. "Alright."

I stood up. I couldn't keep my hands to myself a moment longer. I reached out and grabbed his waist, loving the feeling his body against mine as he pressed close.

His hands were limp by his side and he stared at me as though waiting for a command.

"Put your hands on me, Caden."

He lifted his arms slowly and placed his palms on my elbows in an awkward move that would have made me laugh if it was a less important moment.

"Kiss me."

He went up on his toes without hesitation and pressed his lips to mine. His flavor exploded into my mouth and I moaned. I needed this so much, but I had to hold back my hunger, for mine was a man's and an Alpha's. His was not.

Or not yet anyway.

As far as sexual hunger went, poor Caden was like an abused teenager, with no idea of what was going on in his body. But I held tight to the faith in the stories I had heard. That the Omega's sexual appetite would be one to appease any Alpha.

I moved my fingers down over his lean hips and caressed his arse with my hands. I slipped my tongue between his lips, tasting the inside of his mouth and moving my lips on his until I felt a response. Caden gripped tight to my arms and lifted his tongue to meet mine. I pulled back and his eyes flew wide in surprise.

I grinned at him with what I hoped portrayed lustful intent. "Let's take this to the bedroom."

I bent over and hefted the tiny Omega over my shoulder.

"Woah," he called out and wriggled in my grip. I smacked him on the arse, my hand hitting more bone than muscle, and I winced.

He stopped moving immediately.

I was going to have to be careful with him until he got stronger. I placed him down gently on the bed and stripped him of his shirt and pants, and his skeletal frame shook with cold.

"Climb into bed," I said and he scrambled back and beneath the covers.

I pulled at my shirt and jeans, my cock springing free from its confines, thick, throbbing and alive.

"You're so big, Max. I..." Caden's eyes ran over me and I could see the admiration in his gaze. I had seen the men who had ruled him, and poor Caden's estimation of what a man should be, was sorely lacking.

"You need to build some muscles too, Omega. I can't wait to see how strong you can get."

I prowled around the bed and climbed onto the mattress. Caden shuffled to the side as I slid beneath the covers to join him.

He turned over and moved beneath the blankets. A move I was pretty sure meant he was going to go down on me again. I pushed him back against the pillows. "It's time to stimulate you, I think. Teach you how incredible you can feel."

I reached for his cock and ran my hand up and down his length. He gasped, stilling like a deer in the headlights.

I pulled my hand back, licked my palm to slick it up, then placed it back on his shaft. I wanted to make him feel as good as I did. Feeling him next to me had my cock throbbing and my hormones racing like a formula one car.

This time when I moved my hand on him, Caden relaxed into me. Melting like butter on toast. Satisfaction rippled through me as he stared up at me with wide open eyes, wonder and awe clear in his gaze. Then he began to move with my hand. It was the hottest thing I'd ever seen.

As his cock filled my palm, he bucked and moaned. I captured his sexy sounds with my mouth, loving the way he grabbed for my arms and this time met my kisses with enthusiasm.

His cock stirred in my hand, lengthening and thickening. I'd only had a few encounters with males in the past. Brief one nighters that had filled the lonely voids of time. But feeling my mate beneath me was the biggest turn on of my life. My heart was pounding, my own cock thick with blood.

I shuffled down his thin body and took his swollen cock into my mouth, a first for me. He smelled of our flower soap and the groan that shot around the room heralded an early orgasm.

"Max!"

I pulled my mouth off and milked his cock with my hand. Caden cried out long and hard. White, thick streams of cum pulsed out of him all over my hand and his abs.

Caden shuddered and shook, his belly convulsing with the strength of his orgasm.

I pulled back from him and knelt on the mattress, looking down at the gorgeous sight of the man who should be my mate. His heavy eye lids at half mast, his face a mask of bliss.

"Flip over. I want to fuck you."

Caden rolled over and pushed back onto all fours, opening his thighs for me.

I worked my cock with my hand, spreading his sticky cum all over the length. I rubbed his winking little star with the same white stickiness and pressed a finger into him.

He moaned again and pushed back against my hand, his arse tight around my digit.

"Work your cock for me, Caden. Get hard again. Put your hand on yourself, go on."

Caden shifted his weight so that he could reach beneath himself and gasped as he touched his cock for me.

"Good boy. Beautiful boy," I praised him.

I shuffled forward, breathing deep for control. My wolf howled inside of me. Obviously, he wanted me to lean forward and bite my mate and bind him to me for all time.

The instinct to possess him was intense, so instead I focused on the desire flooding my body like a firestorm. The tingles of impending orgasm were already teasing the backs of my legs. My balls ached and my gut clenched.

I smeared some of my own pre-cum onto Caden's arse and drew my cock to the entrance of his body.

Slowly, slowly.

I bucked my hips and pressed into him. He gasped and stilled, shaking as though terrified.

"What's wrong? Is it hurting? Should I stop?" I put my hands on his hips and readied myself to pull out of the hottest, tightest, most desirable body I'd ever encountered.

"No. Don't stop. Please," Caden begged, holding onto my thigh where he could reach and held me to him.

I knew it must be hurting. Having never had it done, I could only imagine that its normal for some discomfort, but I was determined to make it good for him.

"Relax. I won't leave. I'll go slow."

I moved in another inch and then out again. *Fuck that took some control.* He pressed back and I gave him more of my length, until his hot, tight body gobbled up my cock.

"Oh fuck, you feel so perfect," I groaned out, gripping his thin hips as gently as I could.

I ached to just let the animal in me take over, and fuck him into oblivion. My mind threw up pictures of me sprawled on top of him, pounding him into the mattress. But I clung to the last vestiges of control that I had. Scaring him, or even worse, hurting him, was the last thing I want to do.

"Pull your cock with me, Caden. I'm going to ride you."

I begin to move faster and thrust into him harder. Caden's groans and moans fill the air. Sweat gathered on my brow as I fought off the need to cum.

Then I hear it. The catch in his throat. The tightening of his arse around my shaft. He starts to cum once more, the jerking of his body giving mine the sign that it's time to let go of all control.

My eyes dropped to slits as I roared out my orgasm. Hot spurts pulsed out the end of my cock and hot ecstasy rippled through my whole body. As the last tingles of pleasure reach the tips of my toes, I fall to the bed, rolling to the side to avoid crushing my small mate.

"That was so different." Caden pants, his face mashed into the pillow. His blond hair spills over his features.

I can't stifle the laugh that rises, happiness filling up my chest. "In a good way?"

Caden raises his head, staring at me with those intense eyes. "In an amazing way."

I stretch my arms above my head and enjoy the deep satisfaction that came with knowing that my lover is truly happy. When I looked back at Caden, his eyes were shutting and his face was relaxing into sleep.

"Go to sleep, beautiful boy, and when you wake you're going to have a massive breakfast and start your first day as a true member of our pack."

I kissed him on the forehead and pulled the blankets up. Tonight was the first night with my mate in my bed, and it was by far, the best day of my life so far.

CADEN.

Life was so good. Every day, or at least for the past three weeks, I woke up to a hot man, hot sex, and a hot meal. It was a heaven I hadn't dared to dream of.

"Caden, how are you today?" Tenille, Max's mother, asked me as I ate my lunch with her. *Lunch*, such a novel concept to eat more than once a day.

"Wonderful, thank you. This food is amazing." We had fresh fruit and vegetables from the garden, and there was always meat from the hunting parties. "I can't believe we have so much meat all the time."

Tenille laughed. "Well, my husband, and Max after him, have done a good job at working out sustainable ways for us to live. If we didn't have to deal with those vampires, we would live carefree."

My mood dropped instantly. "I don't know much about vampires. We never had to deal with them much at our pack, which is strange."

Tenille looked away as though bashful. "Well, ah, vampires do prefer clean and healthy sources to feed from. Being well fed, our blood seems to attract them more."

A chortle burst from my throat. "That's funny. My old pack was actually safer because of how unhealthy we were. Ha!" I continued to laugh and consumed the food in front of me. Max loved to feed me, and when he went out, he put his mother in charge of me, saying I needed to be fattened up.

I didn't disagree with him. The difference between my body and his was so marked that I looked like a skeleton compared to his muscular, godly body. I was determined to change that for him and be the Alpha Mate that he said he wanted in me.

Not that he had mated with me yet, but he would soon. I was sure.

"That's probably true...in some ways," Tenille said as she smiled at me. So warm, and kind. Much like my own mother had been.

I finished my food and cleaned away the dishes like they showed us how to.

"Can I do anything for you. Tenille?"

"Well, you can go and harvest some more herbs for me." She handed me a basket. "The garden is at the back of the units to the left. Just pick a little bit of everything if you can."

"Of course."

I wanted to be helpful, as much as possible. That was the deal with Max that I had. I left the house with the basket in my arms and let the smile that had been hanging around for days, stretch across my face.

Part of me remained terrified that this was some sort of strange dream that I had yet to wake up from. But the other half was so happy, I just couldn't seem to stop myself from luxuriating in the time I had.

The garden was small and well kept, I stopped and stared for a moment, soaking it all in. In this world with no humanity, and very few beings left on the planet, I couldn't believe that such a little Eden still existed.

"What are you doing here?" came a growled question and I jumped, instinctually lifting my arms to cover my face.

"Tenille asked me to fetch some herbs," I managed to get out.

When no response came, violent or otherwise, I lowered the basket and saw the face of the big Beta that helped Max with hunting some days. "Oh, hi Barry."

"Omega," Barry said, his lips lifting up into a sly grin as his eyes ran the length of me. "Please continue what you were doing."

A weird shiver coursed down my spine and I turned away to do as I'd been asked by Tenille. There was something strange about that Beta. He didn't fit in here. He reminded me a lot of the Alpha's I had at my old pack.

"You're hot, you know that?" Barry asked suddenly and I jumped.

"Oh, thank you." What else could I say? I picked some of the rosemary and the other plant that I knew Tenille liked for her cooking.

"Max left you alone again? I really do need to speak our Alpha about his treatment of you. If you were mine, I'd never let you out of my sight."

I shivered again from the strange tones in his voice and plucked more herbs, the bristly plants tickling my fingertips. "I can't hunt, so I'm not much use to you guys out there."

Although part of me wished that Max would involve me in more. I was still a male after all.

"Oh, I don't know about that. You're getting stronger by the day, and after all, you are still a man. Aren't you?"

Had he just heard my thoughts?

I straightened up and stared at the big, bulky Beta. "Of course I am."

"Then I don't know why you let Max tell you what you can and can't do."

I frowned and made a quick trip around the plants to make sure I'd got some of everything. I didn't like where this was going.

"Because he's the Alpha."

"Yes, and that's why you're with him, isn't it Omega? You wouldn't choose him if he were a Beta like me."

"Of course I would," was my immediate response, but when Barry laughed, I had to look away as my cheeks burned.

I didn't know how I would feel or who I might have ended up with, if I'd been given a choice. Although Max said I had a choice, I wasn't allowed to speak to any of the others wolves, so I had no idea what I was choosing or who.

I adored Max. He was kind, and sexy, and so generous with me. But there was something to be said for true freedom and Barry was right, I didn't have much of that.

I left the small garden and made to walk past the Beta. He grabbed me roughly and I fell against him, any strength I'd had flowing away with years of submissive conditioning.

"You know Max will be rid of you as soon as you do one thing wrong, Omega. I'd be very careful," Barry said, his voice smooth, like the sheets I now slept on.

"What do you mean?" I asked, though my voice trembled and a strange part of me rejoiced in the violence I felt within Barry's frame. This was comforting in its familiarity.

"Max has fucked half the women and men in this pack. He gets rid of them as soon as he's had his fill. Don't think you're anything special." The vile words were accompanied by a sneer and a groping hand at my arse.

I gasped, hot horror flowing over my body. "But he says he wants me as his mate."

Barry turned me in his arms and grabbed hold of me tight. He stared down at me, his face a horrible mix of domination and cruelty. A look I knew well. "Ha. You didn't believe him, did you? I mean, has he done it yet? How many times has he taken you to bed? Has he mated you?"

"Well...no."

And why was that? He'd had plenty of opportunities. I had displeased him the other night in bed by not responding how he wanted me to. Maybe, that was the reason for holding out on me? I was still learning, but did that mean I wouldn't get the chance to show him what I could be?

"Of course not, and he won't. He still wants a woman as a mate. He wants kids and a family. He's an Alpha. I think he's a dick head. Who needs any of those kids around the place? They make the pack weak, vulnerable. If I had you, I wouldn't care about not having any children. I'd never take my hands off you."

Cold shock hit me square in the face and my mind began to numb to reasoning. "I hadn't thought about that." I bit my lip to stop it trembling as all the reasons why Max hadn't mated me yet became clearer in my head.

I'm not good enough...

"An Alpha has to have pups. After all...who's going to continue the line if Max doesn't?"

A quiet voice in my head still protested the change I was about to make. I was half in love with Max already, and I was sure he felt something for me too. "But he said..."

Barry's hands dug into my arms and his voice sounded hard. "Don't believe anything Max says. He's too nice a guy to tell you the truth. He wouldn't want to hurt you. He's probably been trying to spare your feelings while you get better. And you do look a hell of lot better, Caden. I'm loving this flesh on your bones."

Barry ran his hand down the side of my face and I forced myself not to flinch. I knew that tone and I knew what he wanted. But how could I betray Max like that? He'd warned me what would happen if I stepped out of line.

"I can't, Barry. You know what the Alpha will do if he finds us together."

And that's if I can get through it myself. I may have spent years in a pack where I traded my body for safety, but I wasn't in that world anymore. *I'm not sure I can still do it.*

"He won't find us together. Don't worry. He's too busy playing with Connie in the forest. "

"What?" I gaped at him, jealousy spearing me through the chest. Connie was a tiny little blonde with massive breasts and swinging hips that made all the men around her stare. I'd seen her, and I didn't like her.

"You didn't think you were the only one he was fucking. Seriously?"

Hot tears stung my eyes as Barry's words circled around in my head. *Yes, I did. I thought he loved me.*

"I should go back." I wanted to get away from here. I needed to lick my wounds, pull myself together. I'd never thought about what Max would be doing behind my back. He'd demanded my loyalty, but he'd never spoken of his own. Of course he wasn't being faithful.

Seemed like all the Alpha's were exactly the same.

"Come with me," Barry said, lifting me up and carrying me into a nearby house. He closed the door and slid his hands beneath my T-shirt as he placed me back on the floor. He ran his rough hands over my abs and down to my crotch where my cock wasn't interested in him at all.

"What are you doing, Barry?" I knew the answer of course, and as my control slid away and my old personality slid into place I wanted to cry for the pain in my heart.

"I'm offering to take his place. Leave him and come live with me. I'll look after you better than he ever did."

Barry's tongue was inside my ear and I sunk against him, all resistance gone. I was alone once again, doing what I needed to do to survive. It couldn't be too bad, surely?

"But... Alright. What would you like me to do?" I could feel the cold calm encompassing my body once more. Like some sort of horrible plague consuming my once-warm flesh.

I had a safe place inside my mind for moments like this. I could retreat there until it was over.

"Get on your knees and suck me."

Of course. It's always that.

"Okay." I sunk down and opened my mouth, acid burning in my

gut like the old days. He opened his jeans and took out his cock, the horrible thing purple and veiny.

The door banged open with a loud clatter. "What the fuck are you doing?"

Nooooo... I launched myself backwards, scrambling like a crab across the room. Away from the heated anger of the Alpha behind me.

Max charged forward and fear froze the breath in my throat. But he wasn't going for me. Barry's head slammed back into the wall again and again. Max's fist ploughed into his face over and over. I crawled back as far as I could go, until my spine pressed against the wall. I watched as Barry's blood splattered across the walls and over Max.

Finally, his arms shaking from the stress, Max stepped back and away. Barry slid to the floor like a bag of potatoes. A bloodied mess. Max turned towards me with his damaged fists clenched and his nostrils flaring.

Fear made my throat close up and my heart race like a bongo drum. "Oh please. No."

He was going to kill me.

"Go home. Now," Max growled out, his eyes slanted yellow like the wolf.

I scrambled to my feet and ran as fast as I could.

*M*AX

My teeth were shifting, cutting into my soft lips and making my blood boil. My wolf screamed at me for release and like it or not, I was going to shift. No choice now.

Barry the bastard was in bad shape. His only hope was his shifter blood healing him as fast as possible, and a surgeon. Part of me didn't want to call for help. The lying, scheming bastard had done this on purpose, but he was still a member of our pack, and I was no murderer.

I stumbled to the door and called out to the only Beta I could see. "Nate!"

He ran to me, "Alpha. What's happened?"

From the startled look on the Beta's face, I must look an utter mess, but I had no time. My arms and legs were changing.

"It's Barry. Get the surgeon. Now. He's..." A groan ripped through me as pain rippled along every nerve cell in my body. Fighting my shifter demanded a payment and he was taking it in blood.

"He's...dying. Get help."

Nate nodded and ran. I let my humanity go. I fell to the ground. My arms turned into fur-covered legs. My face became the pointed mask of a wolf.

I began to run, the front gates opening for me as I moved towards them. I needed to get out of the confines of the pack's walls, and for once I didn't care who I found in my travels.

Vamps, werewolves...

Bring. Them. On.

My muscles clenched and tightened. Angry, red bubbles filled my mind and clouded my thoughts. The betrayal, something I had never experienced before. Why would an Omega betray me? A true Alpha.

Caden was my mate; I was his. Why would he do this to me?

Do the one, and only thing, I cannot forgive.

He's destroyed everything.

My thoughts became a mess of animal growlings as I ran.

It was nightfall before I returned home, and although I sensed a new coven of vampires in the area, I saw no stirrings of real beings. I found none hiding, though I looked. They were usually easy to sense during the day in their underground caves. We'd killed many that way.

But not today. I could smell them but I couldn't find them, and I was intensely regretful of that.

When I finally returned home, my mind was blank and a frown twisted my lips. I hadn't been this angry since those early years when my father died and the grief seemed to take away some of my humanity. I'd clawed it back. Fought so hard for so long to be the good person I'd always been.

The bastard was back. And I had my mate to thank for that.

He was on the floor in the dining room. Curled up on the floor asleep.

Good. He could stay there from now on. Or the couch. I didn't care. If he chose another man over me, then he'd never sleep with me again. I couldn't bear to be near him.

I got into the shower and had a cold wash, getting rid of the heated sweatiness over my body.

My thoughts line up like a list.

My mind remained empty of everything except the need for retribution.

Barry had already received his payment, but what to do about Caden?

I went to bed and tried to sleep. Even with all the anger swirling in my gut, I wasn't sure I could bring myself to hurt Caden. Nor throw him out to live with another in the pack.

If I left him to his own devices, he'd be gobbled up by my Betas and I wasn't ready to do that yet.

As the dark hours of the night wore on, some common sense came back to me.

Caden was an abused teenager. He hadn't grown up the way I had in a loving home. But that didn't excuse what he'd done today. And the why still eluded me. Why would he go to Barry after all I had promised him?

I tossed and turned all night, and although a part of me still wanted Caden desperately, my wolf was uncompromising.

I could never accept him as my mate now.

CADEN.

What have I done?

I woke up in the morning still on the floor. My head is full of hateful, black dreams. My cheeks are wet and I'm cold enough to shiver.

I mentally slapped myself and remember where I've come from. I now have a house to live in. *A house.* I'm no longer hungry or abused. I have nothing to complain about. Not yet anyway. There's no way of knowing what my punishment from Max will be.

My heart aches for what I've lost. The warmth and comfort of the Alpha. Max.

On cue, my stomach grumbles and lurches, and the door opens with a swish.

Max walks into the room, steps around me, and goes into the kitchen. He bangs around a while, cutting something up while I slowly unfurl myself and straighten until I'm finally standing.

I can't look at him.

He must hate me.

He puts something down on the bench a foot from where I am, and I flinch.

"Eat," He barks at me and my head shoots up.

In front of me is a plate, a slab of their bread and some sort of honey or yellow jam on it. My mouth waters, as do my eyes.

"But..." My lip trembles and I bite it to stop the inevitable flow of tears.

"But what? You think I'd stop feeding you because you're not my mate anymore? You're still a part of this pack, Caden. So eat. You need to get stronger."

The harsh words may as well have been a cane to my back. But I deserved the whip of words. So much so.

I stepped forward, my heart throbbing with pain as his words sunk into my head. *Not his mate anymore... not his mate anymore...*

I picked up the bread with trembling hands and brought it to my lips. The sticky sweetness made me groan in appreciation as it went across my tongue, and I managed to swallow it down.

"How did you get such a thing?" I ask quietly.

"After the initial deaths, we went in search of food and raided a lot of local supermarkets. My father and I hid a lot of the foods that would last. We still have a supermarket of sorts, buried underground." His hard face softened for a moment, a proud smile quirking up his lips.

"Your pack has done so well, Max," I managed to say, though I trembled with the strain.

He shrugged, chewing on his own bread. "We've done better than most."

We stood in silence until the food was gone. Max whisked my plate away, rinsed them in the sink, then set them to dry. I watched carefully, noting how he liked things done.

"Go find my mother. She'll give you your chores for today. I'll see you tonight." He walked past me without a touch, and a whimper rose in my throat at the lack of affection. It was amazing how quickly I'd come to yearn for those things that I'd never had before.

I was left in the empty room, swaying like a tree in the wind for a moment, my mind blank, coldness filling me up. Lost.

Then a door slammed and I jumped. I turned towards the noise, my heart racing and my mind finally in gear. I muttered to myself, trying to push some will power into my body. "Okay. All right. Come on Caden, you can do this. Tenille. I need to find Tenille."

I forced my lazy, heavy limbs into action and raced out of the house. I stepped into the warm sunshine and went looking for Tenille. If I even had the slightest chance of winning Max back, it would be through doing what Max asked. And that started with Tenille.

Luckily, I found Max's mother by one of the smaller units, holding a baby I didn't recognize. He was fat and had red cheeks, his eyes wet from crying.

"Hi, Tenille... Max told me to find you and ask for a job."

Tenille looked me up and down, her mouth tight and her eyes hard. "You really fucked up yesterday, Omega."

I fell back like she'd punched me in the gut. "Ah... um..." What could I say to that?

She moved the baby on her hip and jiggled him with the ease of a practiced hand. "Caden, you don't realize what you've done."

"I—"

She cut me off. "No. You don't. You haven't just angered the Alpha that took you in and caused massive injuries to Barry. Although to be honest, he had it coming for a long time. Max can be soft about some things. And disciplining his pack is sometimes hard for him. I would have thrown Barry out on his arse years ago."

I could only nod. I had the same feeling, though I couldn't say that aloud after what I'd done. "He...ah..."

"Seduced you. Told you that Max didn't want you. Convinced you that you needed him."

I gaped at her. "How did you know?"

She rolled her eyes. "Because I know Barry, and I can tell by looking at you what sort of life you've had, young one. But that's not a good enough excuse for what you did. Max did nothing to deserve your betrayal, and I'm afraid you've not only damned your own life, but his as well."

"I can make it up to him. I can…" I'd never met a man who wouldn't take me back after I did something wrong. There was always a key phrase, or some sort of torture I could inflict on myself to make it up to him.

Surely Max would be the same?

She shook her head and stared at me sadly like she could read my mind. "Max is not like other men, Caden. You won't be able to wiggle your arse and fix everything. But you still don't understand, and that's probably because no one ever told you what you are."

Yes, they had. "I'm an Omega."

She nodded, but blew out a breath as though she were becoming impatient. "Yes, you are. And did anyone ever tell you what sort of mate you would have?"

My mind recited all the things my mother and grandmother had said to me. My stomach clenched as I also recalled all the horrible things the Alpha's of my last pack had said I was useful for. But no, I couldn't remember anything about my mating.

"No. I didn't expect a mate at all. My parents were Betas and they didn't know. They said that I would be revered for my sex drive, so I kinda concluded that's all I was good for." I swallowed hard as I spoke the words that had tortured me for so long. "My grandmother told me to stay alive. At any cost."

Tenille nodded, still frowning. "And there was a reason for that. No disrespect meant to your grandma, but she should have told you the full reason. An Omega is special, very special. You are rare among our breed. You are designed to be the Alpha Mate of this pack, to my son."

Was she serious? "Really?" *I'd thought Max just liked my arse.*

Why hadn't anyone told me that I was more than a non-shifting piece of sex that was no use to the pack in any other way?

"Yes. And more than that, when properly mated you will give Max strength, unlike anything he has ever known. You will amplify everything he is. His power, his size. But without it, he will be vulnerable."

"I can do that now!" Excitement pulsed through me for the first time today. If I could truly enhance the natural abilities of an Alpha, I would have a purpose. A reason to live, and Max would keep me around. Forever.

"No. you can't. Max has to accept you, bond with you wholly. He doesn't trust you now, and that's what I'm trying to tell you. You may have just damned both of you forever."

No, I couldn't accept that. I hadn't actually done anything wrong, thanks to Max's timing of finding us. Thank God. Surely, I could explain that and everything would be alright again? "But I can fix it."

"I'm not sure that you can. My son is proud. Too proud. I'm sorry. For both of you." She shook her head and offered her knuckle to the crying baby. He sucked hungrily on her hand.

If an Alpha Mate was saying this to me, could she possibly be right? That there was no way I could fix my mistake? My knees buckled and I stumbled forwards, crashing into the wall.

Pain splintered through my crushed arm and I gasped as my chest tightened. "Oh my God." I couldn't breathe. Air wheezed in and out of my lungs until my chest heaved and the black spots crowded into my eyes.

A steady hand ran the length of my arm and squeezed my forearm, giving me an anchor in the storm. "Stop panicking. If you have any hope of being my son's mate, then you need to pull yourself together. Be strong. An Alpha Mate is the best of the pack, not the worst."

Her strong words pulled my mind back from the darkness, and the sunshine flowed in once again. She was right. There was no hiding in my weakness any more.

"I want to be better for him, Tenille. I do. I want to be everything Max deserves."

She gripped my hand hard, the first tendrils of a smile filtering onto her face. "Then you better be ready to work bloody hard,

Caden. Because if you were in the police force, and Max was in charge of you, he would have had you drawn and quartered for yesterday."

I stared back at her. "Been there and done that. I can survive anything if it means having a life with Max." I didn't want to go into any details. But physical pain was the least of my worries.

"That's the spirit, Caden."

I needed to stop making excuses and accept what I'd done. I made a horrendous mistake yesterday. I had been talked into betraying Max, and if I thought about it, I hadn't put up much of a fight either. Where was my loyalty? Max was the best, most thoughtful, and generous Alpha I'd ever met, and I wanted to be good enough for him. I did.

Whether I could be, was a different story.

"What if I'm just not cut out to be an Alpha's Mate, Tenille? I mean...he deserves the best, and my past has made me so damaged. I'm not sure I can fix it all. He should have a woman, someone to give him children..."

I released all my fears at once, speaking to her as though she were my own mother.

She held tight to my hand. "Max doesn't have a choice now. His wolf wants you, identifies you as his mate. He'll want no other now. So you either get rid of all that doubt and bull shit that's been holding you back, or you let Max go through this shitty life alone."

The horror of that image struck me through the chest, hardening my resolve.

I wasn't good enough for him yet, but I could be. I was sure of it.

"Okay, Tenille. Give me another job, one worthy of the next Alpha's Mate." I didn't want to be a scavenger anymore. Surviving day to day with no future in sight.

Tenille raised an eyebrow and stared at me as though she were issuing me a challenge. "You know what should be done, Caden. Go do it. Don't ask me."

I nodded and gave her as big a smile as I could manage.

Food needed to be organized for dinner, the children needed to be attended to. There were also some maintenance jobs for some of the houses.

Tenille was right. I *did* know what needed to be done. I didn't know all the ins and outs of everything yet, but I would learn, and if that meant I could claw my way back into Max's favor, then I'd do anything.

I went straight to the kitchen and meal prep area and spent the rest of the day there.

The hunting party didn't arrive home until the sun was setting and I was ready to greet Max with a hot meal and everything I had in me to give.

~

MAX

They were here. I could smell them like the dank death that encased their souls. "Move! Now! The vamps are here!"

The hunting party ran for our pack's home. We could stay and fight them outside the walls, but what would happen to our families on the inside if we missed some that snuck across the walls?

We barged inside and I pushed the gates shut again, slamming the huge locks home. I screamed to my men. "Protect the children. Don't open the doors. No matter what." The men ran to their homes, stripping their clothes off as they went. Wolves appeared everywhere as my pack transformed, ready for battle.

A fight with the vamps was always lethal for us. We had the UV lights which were effective in slowing them down, and we had our strength. But so did they. We would lose men tonight, and if we were unlucky, women and children too.

They were too strong, and fast. I lost too many good men last year. I wasn't sure how we would get through this one with even more women and children to protect.

Caden came running towards me and my wolf leapt to the surface.

"Get back, Caden. Go inside. Now."

"Why? What's happened?"

As though in answer a, ungodly shriek sounded from above. We twisted to see the three black figures take out one of our UV lights that weren't even turned on yet. "Fuck. There's a lot of them." *And they know we have the lights. Damn it!*

"What is it?"

"Vampires. Go. Quick. Now." I pushed at him but he held his ground.

"I want to help you," Caden yelled, the noise around us picking up in volume as the wolves began to howl.

My teeth were descending and my eyes were shifting, the world around me becoming one of black and white. "No Caden. You can't fight. Run. Go now."

Caden nodded once, his eyes filled with worry. Then he ran for home.

I turned back towards the front gate and took a deep breath as my wolf leapt up to take my place. Something shivered deep inside of me as I pushed him back down. I needed to do one more thing, and for that I needed my vocal chords.

I recognized that shiver inside of me. It was fear. And that was Caden's fault. He made me weak. I'd never been afraid before now. Even with the severing of our ties, I didn't want to die. I didn't want to leave him alone in this world.

I grabbed onto the anger that rose like the mist in the morning and faced the danger coming at our gates. They would not get through.

One of the young Betas was by his post at the gate and I yelled at him, "Turn on the lights!"

He flicked the switch and the houses flooded with bright light, temporarily blinding us all as it became daylight at dusk. There were screams from the vampires as they collapsed to the ground, writhing in pain as we used their main weakness against them.

"Kill them!" I screamed as my wolf took full control of my body. I fell to the ground and a growl ripped through my mind as I became the Alpha wolf of my pack. The vampires that were still moving hopped over our fences and charged.

I bounded forwards, leaping for the nearest female vamp with sharp teeth as she swung a clawed hand at me. I wove around her fighting stance and clamped my jaws around her throat, ripping out the blackened blood and throwing her to the ground.

Our UV lights were exploding around me. Crashing to the ground and bringing with them, darkness. The vamps' playground. The vampires were throwing the lamps to the ground. Smashing them but dying themselves. Sacrificing themselves for the rest of the group.

I leapt for a half-burnt male, ripping out his shoulder. Feeling the crack of bone and the rip of flesh between my teeth. Fear coursed through me as I watched them working together. I'd never seen such a dedicated, group attack before. A pack of three vamps ran through the yard and before I could run that way, they were taken down by four of my wolves. Another two bounded across the roof tops of our houses to take out the final lights.

I raced through the yard, growling and biting anything that moved. Some of the fallen vamps were still reaching up from the dirt and I clawed their heads as I ran through.

A female vamp broke a window and tried to get into one of our houses. I charged forward and grabbed onto her leg. I gripped hard and tore her backwards. Away from my family.

Another vamp launched at me, tearing at my side.

I didn't let go of the one trying to get into my mother's house, but the one at my side worked her way up to my neck. I finally fell. Hot, searing pain ripped through my chest as blood poured down my side.

Fuck. No.

I bit down harder, snapping the leg off the vampire I held, and twisted to try to get the other one off me. The vampire at my side clung to my neck like a leech. Sucking my life force as though its life depended on it.

"No!" I heard a scream from around me and a massive white light flashed at us at short range.

I couldn't see but that light was going to save me. I sent up a prayer to whoever was behind the artificial sunshine and swung hard at the vampire slowly killing me. The vamp fell back and away. Some of the pain eased and I collapsed onto the ground. I heard one of my pack members behind me finish the job I couldn't.

Thank God. There shouldn't be too many left now. Hopefully.

"Max. Max! Get up. Quick. We need to get you to Maree."

It was my own little terrified Omega who'd run to me with one of the lights. How he got it working I had no idea.

I tried to speak, but nothing came out. Blood pooled beneath me like a running river. Caden had to get away. There could be more vampires around.

"Help! Please hurry!"

No. You're the one that needs help. Please, Caden. Run...

Arms lifted me up off the muddy ground and pain ricocheted through my tired body, draining me of all life, sight and sound. The blackness engulfed me.

CHAPTER 7
CADEN.

They worked on Max for what seemed like days. Stitching him up, wrapping up his wounds. But it must have only been a few hours, because he was home resting in bed before the sun came up the next day.

Massive internal bleeding and damage to his carotid artery, Maree said. Which normally, would be curable in an Alpha male of Max's strength and youth. His shifter genes meant that he healed at a phenomenally fast rate. It was the vampire poison that was the problem. That was what would kill him. And soon. Vampire venom was lethal, and fast acting.

Don't know how he's still alive, they all said.

Well I sure as hell knew. He was the strongest, best Alpha that I'd ever known. He'd live. He had to.

There was no way on Earth I was living without him. But how to get him to forgive me after everything that had gone on?

"How's my son doing?" Tenille asked as she stepped into the room, a pot of warm soup in hand.

"I...don't know," I answered, not sure what to say.

"He's still alive, Caden. Focus on that," she said, setting down the food.

"True, but I don't know how long for. Or if he'll forgive me if he does wake up."

Tenille handed me a large mug with steaming hot soup in it. "Drink it all. Max would hate for you to get any thinner than you already are."

She wanted me to eat at a time like this? She had to be kidding.

"How's the rest of the pack, Tenille? Maree seemed to be running from house to house last night helping people."

Even in my state of panic, I'd still noticed the way our surgeon had tried to help all the others.

Tenille sighed heavily. "We're down six men. One of the vampires found Barry too and drained him."

Her gaze ran over me for a reaction and I struggled not to smile. Instead I shrugged. I was glad he was dead.

"And the U.V. lights? Can they be fixed? Do you think they'll attack again soon?"

I'd known nothing about vampires, but I'd learnt quickly last night. Those lights were the best weapon we had against the foul creatures.

"Some of the younger Betas are working to fix them now. We have globes in storage, hidden. But hopefully, we won't need to use them again soon. Last night's attack was a very large coven. The biggest I've seen in decades. There shouldn't be many of them left around here. Not for a while anyway."

"That's good...." My throat cracked, unable to remain calm a moment longer.

"What am I going to do, Tenille? I mean, without him, there is no pack for me now. I feel like my heart is broken." If someone had told me that a vampire had crushed my ribs in an attack, I would have believed them. Everything inside me felt bruised and sore.

"Then you have chosen him for your mate, finally. Though unfortunately, it may be too late." Her voice was sad as she reached over and lovingly stroked his face.

I watched her and as I did, anger rose inside me. Why did everyone keep saying that? How was Max going to find the strength to live if everyone kept giving up on him?

"No! It can't be! I refuse to believe that."

I went to place the soup back on the table, but Max's mother glared at me. I lifted it to my lips and swallowed it down. Still hot, nourishing, and thick. My stomach lurched in rejection, but I swallowed repetitively until it settled. She was right. Max would be angry if I didn't eat.

"Caden. Max has cut you off as his mate. You won't be able to save him."

My teeth clamped together and I glared at her. "Don't you dare say that to me. I'm going to find a way."

One of her eyebrows rose high in taunting question, then she swept out of the room.

I couldn't control my breathing. My heart ached liked it had been cracked open with a hammer. My teeth ground together and my jaw ached. Why did everyone just want to give up on him?

"Eat, Caden." Max's weak voice broke through the red haze in my mind.

I jumped forward, my knees banging into the bed frame as I grabbed for Max's arm. It was stone cold and I gasped as I clung to him. Oh God. He was on death's door.

"Max. Max! I am so sorry. For everything! I should never have let Barry talk me into going with him. I was weak, so weak. And stupid. And a coward. But I don't want to be that anymore. I want to be yours. And be worthy of you. Please. Please fight this and I'll prove to you that I'm the person you need."

Max turned his head away. "I'm going to die, Caden. Just go. You'll need to learn to live without me. I won't last the week with this poison in my blood."

My throat closed up with pain as though someone had pressed their foot into my trachea. "No. Please…"

"Go away." Max pulled his arm away from me and I moved back, watching the blue veins of his neck begin to bulge and ripple with the poison flowing through him.

"But we've got time… we could."

"No." Max's voice cut me off. "I'll make sure the pack is in order, but I'm not going to spend the last few days of my life fighting with you. Stop. It's done."

Somewhere inside of me, a part of me stood up and screamed. I jumped to my feet and let the strong voice inside me have its way. "No! You will not die! I'm sorry. More sorry than I can say. Don't give up on me Max. Please don't…"

I could see the infection spreading and backed away to the door. "I'm going to find a cure for you. Just hold on. Please."

I turned and ran outside, into the sunlight that mocked me. How could the sun rise on a day when Max was hurt? Dying? Where was the darkness? There should be clouds blocking out the sky.

What was I going to do? What could be done? Surely there was a way.

I ran towards the houses where I knew Maree usually spent her days and burst inside. "Maree! Maree! You need to help me, please. Tell me what to do to fix Max. There has to be something I can do."

Maree was mixing something in a bowl and stared at me like I was mad. "I've done everything I know how to do, Caden. If there was something you could do, I would have told you already."

She was so calm. Too calm! Didn't she know what this would mean for the pack? It could mean anarchy! Who would be the next Alpha if Max died? It would be like our old pack all over, and I couldn't live through that again.

"I know that, but please, can't you think of something? We can't lose another Alpha. Tenille told me of the Omega mating, that it has some sort of purpose, some power that…" I couldn't finish that sentence. I didn't know enough about the superstition and now that I was repeating it aloud, the idea that I might have the power to heal him seemed preposterous.

Maree's face seemed to fall. "Well, I do know that a mate of an Alpha has some healing powers, an Omega especially. But you aren't Max's mate, and he probably couldn't go through with the bonding now anyway."

Let's see about that. "What does a mating require, Maree?"

The surgeon's face grew rosy and I suddenly knew at least part of what had to be done.

"We have to have sex? That's it?"

It couldn't be that simple or we would be mated now.

"Well, yes. But there's a lot more to it than that. Your hearts have to be in agreement. You both must want each other, need each other, choose each other. It has to be a true mating, of the minds, hearts, and bodies."

Well, that was what I wanted. "I can do that."

She put her hand on her hip and stared at me. "You can't if he's unable to...fuck you, Caden, and he grows weaker by the hour. I've told him that he probably has a few days, but I'm not sure about that either. I've never seen Vampire poisoning's that haven't killed the host instantly." She took a long breath then blew it out slowly. "Not to mention the fact that Max has not accepted you yet. That could take months to repair. And to be honest, I'm not sure he will ever forgive you for what happened with Barry."

Now it was my turn to have my cheeks flame with heat. "I..." I swallowed hard, pushing away the feelings of inadequacy and shame. "I don't care. I can make it up to him. I can."

Maree stared at me hard. "I'm not the one you have to convince Caden. As far as I'm concerned, as a surgeon who's seen everything, and a wolf born female mate of an Alpha who couldn't save him, Max is done for."

My fists tightened and I could feel the muscles in my back bulking and grabbing with strength.

She swallowed hard and her expression softened. "But if you

think you can save him, then you better do something soon. Because without a miracle. He's going to dead by the next full moon."

I stumbled away once again and stood out in the court yard. The wind picked up and the clouds danced across the sky, a rumble threatening the sunshine of the day.

Yes. Thank you.

I closed my eyes and held out my hands in acceptance of this moment. People around me ran for the safety of cover.

Me. I stood there and waited. For the lightening. For the thunder and the rain. Bring on Heaven's gift that would cleanse me of all my bad choices.

The cold water hit like a hundred little needles on my skin and the crashing of the thunder rolled in. I opened my eyes and watched the streaking yellow dance through the sky.

I'd spent too many years hiding from the elements. Being scared of the world around me. That wasn't going to happen anymore. I let my arms fall to the sides of my body as peace descended over my mind like a blanketing cloud.

My body floated over to the house that Max had taken me into. His home. A place he had kissed me tenderly, fed me, cared for me. My nose stung with impending tears as I moved through the clean kitchen and into the bedroom that reeked of death.

I stripped the bed covers from Max's body and tugged them to the floor.

The purple and red veins of infection had woven up and down Max's arm, spreading across his neck and into his jaw. The vampire's poison was taking over his body and if I couldn't find a way to save him, the pack was right. He would be dead within days.

"What are you doing, Caden?" Max's confused, weak words strengthened my resolve.

I stripped all my wet clothes off and dumped them on the floor. Then I jumped on top of his beautiful body, my hair dripping down my back.

His eyebrows furrowed as he stared at me. "I don't want this, Caden."

"Why, Max? I need you. Please. Mate with me. Let me be yours."

A muscle ticked in his jaw as he glared at me, real strength still behind his blue eyes.

Good. You haven't given up yet.

"No."

Stubborn man. His life was on the edge of death and he would rather die being righteous than give me another chance.

"Feel me, Max. Please. Feel my power. Feel my love for you. My admiration. My fear that you'll die and take my heart along with you. Please, tell what you want me to do to get a second chance."

Max shook his head and dropped his gaze to my hands that were pressed to his chest. My honesty obviously confused him. "But you... I already tried this, Caden."

I had to be more honest. Put my heart really on the line.

"Max, you don't know what my old life was like. I've done so many things that I'm not proud of. Men used me, every day, every night, any time they liked."

Max turned his face away, his jaw tight and clenching with anger. "I don't want to know."

And that was why I'd never told him. I wanted to be a new person when I stepped into this pack. Forget everything. But the other day with Barry had shown me that I still had so many scars I needed to heal within myself.

Fear wove through me like a poisonous vine, making my hands tremble as I exposed my soul for him. "I was thirteen when I promised my grandmother that I would do anything to survive. And I did. But I don't want to be that man anymore, Max. I want to be an Alpha Mate. I want to be the best person I can be, in this fucked up world. But will you...can you accept me for who I've been? The terrible things I've done to survive?"

When Max turned back to look at me, his blue eyes sad, I felt the first flicker of hope. He didn't say anything so I took the opportunity to keep going.

"Can you Max? Can you accept that I made a big mistake, that I let Barry convince me that you'd never mate with me? Never keep me?"

His eyes widened in surprise. "Is that what he said?"

"Yes. Among other things. And I thought I only wanted to survive. But I don't want to just *exist* anymore. If you don't want to live, then neither do I."

Yes! That's it! If he hates me then this will reveal all.

An idea flooded my brain and I ran into the kitchen and grabbed the biggest knife I could find from the kitchen, sharpened to a dangerous point thanks to Max's skill with a blade. I walked back into the bedroom and sat down next to him, the soft light in the room glinting off the blade.

"What are you doing?" Max asked, twisting to look at what I was holding.

"I want to give you my blood. If yours is poisoned, surely I can replace it with mine and you can live."

That got him moving. Literally. He went to grab the knife from my hand.

"What are you doing? This could help you. Do you have any needles or tubes? Otherwise, I can just pour it into your wound."

"No!" Max sat up, wincing at the pain in his body as he tried to grab the knife once again.

I clung to whatever courage I had and stared down at him, taking the biggest chance of my life. "Mate with me. Please. Save yourself so that we can live together, love each other. Let me apologize to you every day for what I did and I'll do whatever penance you deem worthy."

Max relaxed back against the pillows, his face a twisted mask of pain. "I don't want that."

"What do you want, Max?"

He stared at me long and hard, his eyes burning with the yellow of his wolf. "I want a real mate. A team player. A partner. I want to be able to trust you, love you, share the responsibilities of the pack with you."

"Yes! I want all of that too! Please forgive me for my scars. My past has shaped too much of me. But that stops today. I want to be a whole new man."

Max's face softened. "Well, not all new."

I threw the knife down onto the bed and jumped on top of Max once again. "Make love to me, Max. Mate with me, please. Live for me."

Max lifted his arms and put his hands on my face, holding me close.

I pressed my lips onto his and tasted my own tears. I didn't know what I had to do to save him. But I would follow my instincts and my heart. Hopefully I would reach that magic precipice where I could save him.

Max snuck his tongue into my mouth and I sucked on his flesh, loving the possessive streak in my Alpha. Even as he lay here broken and dying, he was the one taking over the kiss, grabbing my arse and hauling me against him.

I worked down his body, kissing every inch of muscle and hardness until I reached his cock. It lay against his thigh, thickening beneath my gaze. I took him into my mouth, an ash type taste sliding across my tongue.

Oh God, no. Tell me it's not too late.

I closed my eyes and pushed the fear away, focusing on what little bit of life was still there.

His cock stirred in my mouth and I sucked harder, loving the head with my tongue as I worked him up and down. I reached beneath him and slid my fingers over his gorgeous, tight arse. He lifted his legs so that I could play with the perfect little hole. I tapped on it and slid the tip of my finger into him, loving the way he gasped and bucked beneath me.

I hummed with happiness to feel the salty precum slide down my throat. Max's thick thighs pressed against my head. Yummy.

I crawled up and over his body, kissing along the infected area of the vampire bite, thinking only of how much I wanted him to live so that we could start our life together.

I straddled my big Alpha and kissed him once again. His hands roamed over my body and found my cock. Max pumped me with expert skill until I was writhing against him, fucking his hand and wanting him inside of me.

Max's cock was spilling out pre-cum like a waterfall. I reached back, collected it, and spread it over my arse in preparation for him.

"I need you inside me. Please."

Max nodded, grabbed my hips, and positioned me over his cock.

"Do we need to say anything, Max? To make the mating work? I want you so much."

I groaned as I bounced on top of Max's cock, working him slowly inside of me. Inch by delicious inch I descended. Taking him in.

Max shook his head with a growl and exposed his teeth, his wolf jumping to the fore front. I tilted my head to the side, exposing my neck for him as I pushed all the way down.

Pain burned in my body as I accepted his full length. Max leaned forward, grabbed me, and bit me hard. Stars exploded inside my head as I let centuries of breeding control my actions. I squeezed Max as hard as I could, milking his cock while he cried out against my neck.

He came inside of me. Hot streams of seed squirting into my body as my own cock painted our bodies with cum. I couldn't see, couldn't speak. Could only feel the pulses of love and ecstasy between us.

As Max fell away my eyes opened and I stared down at the wound that remained black.

I took the knife from where it still lay on the bed and cut open my hand.

There was no pain as I let the blood flow. This was a good idea, I knew it. Somehow.

"What are you..."

I pressed my hand to Max's open wound, forcing my own blood into his body while we were still joined. Max cried out, this time in pain as his back arched and he trembled beneath me.

Oh, please, please, please...let this be the right thing to do.

I withdrew my hand from the wound and added the second hand to the site, blood still pouring between my fingers. I squeezed at the infection until Max's blood ran black, all down the sheets and over the bed.

I could only hope the infection would clear and the strength of the Alpha would return, stronger than before.

Our eyes met and my breath caught with the intensity in his gaze. Stars started to twinkle behind my eyes and I lay down on Max's body, holding him as tightly as I could. Willing him to push through this.

The blackness crowded in and I let go of reality.

I must have passed out because when I came to, Maree was there, hovering over me with a knowing smile. I looked around. I was still in Max's home and when I lifted my hand, it was bandaged up. I glanced to the side, Max was still there, and his color was better.

I reached out. He was warm to the touch.

Tears tingled in my eyes. "Is he okay?" I croaked out, my throat cracking with the strength required to speak.

Maree nodded. "Yes. I think so. You'll both need some rest, but you should be fine."

I let myself float back into unconsciousness. My dreams were full of cold, dark places and I shook as I came awake. But there was no cold earth beneath me. No abusive man on top of me. There was only Max. His warm body curled around mine. His lips at my ear.

"Wake up, beautiful boy. It's a new day."

I turned towards him, wrapping my arms around his bandaged chest.

"We did it."

"You did it," he said, kissing my lips gently. "I didn't think there was anything on Earth that could bring me back from the brink of death like that."

I grinned up at him. "I was told that an Omega had special powers if he loved his Alpha more than anything in the world."

Max chuckled. "Oh really? Well, aren't I a lucky wolf then?"

I smiled as Max tucked me beneath him, climbing on top of me, and sliding between my open thighs.

"I'm the lucky one, my mate."

And as Max went about showing me how loved and lucky I was, I made a secret pact with myself. One to ride over the one I made to my grandmother. One to hold onto for all time.

A pact to love Max and serve his pack, until death did us part.

THE END

Thank you so much for reading The Omega Shift, I hope you enjoyed it.

Book 2- Saving the Omega is available for download: HERE

Or read on for a sneak peek.

CHAPTER 8
ANGUS.

They were at it again. Fighting.

Though, could you really call it that when one man was doing all the yelling and hitting, while the other stood there, or often knelt down, and just took it?

I shook my head and turned away from the sight that turned my stomach almost every day. How could Sam treat his mate in such a way? Clayton was such a beautiful boy, and I'd never seen him do a thing wrong by Sam.

Anger rippled in my gut as I fought the need to intervene. He wasn't in my pack, so technically I shouldn't. But how could I just stand by and watch this happen?

It's not your place. Get moving.

I forced myself to look away from the sight of the young man cowering against the fence surrounding Sam's pack's property.

Clayton wasn't my concern. I had enough to deal with to keep my own pack safe, but what I wouldn't give to bring the boy over to us. To keep him safe. My wolf inside my mind howled at the injustice, making my arms vibrate with the strength it took to keep him down.

I forced myself to lift my feet, turn away and trudge towards my workstation. If Clayton had been my mate, I'd never treat him that way. I'd never treat anyone that way.

I nodded at Jeff and Dave, two Beta's from my pack, as we walked up the hill towards the power station. The rest of my pack trailed behind me.

In this new world, a world that had gone to hell, I was nothing.

Nothing but the strongest man in the whole bloody town. What did that mean, though, in a place where vampires ruled by fear and force, and my pack was on the bottom of the ladder because we didn't suck up to those blood suckers?

The vampires were a problem we needed to remedy. In the decade since our world had changed forever, I lost most of my strongest men to the pack wars.

Ten years ago, a paranormal being released a virus into the world that killed off every human on the planet. Some said he was a shifter, or a demon. The vampires, of course, believed he was one of theirs, power hungry creatures that they were.

Maybe he was a half-breed that hated us all equally? I didn't know. What I did know was that he had been crazy to attempt what he'd achieved.

Absolutely fucking crazy.

I still couldn't believe he'd succeeded in making Earth a paranormal planet. Whoever thought our lives would be okay after killing off most of the population of Earth had been sorely mistaken. We'd been left with a rotting world, full of dead human bodies, and a chaos of fighting paranormal beings. Each faction wanted whatever land and power there was left to claim.

In some parts of the U.S, I'd heard the fighting still continued, but here, in what had been beautiful San Francisco, we'd worked out a pecking order of sorts. Unfortunately, us wolf shifters came out somewhere in the middle.

I was once the Alpha of a powerful pack. The Highland Wolves. We had good jobs and we worked well in the human world.

So, when everyone around us died, and all the shifters and

vampires that were left began fighting for whatever power was left, we fought too.

To the demise of almost everyone I loved.

What was left of my pack now lived in dilapidated homes in an apartment block we'd cleared out of the humans. At least we were all together.

There were no shops anymore. No supermarkets. Barely enough clean water for everyone, but that wasn't something I needed to worry about. That was the feline shifters' job.

Thanks to us Highland Wolves who kept the power station running, the city had a little electricity. It was a physically laborious job, but it kept my mind from wandering too much to the old days.

"Hey, Angus." Silky stepped up next to me, her slinky smile a ghost of the woman I'd once known.

"Hey," I returned and rubbed my arm along hers.

Silky, a female of our bloodlines, lived in the apartment above mine. None of the females shifted in our packs, not that we could do so now anyway. The vampires had made all animal shifting illegal.

She kept my bed warm most nights, but there was little between us except the urge to stay alive. Affection was essential for any wolf, but as an Alpha, I felt the lack of true affection keenly. I had dreams of being surrounded by my children and the pack, gathering their bodies and pulling them atop me to prevent them from being cold.

As an Alpha of my pack, I'd been told since birth that I would have a fated mate and I looked forward to the day that I would meet the one person meant for me.

That had been before the end of our world, and the end to all good things in our lives. Perhaps my mate had already been killed? Or she lived on the other side of the States? Either way, I'd resigned myself to the fact that I would never have a true mate now, and kept forcing myself to bond with Silky, or whichever female begged for my attention. However, it was a cold, nasty business, and I knew to my core that this wasn't how life was meant to be.

I lifted my head and looked up at the looming building ahead of us. My pack's job for the day, every day, was to keep the electricity station running. Which meant physical labor for all of us, but it was for a good cause.

The other shifters performed other jobs and if they didn't work, the vamps made sure they paid for it in kind.

The vampires still needed blood to stay *alive*, and although humans were their favorite meal, no more of those existed. Which meant we either did our job, or they fed on us. They said our children tasted the sweetest.

I had the bite marks to prove how often I'd gotten in the way of the vamps trying to feed on one of our kids. Luckily, I was too valuable to them to drain, and I didn't think they liked the taste of me too much. The distaste on their faces always appeared comical after a feed of my Alpha blood.

As an Alpha, it ate at my pride that I would be food for the vampires that ruled our town. But they kept us on a short leash with their threat against our children, and I had to admit that they did keep an order to things.

Before the vamps moved in, the shifters were killing each other.

At least that had all stopped.

"Do you think we'll ever get out of here?" Silky asked as we stepped into the old power station.

Most of the machinery didn't work anymore, so we needed to move the machines and cogs by hand. An arduous and painful task.

We provided the town with enough power to cook the food for us all, and generally kept our homes warm for part of the night.

"Honestly, I don't know. If I knew of a safe place we could go, then I'd be gone in a shot. And I'd be taking you all with me."

"But what about the vampires?" she asked.

I shrugged. I hadn't decided yet if the vampires were the best of the evils at the moment, or not. Either way, my pack should not be living under the rule of anyone.

"We have twelve hours of sunlight every day when they can't touch us, Silky. We just need a plan."

The vampires had their daylight watchers. Cougar shifters. Nasty beasts. But even the cougars would be hard pressed to match us in a fight, especially if the wolf shifter packs combined.

Silky nodded and lifted a basket of coal up from the ground.

"Well, let me know when you have a plan. Anywhere has to be better than this."

She turned away to her task and my gaze flashed over the white scars on her neck. She'd taken many vampire feedings too, over the years.

Anger rolled in my gut like a storm and I clenched my hands into massive fists. Fuck it. We had to get out of here and soon.

With every passing day, I could feel my wolf rising to the surface to fight for my pack. To correct the injustice that was now our world.

But if we escaped, would it be to a world that was better, or worse, than this one?

I forced myself into the monotonous rhythm of heavy work, wishing myself back to the days of fire-fighting. I'd loved my job, and thanks to my superior strength and instincts, had been on my path to be captain.

That was never going to happen now.

"You coming over tonight?" I asked Silky, as we trudged back down the hill after sun down. It had been a few days since she'd graced my bed, and I could feel the increased levels of testosterone in my blood needing the release.

The vamps would be up and it would be feeding time. For everyone.

"Maybe not tonight. I'm on babysitting duty for Teri and Martha. Tomorrow though?"

I gave her a smile and a nod. "Sure."

The women all shared child-raising responsibilities, even those that had none themselves. Our pack still looked after one another, which was soothing to see. Not everything was broken in this world.

"Seriously. Doesn't he have anything better to do?" Silky's voice was full of disgust as we arrived back at our building.

I didn't want to look, but as the sounds of flesh being pummeled caught my hearing, I had to see how bad it was.

Sam was at it again. Beating on Clayton in the most sadistic way. Pulling his hair and dragging him around the dirt that lay at the front of their building to degrade him as much as possible.

A yelp and a scream had me turning towards them rather than walking away as I normally would have. Sam swung a lump of wood, and was beating Clay on the back while the young man tried to protect himself by curling into a ball. The thump of the plank against his back had me cringing hard.

Nobody moved.

Heat seared along my veins, anger building in me liking a rising storm.

Another helpless cry from Clayton filled the air. Another disgusting display of brutality as blood covered the wooden bat Sam raised high in the air once again. This had to stop, and if no one else was going to save him, then the time had come for me to.

"Stop. Now," I growled out and stormed across the road.

Stay down. Stay down.

"Angus! No."

I heard Silky's warning, but I was way past caring. I pulled open the old gate that marked entrance to Sam's apartments and tightened my hands into fists.

Sam raised the lump of wood again, his face a grotesque mask of anger as I charged forward. I put both hands out in front of me, aiming for his chest. I ran straight into him and knocked him to the ground.

I stood in front of Clayton's bloodied form and clenched both fists tight.

Stay down. Stay down, I urged my wolf.

Shifting was forbidden by the vamps. They said it was to keep the peace, but I knew it was because we were stronger than them in wolf form. They had one thing over us though. Their bite was deadly to us when we were in wolf form, so I didn't know why they bothered with the rule.

Sam rolled and got up from the ground. His breath reeked of cheap alcohol and blood splattered over his bare chest.

Not his own, I was sure.

"Oh, lookie here. We have an Alpha fight, do we?" Sam sneered and I stood up from my crouched position.

Clayton moved from behind me, the strong pup crawling away to a safer distance.

I focused back on the man in front of me. "You're not an Alpha. You never were."

Alphas were born, not made. And Sam got the title out of luck of survival. Not because, like me, he was the son of an Alpha wolf.

Sam snarled at me. "Well, I'm the only one my pack has, and that means I do what I want, when I want."

My wolf receded into my mind and I breathed a sigh of relief as I focused on the pathetic man in front of me. "Yeah, I know what that means. You sit at home, lazy as fuck, as your pack does the work you should be doing. Meanwhile, you beat the shit out of your mate every day. Yeah, great Alpha you are Sam. Our ancestors would be disgusted."

I spat on the ground for emphasis and heard the growl roll through my opponent.

Sam's eyes opened and his nostrils flared like a racehorse. "He's mine," he declared, speaking of the mate he abused so often.

Clayton's whimper from behind me broke my heart in a way I couldn't describe. Pain shot through my core and fire burst along my spine. My vision disappeared and I saw red for the first time in my life. "No," I growled out through the haze that clouded my brain. I shook myself and focused hard to see the other wolf's face.

Sam's eyebrows rose comically high. "What did you say?"

He seemed more shocked than anything, and for the first time in my life, I did something really stupid.

"I said no. You cannot have him. Not today, not any day. I'll take him back to my pack and the women can look after him."

Sam's mouth contorted into a frown and his eyes began to change. The iris disappeared as Sam's pupils dilated. He was about to do something monumentally stupid, and probably get us both killed.

I glanced over to where Clayton lay tightly curled up in a messy ball, and I couldn't find an ounce of regret if that was what came out of today. I looked back at Sam, and just as I had assumed he would do, he'd gone down onto all fours. He was going to shift, and he'd kill me if I stayed in human form.

The growl that rolled through his chest as brown fur sprouted from his back, made my black-coated Alpha race to the forefront of my mind.

My eye sight changed to that of my wolf and I swallowed hard the answering growl that rose.

"What is this?" a calm voice said next to me, and I pulled my wolf back inside with every ounce of strength I still had.

I stood up straight and looked the vampire elder in the eye. "A disagreement, Vincent."

Sam was too far gone, and in complete wolf form now.

"Wonderful," Vincent purred, his once brown eyes now glowing red. "Then I think I can end the disagreement once and for all."

He flicked his wrist in the air, sentencing Sam, and I moved back. At the signal to feed, ten hungry vampires surrounded the brown wolf.

Told you. Beta.

Alphas were always black. And no one, not even an arrogant try-hard, could change those genetics that told the world who we were.

Sam's wolf snapped his jaws as he crouched lower to the ground. He looked as though he wanted to attack back, but he'd lose this battle.

The vampires descended on him in a fury of sharp teeth and clawed hands. Sam's wolf whimpered and then I heard the human scream out, his body naturally shifting back to his human form as the pain overwhelmed him. They continued to feed far past their usual time, and a sinking feeling hit my gut. This wasn't a feeding, this was as execution. And there was nothing I could do.

I stepped back and pressed against the wall of the building, Clayton's whimpers growing louder and louder beside me.

"Shhhh," I soothed him, squatting down and reaching out for his bloodied shoulder.

He flinched and cried out as I made contact, so I took my hand straight back.

"Don't draw attention to yourself. Stop. I won't hurt you," I urged him.

Although Vincent and I had come to an agreement a long time ago for a relative peace between us, these vampires were unpredictable and vicious creatures

Finally, the frenzy stopped and there was little more than a bag of bones and rotting flesh in a pile on the dirt. The vampires laughed between themselves and wiped their mouths with their sleeves. They hadn't fed like that in a long time. I couldn't remember the last time.

"I think we need to bring back more executions," Vincent joked, his razor-sharp teeth glistening in the dark.

Shouldn't have reminded them how much they like draining people.

"Angus. Come here," Vincent said, his tone soft and deadly.

I pushed myself up and walked back over to him. Surely he didn't need any more blood tonight?

"Yes, Vincent."

"Tell me what the disagreement was about."

I hesitated, not sure how much to reveal, nor what the outcome would be. But in this world, there was never any certainty, so lying was never a good policy.

"Sam was beating his mate to death and I couldn't stand by and watch it happen. So, I stopped him."

Vincent's eyes flicked behind me and then back. "And you want the boy?"

God, yes. But he's not mine to have.

I swallowed hard against the lustful thoughts that I'd always pushed away. "My pack will look after him."

Vincent lifted his lip in a sneer. "He does not look strong, Angus. He will be of no use to your pack."

They'd weeded out anyone who couldn't keep up with the work we did. I straightened to my full height and looked the vampire directly in the eye. "He's stronger than he looks. He's taken beatings that would have killed other men."

Vincent looked unconvinced, but what could he say to such a thing? "Then he is yours, but make sure he pulls his weight. You know what happens to those that don't serve the community, Angus."

I nodded, clenching my jaw against the retort that sprung to mind. There were many in the community, like Sam, who were lazy drunks. But my pack was strong and we drew the most interest, and thus the most ridicule.

"Not a problem, Vincent."

"Make sure you do, because I will hold you personally responsible for him."

I nodded at the thinly veiled threat and the vampires disappeared into the night like they'd never been. I exhaled in a long sigh and turned back around.

Clayton was still where I'd left him. His bedraggled hair fell over his battered face.

"Come on, little one. You're coming home with me."

He didn't move, and I could almost feel his pain as the blood continued to drip down his back.

"Can you walk? Or would you like me to carry you?"

He shook his head and awkwardly climbed to his feet. His shoulders were unbalanced and hunched. The bones in his back protruded as though the skin could barely contain them.

I swallowed hard against the pity and shame that rose in my heart. What sort of monster did this to a defenseless Beta? If that's what he was. I'd never really thought about Clayton's origins before.

"This way." I gestured to our building that lay opposite the one he'd lived in.

Clayton hobbled across the road and into my building wearing only a pair of tattered pants.

I passed by Silky, who shot me a worried look. "Are you going to look after him?" she asked.

I nodded once. "I'll send for you if I need some help."

God only knew how he'd deal with an Alpha caring for him after that asshole of a Beta had treated him so badly.

"Good luck then," she said, her face full of something I couldn't quite read. Sadness perhaps?

I smiled back at her. "Thanks. I'm going to need it."

Download: HERE

SAVING THE OMEGA

NEW WORLD SHIFTERS BOOK 2

CHAPTER 1
ANGUS.

They were at it again. Fighting.

Though, could you really call it that when one man was doing all the yelling and hitting, while the other stood there, or often knelt down, and just took it?

I shook my head and turned away from the sight that turned my stomach almost every day. How could Sam treat his mate in such a way? Clayton was such a beautiful boy, and I'd never seen him do a thing wrong by Sam.

Anger rippled in my gut as I fought the need to intervene. He wasn't in my pack, so technically I shouldn't. But how could I just stand by and watch this happen?

It's not your place. Get moving.

I forced myself to look away from the sight of the young man cowering against the fence surrounding Sam's pack's property.

Clayton wasn't my concern. I had enough to deal with to keep my own pack safe, but what I wouldn't give to bring the boy over to us. To keep him safe. My wolf inside my mind howled at the injustice, making my arms vibrate with the strength it took to keep him down.

I forced myself to lift my feet, turn away and trudge towards my workstation. If Clayton had been my mate, I'd never treat him that way. I'd never treat anyone that way.

I nodded at Jeff and Dave, two Beta's from my pack, as we walked up the hill towards the power station. The rest of my pack trailed behind me.

In this new world, a world that had gone to hell, I was nothing.

Nothing but the strongest man in the whole bloody town. What did that mean, though, in a place where vampires ruled by fear and force, and my pack was on the bottom of the ladder because we didn't suck up to those blood suckers?

The vampires were a problem we needed to remedy. In the decade since our world had changed forever, I lost most of my strongest men to the pack wars.

Ten years ago, a paranormal being released a virus into the world that killed off every human on the planet. Some said he was a shifter, or a demon. The vampires, of course, believed he was one of theirs, power hungry creatures that they were.

Maybe he was a half-breed that hated us all equally? I didn't know. What I did know was that he had been crazy to attempt what he'd achieved.

Absolutely fucking crazy.

I still couldn't believe he'd succeeded in making Earth a paranormal planet. Whoever thought our lives would be okay after killing off most of the population of Earth had been sorely mistaken. We'd been left with a rotting world, full of dead human bodies, and a chaos of fighting paranormal beings. Each faction wanted whatever land and power there was left to claim.

In some parts of the U.S, I'd heard the fighting still continued, but here, in what had been beautiful San Francisco, we'd worked out a pecking order of sorts. Unfortunately, us wolf shifters came out somewhere in the middle.

I was once the Alpha of a powerful pack. The Highland Wolves. We had good jobs and we worked well in the human world.

So, when everyone around us died, and all the shifters and

vampires that were left began fighting for whatever power was left, we fought too.

To the demise of almost everyone I loved.

What was left of my pack now lived in dilapidated homes in an apartment block we'd cleared out of the humans. At least we were all together.

There were no shops anymore. No supermarkets. Barely enough clean water for everyone, but that wasn't something I needed to worry about. That was the feline shifters' job.

Thanks to us Highland Wolves who kept the power station running, the city had a little electricity. It was a physically laborious job, but it kept my mind from wandering too much to the old days.

"Hey, Angus." Silky stepped up next to me, her slinky smile a ghost of the woman I'd once known.

"Hey," I returned and rubbed my arm along hers.

Silky, a female of our bloodlines, lived in the apartment above mine. None of the females shifted in our packs, not that we could do so now anyway. The vampires had made all animal shifting illegal.

She kept my bed warm most nights, but there was little between us except the urge to stay alive. Affection was essential for any wolf, but as an Alpha, I felt the lack of true affection keenly. I had dreams of being surrounded by my children and the pack, gathering their bodies and pulling them atop me to prevent them from being cold.

As an Alpha of my pack, I'd been told since birth that I would have a fated mate and I looked forward to the day that I would meet the one person meant for me.

That had been before the end of our world, and the end to all good things in our lives. Perhaps my mate had already been killed? Or she lived on the other side of the States? Either way, I'd resigned myself to the fact that I would never have a true mate now, and kept forcing myself to bond with Silky, or whichever female begged for my attention. However, it was a cold, nasty business, and I knew to my core that this wasn't how life was meant to be.

I lifted my head and looked up at the looming building ahead of us. My pack's job for the day, every day, was to keep the electricity station running. Which meant physical labor for all of us, but it was for a good cause.

The other shifters performed other jobs and if they didn't work, the vamps made sure they paid for it in kind.

The vampires still needed blood to stay *alive*, and although humans were their favorite meal, no more of those existed. Which meant we either did our job, or they fed on us. They said our children tasted the sweetest.

I had the bite marks to prove how often I'd gotten in the way of the vamps trying to feed on one of our kids. Luckily, I was too valuable to them to drain, and I didn't think they liked the taste of me too much. The distaste on their faces always appeared comical after a feed of my Alpha blood.

As an Alpha, it ate at my pride that I would be food for the vampires that ruled our town. But they kept us on a short leash with their threat against our children, and I had to admit that they did keep an order to things.

Before the vamps moved in, the shifters were killing each other.

At least that had all stopped.

"Do you think we'll ever get out of here?" Silky asked as we stepped into the old power station.

Most of the machinery didn't work anymore, so we needed to move the machines and cogs by hand. An arduous and painful task.

We provided the town with enough power to cook the food for us all, and generally kept our homes warm for part of the night.

"Honestly, I don't know. If I knew of a safe place we could go, then I'd be gone in a shot. And I'd be taking you all with me."

"But what about the vampires?" she asked.

I shrugged. I hadn't decided yet if the vampires were the best of the evils at the moment, or not. Either way, my pack should not be living under the rule of anyone.

"We have twelve hours of sunlight every day when they can't touch us, Silky. We just need a plan."

The vampires had their daylight watchers. Cougar shifters. Nasty beasts. But even the cougars would be hard pressed to match us in a fight, especially if the wolf shifter packs combined.

Silky nodded and lifted a basket of coal up from the ground.

"Well, let me know when you have a plan. Anywhere has to be better than this."

She turned away to her task and my gaze flashed over the white scars on her neck. She'd taken many vampire feedings too, over the years.

Anger rolled in my gut like a storm and I clenched my hands into massive fists. Fuck it. We had to get out of here and soon.

With every passing day, I could feel my wolf rising to the surface to fight for my pack. To correct the injustice that was now our world.

But if we escaped, would it be to a world that was better, or worse, than this one?

I forced myself into the monotonous rhythm of heavy work, wishing myself back to the days of fire-fighting. I'd loved my job, and thanks to my superior strength and instincts, had been on my path to be captain.

That was never going to happen now.

"You coming over tonight?" I asked Silky, as we trudged back down the hill after sun down. It had been a few days since she'd graced my bed, and I could feel the increased levels of testosterone in my blood needing the release.

The vamps would be up and it would be feeding time. For everyone.

"Maybe not tonight. I'm on babysitting duty for Teri and Martha. Tomorrow though?"

I gave her a smile and a nod. "Sure."

The women all shared child-raising responsibilities, even those that had none themselves. Our pack still looked after one another, which was soothing to see. Not everything was broken in this world.

"Seriously. Doesn't he have anything better to do?" Silky's voice was full of disgust as we arrived back at our building.

I didn't want to look, but as the sounds of flesh being pummeled caught my hearing, I had to see how bad it was.

Sam was at it again. Beating on Clayton in the most sadistic way. Pulling his hair and dragging him around the dirt that lay at the front of their building to degrade him as much as possible.

A yelp and a scream had me turning towards them rather than walking away as I normally would have. Sam swung a lump of wood, and was beating Clay on the back while the young man tried to protect himself by curling into a ball. The thump of the plank against his back had me cringing hard.

Nobody moved.

Heat seared along my veins, anger building in me liking a rising storm.

Another helpless cry from Clayton filled the air. Another disgusting display of brutality as blood covered the wooden bat Sam raised high in the air once again. This had to stop, and if no one else was going to save him, then the time had come for me to.

"Stop. Now," I growled out and stormed across the road.

Stay down. Stay down.

"Angus! No."

I heard Silky's warning, but I was way past caring. I pulled open the old gate that marked entrance to Sam's apartments and tightened my hands into fists.

Sam raised the lump of wood again, his face a grotesque mask of anger as I charged forward. I put both hands out in front of me, aiming for his chest. I ran straight into him and knocked him to the ground.

I stood in front of Clayton's bloodied form and clenched both fists tight.

Stay down. Stay down, I urged my wolf.

Shifting was forbidden by the vamps. They said it was to keep the peace, but I knew it was because we were stronger than them in wolf form. They had one thing over us though. Their bite was deadly to us when we were in wolf form, so I didn't know why they bothered with the rule.

Sam rolled and got up from the ground. His breath reeked of cheap alcohol and blood splattered over his bare chest.

Not his own, I was sure.

"Oh, lookie here. We have an Alpha fight, do we?" Sam sneered and I stood up from my crouched position.

Clayton moved from behind me, the strong pup crawling away to a safer distance.

I focused back on the man in front of me. "You're not an Alpha. You never were."

Alphas were born, not made. And Sam got the title out of luck of survival. Not because, like me, he was the son of an Alpha wolf.

Sam snarled at me. "Well, I'm the only one my pack has, and that means I do what I want, when I want."

My wolf receded into my mind and I breathed a sigh of relief as I focused on the pathetic man in front of me. "Yeah, I know what that means. You sit at home, lazy as fuck, as your pack does the work you should be doing. Meanwhile, you beat the shit out of your mate every day. Yeah, great Alpha you are Sam. Our ancestors would be disgusted."

I spat on the ground for emphasis and heard the growl roll through my opponent.

Sam's eyes opened and his nostrils flared like a racehorse. "He's mine," he declared, speaking of the mate he abused so often.

Clayton's whimper from behind me broke my heart in a way I couldn't describe. Pain shot through my core and fire burst along my spine. My vision disappeared and I saw red for the first time in my life. "No," I growled out through the haze that clouded my brain. I shook myself and focused hard to see the other wolf's face.

Sam's eyebrows rose comically high. "What did you say?"

He seemed more shocked than anything, and for the first time in my life, I did something really stupid.

"I said no. You cannot have him. Not today, not any day. I'll take him back to my pack and the women can look after him."

Sam's mouth contorted into a frown and his eyes began to change. The iris disappeared as Sam's pupils dilated. He was about to do something monumentally stupid, and probably get us both killed.

I glanced over to where Clayton lay tightly curled up in a messy ball, and I couldn't find an ounce of regret if that was what came out of today. I looked back at Sam, and just as I had assumed he would do, he'd gone down onto all fours. He was going to shift, and he'd kill me if I stayed in human form.

The growl that rolled through his chest as brown fur sprouted from his back, made my black-coated Alpha race to the forefront of my mind.

My eye sight changed to that of my wolf and I swallowed hard the answering growl that rose.

"What is this?" a calm voice said next to me, and I pulled my wolf back inside with every ounce of strength I still had.

I stood up straight and looked the vampire elder in the eye. "A disagreement, Vincent."

Sam was too far gone, and in complete wolf form now.

"Wonderful," Vincent purred, his once brown eyes now glowing red. "Then I think I can end the disagreement once and for all."

He flicked his wrist in the air, sentencing Sam, and I moved back. At the signal to feed, ten hungry vampires surrounded the brown wolf.

Told you. Beta.

Alphas were always black. And no one, not even an arrogant try-hard, could change those genetics that told the world who we were.

Sam's wolf snapped his jaws as he crouched lower to the ground. He looked as though he wanted to attack back, but he'd lose this battle.

The vampires descended on him in a fury of sharp teeth and clawed hands. Sam's wolf whimpered and then I heard the human scream out, his body naturally shifting back to his human form as the pain overwhelmed him. They continued to feed far past their usual time, and a sinking feeling hit my gut. This wasn't a feeding, this was as execution. And there was nothing I could do.

I stepped back and pressed against the wall of the building, Clayton's whimpers growing louder and louder beside me.

"Shhhh," I soothed him, squatting down and reaching out for his bloodied shoulder.

He flinched and cried out as I made contact, so I took my hand straight back.

"Don't draw attention to yourself. Stop. I won't hurt you," I urged him.

Although Vincent and I had come to an agreement a long time ago for a relative peace between us, these vampires were unpredictable and vicious creatures

Finally, the frenzy stopped and there was little more than a bag of bones and rotting flesh in a pile on the dirt. The vampires laughed between themselves and wiped their mouths with their sleeves. They hadn't fed like that in a long time. I couldn't remember the last time.

"I think we need to bring back more executions," Vincent joked, his razor-sharp teeth glistening in the dark.

Shouldn't have reminded them how much they like draining people.

"Angus. Come here," Vincent said, his tone soft and deadly.

I pushed myself up and walked back over to him. Surely he didn't need any more blood tonight?

"Yes, Vincent."

"Tell me what the disagreement was about."

I hesitated, not sure how much to reveal, nor what the outcome would be. But in this world, there was never any certainty, so lying was never a good policy.

"Sam was beating his mate to death and I couldn't stand by and watch it happen. So, I stopped him."

Vincent's eyes flicked behind me and then back. "And you want the boy?"

God, yes. But he's not mine to have.

I swallowed hard against the lustful thoughts that I'd always pushed away. "My pack will look after him."

Vincent lifted his lip in a sneer. "He does not look strong, Angus. He will be of no use to your pack."

They'd weeded out anyone who couldn't keep up with the work we did. I straightened to my full height and looked the vampire directly in the eye. "He's stronger than he looks. He's taken beatings that would have killed other men."

Vincent looked unconvinced, but what could he say to such a thing? "Then he is yours, but make sure he pulls his weight. You know what happens to those that don't serve the community, Angus."

I nodded, clenching my jaw against the retort that sprung to mind. There were many in the community, like Sam, who were lazy drunks. But my pack was strong and we drew the most interest, and thus the most ridicule.

"Not a problem, Vincent."

"Make sure you do, because I will hold you personally responsible for him."

I nodded at the thinly veiled threat and the vampires disappeared into the night like they'd never been. I exhaled in a long sigh and turned back around.

Clayton was still where I'd left him. His bedraggled hair fell over his battered face.

"Come on, little one. You're coming home with me."

He didn't move, and I could almost feel his pain as the blood continued to drip down his back.

"Can you walk? Or would you like me to carry you?"

He shook his head and awkwardly climbed to his feet. His shoulders were unbalanced and hunched. The bones in his back protruded as though the skin could barely contain them.

I swallowed hard against the pity and shame that rose in my heart. What sort of monster did this to a defenseless Beta? If that's what he was. I'd never really thought about Clayton's origins before.

"This way." I gestured to our building that lay opposite the one he'd lived in.

Clayton hobbled across the road and into my building wearing only a pair of tattered pants.

I passed by Silky, who shot me a worried look. "Are you going to look after him?" she asked.

I nodded once. "I'll send for you if I need some help."

God only knew how he'd deal with an Alpha caring for him after that asshole of a Beta had treated him so badly.

"Good luck then," she said, her face full of something I couldn't quite read. Sadness perhaps?

I smiled back at her. "Thanks. I'm going to need it."

CHAPTER 2
CLAYTON.

One more step. Just one more step.

I dragged my bad leg down the cold corridor and bit my lip to stop myself from screaming out against the pain. It was like knives running up and down my thigh. But I'd had worse.

The Alpha—Angus I think his name is—he'd tell me where to go.

When I couldn't feel him behind me anymore, I turned around to see him with that scruffy female he always hung around. Why he chose her for a bedmate, I'd never know.

"Next door on your left," he yelled out to me, and I turned back to my job. To get inside. Away from the vampires, and my old pack who would surely blame me for the death of Sam. A shiver coursed up my spine that intensified the pain in my back. I blinked back the tears and trudged up the hallway to my destination.

It was a horrible thing to admit to, or even think, but I had been so happy when those vampires had come and drained Sam. I'd never been so relieved in all my life. To see that man, a man I had trusted and tried to love, who had beaten me half to death for months, die.

Good riddance.

I lifted my shaking arm and pushed open the heavy door.

The room was clean and didn't smell like our building. Not moldy at all.

I dragged my body inside and stood trembling for the Alpha to inspect me. What would he want me to do in return for this sanctuary?

Nothing I hadn't done before, I was sure. Though I could feel the strain in my muscles and I knew my body was ready to give up, my mind remained unbroken. I didn't think I could cope with another beating like the one I just encountered, but would Angus do that after saving me from the same thing?

"Are you okay?" came the soft question behind me.

I turned around to see Angus step into the room and shut the door.

The lights were on in the living room. A blessing from the pack that had saved me. They made the electricity work in a time where such things were extreme luxuries.

"Ah..." How did he want me to answer that? Did I look okay?

"I'm sorry. That was a stupid question," Angus corrected himself. "Well, I should probably lay out the ground rules for you."

I heaved in a breath and nodded once. This was where he would tell me what I needed to do for my food and shelter.

"No one is allowed to hit you, ever again. Me included."

Huh?

My head came up and I stared at the Alpha, heat rippling through my chest as I finally looked at him properly. He was such a good-looking man. Why had I never really noticed before?

Angus. Like the bull. Short dark hair, a strong jaw, and muscled like a large animal.

"Unfortunately, you'll be required to work with us in the power plant, but I'll work a few extra hours the first couple of days to make up your quota while you heal."

"Sorry? You're going to work...for me?" Surely he hadn't just said that?

"Of course. You can't work in the state you're in, and as your Alpha now, it is my job to protect you."

I snorted, unable to help myself.

Angus sighed. "I can imagine you don't have a very positive view on pack structure at the moment, but you need to know that Sam wasn't an Alpha. He was a Beta, and a sadistic bastard. He should never have been running your pack." He cleared his throat and looked down for a moment. "And on a personal note, I'm so sorry I didn't step in earlier."

I raised my gaze to Angus's again. "What do you need from me, for this...kindness?" I managed to ask.

He was a handsome man. I was sure I would be able to handle his body if he wanted me.

Angus gazed at me with a strange, pitying look. "I told you. Unfortunately, you'll need to work if we're all to eat in this fucked up world."

"Well, of course, but what else?"

Did I really need to spell it out?

I felt sorry for the guy when he finally got it. His eyebrows went really wide and then his mouth moved up and down in shock for a while, like an old cartoon character I used to watch as a child.

"You think I'd demand... Hell no!" Angus spluttered. "No Beta in my pack gets abused like that."

"I'm not a Beta," I explained, because obviously the Alpha didn't know what I was. Hopefully it didn't change Angus's view of me.

He took a step closer and dropped his voice. "What are you then?"

There was only one other option, and he knew it. He obviously wanted me to say it.

"I'm an Omega. A freak. An aberration, if Sam was to be believed."

The complete opposite of what my parents had taught me as a child, but hey, who was I to question the guy beating in to me?

"You're a.... Damn.... That explains it." Angus staggered sideways and crashed into the couch, sitting down on the worn cushions in a way that spoke of true shock.

"What's wrong?" I asked, panic flitting through my chest at the idea that he didn't want me. No one seemed to want me anymore.

"Ah...um...nothing." Angus shook his head as though he'd been hit over the head by a frying pan.

I took a few shallow breaths, waiting for him to move, but he didn't. Perhaps he wouldn't kick me out just yet?

I needed to make myself as presentable as possible. "Ah... May I... wash myself?" I asked, hating to ask anything of the Alpha already, but I was disgusted by the filth on my body.

Despite the fact that I couldn't shape shift, my father's shifter genes were strong in me. I healed faster than most of the pack, and I could already feel my back knitting together in that itchy way it had.

I flinched as I looked down at myself. The blood on my pants was gross. I was crispy and disgusting all over. I didn't want to think about how badly I'd smell to the Alpha on the couch.

Angus jumped up like a fire alarm had gone off. "Yes! I'm sorry, of course."

He was sorry? What for?

"This way, Omega." He directed me into the bathroom, which was the whitest, cleanest bathroom I'd seen in years.

"Wow. Who does your cleaning?"

He shrugged. "One of the women. Those that are in charge of the children clean everyone's homes as well."

I reached out to touch one of the cream tiles and saw the blackened skin and red splatter on my arm, so I pulled it back and didn't touch the clean bathroom.

"We have some hot water, and use this soap if you can. Are there any open wounds you need me to help you with?" Angus asked, and I tried not to flinch when he came too close.

He was showing me nothing but kindness. He wouldn't like me flinching away all the time. But it was hard when he was so big. Bigger than any other wolf shifter I'd met.

Sam hadn't like the way I flinched away from *his* touch, but I hadn't been able to stop myself then.

There was something different about this Alpha, though. I could feel the kindness in him. The strength and the calm. Just like the Alpha who'd led our pack, back before the world flipped on its head.

"Ah... thank you Alpha Angus."

"Just Angus, please," he croaked out.

"All right."

I reached for the taps and twisted them until heavenly warm water flowed. Steam began to rise around us. It wasn't as clean as the water of old, but it was drinkable, and that was enough.

I pushed my disgusting pants down my legs and stepped beneath the spray before I had a chance to be nervous. Angus was still standing there watching me, and although I knew that the wolf shifters were used to being naked around each other, it had been years since the packs had been allowed to shift.

I gasped at the pain sluicing down my skin. Like hot needles, piercing my skin over and over. The heat of the water made my bruises and cuts sting, though I was grateful for the cleansing of my wounds.

I forced myself to breathe deep. In, out. In, out.

My skin was mending. There weren't any more cuts now. I could sense that and needed to stay focused on the healing. Not on the man staring at me.

What must he think of all my protruding bones and lack of muscle? Compared to him I was a literal skeleton. A reminder of how badly I'd been treated for so many years.

I tipped back my head and let the water run through my dirty hair. How long had it been since I'd had a proper wash? A month? Longer?

Would Angus be totally disgusted by me?

I cracked an eye open and risked a glance at him. He was still staring at me, his gaze roaming over my body, but I couldn't see any disgust in his face.

I glanced down at the red and brown muddied water and grimaced. The women who cleaned this bathroom were going to hate me for this mess.

I risked another glance up to see Angus staring at me with a longing.

My first reaction on seeing that look was to cower, but instead I searched out his reactions. Responding to an Alpha correctly was one of the many advantages of an Omega, my mother had always said.

Angus was relaxed, happy even. I sensed no violence in him, and yet there was a lusting scent in the air the reeked of his need.

I threw my head back under the water once more and reached for the soap. It was strangely slippery and as I washed the grime from my arms and scrubbed my hair, I remembered the flowery scents of my childhood baths. This was the closest I'd gotten to such a thing in ten years.

He didn't move, just continued to watch me silently as I became cleaner.

"Would you like a shower too?" I asked, afraid of using all the water.

Angus's mouth twisted up. "I probably should. Been working all day." He reached over his head and pulled his black T-shirt off. The huge muscles in his arms and shoulders rippled in a dangerously sexy way. Then his jeans descended to the tiles and he stood up.

My mouth ran dry as my gaze zoned in on one area of his Gus's massive body.

"Ignore this, okay?" He gestured to the massive erection he had and I nodded quickly.

How could I ignore that?

Despite having an asshole of a mate, he hadn't turned me off men completely. And Angus was one hell of a man.

You must be delusional if you're getting hot over a guy, an hour after your mate was killed in front of you.

The Alpha handed me a light green towel and I took it,

exchanging places with him so that he could scrub himself beneath the warm water.

He turned the taps hard so that I soon felt the cold spray on my face as he doused himself in freezing water. He gasped a little, but scrubbed his skin of its day's dirt, then flicked off the taps quickly. His cock was now at half mast, after its blast of cold water. What a shame...

Total boner killer.

"Should I be apologizing for getting your mate killed, Clayton?" Angus asked, standing there like a God. His muscles bunched with massive strength and water dripped from his skin in a way that made me want to offer my tongue for a towel.

I licked my dry lips and handed him my towel, letting my clean nakedness show through.

He took the towel and dried himself quickly, wrapping it around his waist and covering himself from view.

"No. He was as mean as a snake and I'm not sorry he's gone," I finally answered, lifting my head high.

I knew my face was still a mess, but it would heal. I'd been good looking once, and hopefully I would be again, and then Angus would want me.

A smile spread across his face and my gut tightened with arousal.

Seriously...my healing must have just reached light speed.

"Good. Now, let's find you a place to sleep."

"What do you mean?"

He wanted me to sleep apart from him?

"I mean, this apartment has two bedrooms, so if you want to sleep in the other room—"

"No. No I don't," I rushed to say.

I didn't want to be alone, and the last thing I wanted was for him to find a reason to toss me out. Or worse, hand me back to the pack who stood by while I was abused for so long.

Angus straightened up, his massive shoulders causing a quake in my gut. Fear, or desire, I wasn't sure.

"How old are you Clayton?" he asked unexpectedly.

I didn't hesitate to answer. "Twenty-six."

Which meant I was old enough to remember how good life had been for us all, before that psycho had condemned us to a world of fighting and death. I hoped he was six foot under somewhere.

His shoulders relaxed and he blew out a sigh of relief. "Oh, good. You look a hell of a lot younger than that."

"And you?" I asked him, swallowing the lump in my throat.

This felt like a strange version of a date I went on when I was sixteen.

"Oh...ah, thirty-five. I think. Yeah. You lose track of time in this world."

I nodded. "You're telling me."

"I have a little food if you want something to eat. I'll get some clothes for you too."

I glanced down at my nakedness and nodded. I hadn't even realized I wasn't wearing any clothes. Sam had rarely allowed me to wear anything but a tatty pair of pants anyway.

We walked out into the small, clean kitchen and Gus pulled down some cans of fruit that I hadn't seen in years. The labels were faded and there was dints in the sides, but it was real fruit.

"Wow, you still have things like this?" I whispered.

He shrugged. "Yeah. Thankfully, I didn't hoover it all when we first got here. I knew it had to last."

He pulled a can opener from a shelf, opened the can, and poured it into a single bowl.

He even pulled a spoon from a drawer.

"This is so...civilized." I managed to say, the ghost of a laugh in my throat.

Angus actually did laugh, the noise both jolting to my fried nervous system and soothing at the same time.

"Yeah... we try. Here. Eat." He pushed the bowl at me. "Wow, you're healing up already."

I picked up the spoon with trembling hands. I hadn't eaten this much in longer than I could remember.

"I'll have a little, and then you have the rest."

Angus laid a gentle hand on my shoulder and I jumped.

"No one's going to hurt you, Clayton. Least of all me. And no, that's all for you. Eat, and I'll find you something to wear."

He disappeared and I stared down at the most colorful, nutritious meal I'd had this decade. I dipped the spoon into the thick juice, scooped half a cut peach onto the spoon, then brought it to my mouth. The sweetness burst across my tongue and I closed my eyes as I chewed, relishing the smoothness of the fruit. The clean taste.

Wow. That's amazing.

I ate slowly, my stomach aching painfully with the constriction of muscles around the unfamiliar food.

When he came back, I'd finished less than half. I'd counted, so that I may leave him the biggest portion. He was, after all, twice my weight. At least.

I glanced up at him and reassessed. *Definitely double.* If he was less than six foot six and two hundred pounds, I'd be surprised.

"Here you go," I said, pushing the bowl towards him.

"Nope, I told you it was a treat for you, but if you want to eat it later, that's fine too. It'll keep until morning. Here you go."

I kept staring at the bowl. There was no way he was going to share such an incredible amount of food with me. Surely not.

I twisted around and stood up on shaky legs.

Angus was dressed in another pair of faded jeans and another black tank top. He handed me a pile of clothes that looked very similar to what he wore. Hopefully they were smaller, though it didn't really matter. They were soft and clean.

"Sorry, I only have the one sort of clothes. It's easier. But I think these are a different size. I haven't worn them."

He handed me even more new clothes. Jeans and a top, the material still stiff as though never worn. Tears stung my eyes.

"Where'd you get all this?"

"In one of the raids of a mall. Before most of them were blown up. I took enough for the whole pack, for a life time. It's turned into a bit of a uniform."

I nodded and pulled the top over my head. I'd noticed that. The uniform look of his pack.

Not that I got to see them all too often. They were always working and I was always tucked away somewhere Sam wanted me.

The top was soft against my battered and bruised skin, but I had to sit down to try the pants on. My legs weren't quite strong enough to balance on one foot yet.

"Ah, since we're going to bed, how 'bout you put these on?"

He handed me a soft pair of leggings.

"What are these?"

"An accident actually. I grabbed some sports clothes as I passed by that section in the mall. But most of the pack don't wear them because they're not tough enough. I still had these for some reason. New, as well."

I pulled on the super soft black leggings and groaned as a warm cloud floated over me. "This is heaven, thank you." My body felt nurtured and settled for the first time in years. Unreal. Just like a dream. Hopefully I didn't wake up, back in my old world anytime soon.

"Not a problem. Do you need any more help with your injuries? I might be able to rustle up some cream, or something?"

"No, no. I'll be healed in a couple of days."

Angus cocked his head to the side. "Yeah, I always wondered how you continued to take such a beating from him. You're healing capacity must be off the charts."

I shrugged. "My mom always said an Omega was special, but in this world, I've known nothing but disdain. I can't shift, I can't lift heavy weights."

Angus stepped closer, his blue eyes alight with something exciting. "You are special. Omega's are a rare breed that are meant for one thing..."

The hairs on my arms rose as he stopped, not finishing a sentence I very much wanted to know the finish of.

"What's that?"

The question hung in the air like a ripe fruit about to burst and as Angus licked his lips, I leaned forward for the answer.

"You're meant to be the mate of an Alpha."

CHAPTER 3

ANGUS.

id I really just say that?

The look on Clayton's face was comical as I took his hand and dragged him into my bedroom. The last thing I wanted to do was force him into a sexual situation, but he needed to know the facts.

My wolf rode high in my mind. I could practically feel him on my back.

Was this my mate? The one I'd been waiting for?

Why had he ended up the mate of that asshole, and not mine?

"How did you come to mate with Sam, Clayton?" I asked as we stepped into my bedroom.

I tugged off my clean clothes and lay them beside the bed, ready for the next day. My belly complained of lack of dinner, but I wasn't going anywhere tonight. I had some other cans of fruit if I needed something later.

I pulled back the sheets and slipped beneath the blankets.

Clayton stood beside the bed blankly, his face crumpled in pain.

"What's wrong?" I asked.

He'd been the one to insist on sleeping in my room and not the other.

"Where would you like me? On the floor?" he asked.

I barked out a laugh. "You're kidding me, right? Get in here." I threw back the covers on his side to emphasize where he should lie. "Though if I grope you a little through the night you'll have to excuse me."

The poor kid had gone through so much, the last thing he needed was my horny self forcing him to have sex with me.

He stripped and scampered over, his skinny body vibrating... With fear? No. I could smell his arousal.

"No. That would be fine. My mother always said I was like an octopus to sleep with," Clayton explained.

I chuckled and let him settle into the bed, his posture stiff and uncomfortable on the soft mattress.

"Look, if you don't want me to touch you, Clayton, I won't. I promise. I'd never force myself on you."

His lips lifted in a smile. "Oh, I know that. Tell me more about this Omega mating thing."

He rolled on his side and faced me, and I mirrored him, stuffing two pillows beneath my head.

"Well, most Alpha's mate with females, obviously. Or you wouldn't get the continuation of the line. Except when you get an Omega born into a pack. An Omega is the perfect mate to an Alpha. I was told by my parents that when mated, the Omega amplifies the Alpha's power."

An incredible thing that I'd never really thought about being my destiny. I'd always assumed that my mate would be female.

"Have you ever known a pairing like that?" Clayton asked me.

"No, I haven't. But the stories are legendary."

Clayton's gaze dropped and a sadness filled his face.

"What's wrong?" I asked.

"Sam always said I was like a major energy suck. He

hated....mating with me. Not that I think we ever mated. Not really, not the way you're meant to. Both souls entwined."

I agreed that a true mating would be more than the average, but there was one thing that didn't make sense to me. I didn't really want to ask, because I didn't want to imagine Sam being with Clayton, but I needed to know.

"What do you mean he hated mating you?"

I couldn't imagine Clayton being anything but a pleasure to bed.

He shrugged. "I don't know. That's why he used to beat me so often. He said I made him feel sick, or something. He could barely get it up half the time."

I shouldn't have laughed but I did, and Clayton's face fell.

"No, please don't take that badly, because you are one sexy thing. I'm having a hard time keeping my hands to myself and my cock is thickening by the minute. If he couldn't get it up, that's on him. Not on you."

Clayton's eyes lit up and he licked his full lips.

"Can I see?"

I wasn't sure if that was a good idea, but I was willing to test out my self-control if it meant giving the Omega the compliment he deserved. "Sure." I rolled onto my back and pushed the covers down.

Clayton licked his lips once again in that sexy way that he had. His gaze focused completely on my cock. Which was throbbing and thick and laying against my belly. Precum glistened on the tip.

"You're big," he said, his hand reaching out for me.

I grabbed his arm before he could touch.

"I'm not sure that's a good idea. You've just been badly hurt and I don't want anything from you, other than your affection."

Clayton cocked his head and stared at me. "But I want to touch you. You don't want me to?"

He sounded confused and I had to laugh. Because it was pretty bloody obvious that I wanted him.

"Of course, I do but how 'bout we wait until you're feeling better?" I let go of his arm and his hand wrapped around my shaft.

"How 'bout we don't wait?" he asked.

"But..."

Clayton began to work my flesh like an expert. Up and down he slid his hand. Sparkles of sensation flitted along my nerve endings and my ability to talk shut down. I tried to.

You should stop.

I should be doing you instead.

But anytime I opened my mouth, nothing but a gasp came out. Then a groan as heat tickled over my balls and hit me in the gut.

Clayton moved forward and put his mouth over me. The exquisite pressure of his wet, warm lips and the squeezing of his hands was too much for me.

I groaned and tried to push him off, but I couldn't touch his back and Clayton pressed down with his mouth more. Engulfing me. Heat raced up my legs and my balls ached. Fire exploded in my gut as pleasure pulsed through my cock and my cum spilled into Clayton's mouth in long, amazing squirts. My hands gripped the sheets beside me as Clayton came off, his soft smile one of pure satisfaction.

"Whoa, Clayton. That was incredible."

He sucked on his lips as though tasting himself. "You taste really good."

I laughed. "Thank God for that. Now you?" I asked.

Could I do the same thing for him? I'd never taken a male lover before, but knowing my own body meant I was sure I could do the same thing for him.

"No. I wanted to do that to say thank you for saving me tonight. My body's not ready for anything else."

I didn't like the sound of that. "Well, please don't do that again unless you want to. You owe me nothing, from now on. Clean slate, okay?"

Clayton nodded. "Okay."

Worry crept into my mind like a thief in the night, but Clayton looked more relaxed now. His eyes were shining with a light they hadn't contained before.

My muscles were turning to liquid and my eyes were heavy lidded. We needed to talk about so many things. His mating with Sam, the roles we would need to play for each other. As I stared down at the first piece of happiness I'd found in years, I couldn't bring myself to speak about it all now.

"Come here, beautiful boy." I carefully drew him closer to me and turned us both over so I could cuddle him from behind.

His back was healing much faster than even my body would have with a beating like that. Which was incredible considering my health and muscle, not to mention my Alpha status. Which, by definition meant I was the biggest and strongest of the pack.

Clayton's shifter genes, although recessive, must be very strong indeed.

I put a hand over his sharp hipbone and dragged his butt against my sated cock. He nestled in like he'd always been there and warmth spread through my chest.

Was this what it felt like to be with your mate?

I didn't want to come to any conclusions too soon, but this was beginning to feel like destiny. Clayton felt like home.

"I'm glad I found you, Clayton."

"Me too." He sighed loudly and relaxed into his pillow.

I'd found something very special here and I was going to hold onto him for as long as I could.

When I woke up hours later, the sun was only just rising over the land and I could see Clayton's thin body in front of me.

His shoulders were rising and falling in time with his breathing. He looked so peaceful and beautiful now. His clean hair held a faint red shine to it that reminded me of my Irish grandmother who loved a good story. I believed she would have loved this one.

Clayton jolted suddenly and rolled, falling out of bed. There was a loud thump, and then nothing. Not a whimper. Complete silence.

It was strangely comical.

"You okay?" I called out to him.

His head popped up like an old jack in the box that I'd had as a child and I smiled at him.

"Forgot where you were?" I asked.

He nodded, his eyes as big as saucers as his gaze darted from me to the bed, and back again.

Poor thing. I couldn't imagine how jarring it must be to go from such a horrible existence to one with care and comfort.

Well, maybe I could imagine...

"Come back for a cuddle. I have to go to the power plant soon."

Clayton slowly crawled up the mattress and stiffly turned back around so that I could spoon him once again.

His back was almost completely healed now, which was phenomenal. There was no sign of the beating he took yesterday, except for some slight bruising. There was however, some faint scars from years ago.

Wow.

I could only imagine how bad those injuries must have been to scar up on one with such amazing healing capacity.

I gripped him tighter against me as anger filled my mind like a seething flood. No one, and certainly not a second-rate Beta, had any right to hurt someone the way Clayton had been hurt.

"I won't let anyone hurt you again, Clayton. You know that right?"

The Omega nodded his head and settled gently against the pillows, his muscles softening against my hand. We lay there in the quiet for a while as the sun rose and filled the room with yellow light.

The air around us was still, peaceful. And I never wanted to move. Outside this room there was only work, and frustration. Little to eat, and shifters that had been broken to within an inch of their sanity.

In this room, there was peace, and perhaps a burgeoning connection that could one day transition into real love.

I blew out an annoyed breath, resigned to my fate. I pressed my lips to Clayton's bony back and prepared myself to roll out of bed. I had to. I'd promised Vincent even more power than normal today because of Clayton, so I really needed to get up.

"Gah. Time to move."

I pulled away from his warmth and grabbed my clothes, amazed at how truly reluctant I was to leave him. I'd known him so short a time, and yet I already craved his nearness. That had never happened before. With anyone.

"Wait, I'll come with you."

"No, stay please. Trust me, once you start this life, you'll never stop. So, enjoy your last day of not working."

Clayton rolled out of bed shaking his head. "No, please take me with you."

He grabbed for his shirt and quickly pulled it on over his thin frame. Then he stumbled out of the room, coming back a few moments later with the too-big jeans on his skinny legs.

Determined little thing, isn't he?

"We'll have to get you some rope or something to keep those up," I joked, a memory surfacing. Like a leaf on a pond. My grandfather tying some twine around my waist when I was a little kid. I loved dressing up in his clothes.

I shook my head in frustration, hating my sentimental brain for bringing up painful memories.

Clayton bent over and cuffed the jeans up at his ankles, then rolled the waistband over so that they fit a little better.

Still too big. He looked like a clown, but at least now they won't fall down when he walks.

"I'm coming with you," Clayton repeated, meeting my gaze with his own steely determination. His jaw was set in a way I'd barely seen anyone have the strength to exhibit in years. He wasn't being left behind, and I had no idea why.

"Why are you so determined, Clayton?" I asked.

A misplaced sense of loyalty perhaps? He really owed me nothing. I actually felt like I owed him an apology. I'd roped him in to a debt with the vampires, a life of manual labor.

Clayton bit his lower lip in that adorable way he had and flicked his hair out of his eyes. It really did need to be tamed.

"Because I need to feel useful. To be a part of your pack. Please don't leave me behind, alone."

told him.

He fiddled with his over-sized top and eventually settled on tying the T-shirt in a knot at the bottom corner. Then he walked over to me. "Let's go."

A smile kicked up my lips as pride blossomed in my chest. At any time, even before the world had turned on its head, I would have been proud to have this man as my mate.

"Alright, but you have to tell me why you're so determined to come today."

He sighed. "Well, mostly because I don't know how my old pack is going to treat me now. They're not going to be happy that I got Sam killed, and they're only across the road. They could easily sneak in here when you're up at the power plant and kill me for vengeance."

That was a reasonable fear, considering our packs' rules. An Alpha's death needed to be avenged. But that man was no Alpha.

"You didn't get Sam killed, I did. Well, that's wrong too. He got himself killed. Stupid idiot. He should have controlled his temper better."

Clayton grabbed my arm and squeezed tight. "Please, Angus, don't leave me behind. I need to come with you."

I sighed, my resistance waning. The last thing I wanted to do was take a man who'd been beaten soundly yesterday up to the power station to work. The Omega had no idea how physically hard the work would be for him.

But then again, I'd seen his back myself this morning, and he looked fully restored.

"You're feeling up to it? You sure?"

Clayton gave me a smile that made my heart twinge. His face was so beautiful when it lit up like that. I'd never really thought much about how attractive he was before. I'd known I was drawn to him, but his skin was as smooth as a peach, and his lips called out for my kiss.

"Okay. Come."

I tilted my head and he fell in beside me as we walked out of the apartment block and into the warm sunshine. It was too early for any of Clayton's old pack to be awake, so we made our way up the road to the power station for one of the better days I'd had in a long time.

"You worked hard today, well done," I said to Clayton as we walked back down the hill, covered in grime and grease. He'd gained even more respect from me today, which had been a hard thing to improve on. The small Omega had a gritty type of determination and strength that was at odds with his thin body type and pretty face.

Clayton grinned at me, wiping at a trickle of blood sliding down his arm from where he'd run into one of the broken pipes.

"Thanks. That was actually kinda invigorating. I haven't been able to use my body like that for so long."

He arched his back and stretched out his arms to the sides, the thin muscles rippling with strength.

I ran my gaze over his frame. "You're strong for someone your size."

He chuckled. "And you're the strongest man I've ever seen. Wow. I mean, the work you did today was incredible."

A strange warmth flushed into my face and I glanced away. I could lift anything, and I pushed more metal around than three of the Betas put together, but that was expected from me.

"Yeah, well...thanks. But that's normal for an Alpha. We're designed to be the biggest and strongest so that we can protect our pack against...well...everyone."

A strange lump formed in my throat. I swallowed it down, though my esophagus felt like it was full of razor wire. I'd failed in so many ways over the past decade. So many moments when I'd regretting living. Wishing I'd died along with my parents.

Clayton smiled softly, bringing me back to the present. "It must be hard for you then. To bow down for the vampires."

I nodded, touched by the strong empathy shown by the Omega. No one else had made such an observation. "Harder than you can imagine. In the old world, they stayed away from us. Fed on the humans."

But so much had changed.

"Yeah, life's shit now, isn't it?" Clayton shook his head with a grimace.

I smiled and reached out for him, patting him on the shoulder. I was the happiest I'd been in years. "Not so shitty for me at the moment."

Someone bumped into me as they moved past, shoving me into Clayton.

"Hey..."

Silky shot me a narrowed, angry look over her shoulder as she hurried past.

"What the?"

Damn, she looks pissed off.

"What's with her?" Clayton asked. "Isn't she the one you used to fuck?"

I choked on my laugh. "Pardon?"

How did he know such a thing?

"Oh, well, I've always noticed everything about you. Even if I wasn't supposed to. I... Well..."

I held up my hand to interrupt, stopping his flow of nervousness. Like I had blushed earlier, his cheeks were glowingly pink now too.

"I like that." And I did. I loved the fact that Clayton had been watching me, probably for as long as I'd been watching him.

"Do you think that means that we're mates, Angus?" he asked suddenly.

I put my arm around his shoulders and headed towards the main eating area for whatever they'd made for us today. My beautiful lover against me and my heart light and carefree.

"Maybe, Clayton... Maybe."

CHAPTER 4
CLAYTON.

inner tasted better than it had in years. With Angus by my side, they fed me a proper serving of the strange stew the women made. It was hot, and salty, and filled my stomach so well I could practically feel my muscles bulging with the protein.

Gratitude for Angus's presence in my life flowed over me like a cleansing rain. Yesterday I had been treated worse than any dog I'd ever met, and today I was actually happy. Full of food, covered in the dirt of a good day's work.

Not the dirt from our front lawn where Sam had kicked me.

I couldn't believe how much had changed in so short a space of time, and it was all due to the beautiful man before me. I watched him as he spoke to members of his pack. The attraction that had built between us all day sat low in my belly like a heavy stone.

I loved watching him, no matter what he was doing. His huge muscles had flexed and bulged today as he worked at the power plant. I'd been hard up trying to concentrate on my job while he worked in front of me.

I wanted him.

And that wasn't a feeling I'd had in a long time.

Sam had been a selfish, and sometimes violent lover. I couldn't remember the last time I'd cum with him. But as I stared at Angus, I knew it would be different. That this huge man who looked after his pack so well, would also perhaps look after me.

When I'd finished my food, I sidled up next to him and took his hand in mine. His fingers were roughly callused, and I clung to them.

He turned immediately to me, his eyebrows drawn low in concern. "Are you alright?"

I nodded, nervous energy making my heart pound faster and my throat tighten. "Could we go back to your apartment soon?" I gave him the best suggestive look I could manage, hoping he'd understand what I wanted from him. I even licked my lips.

Angus looked confused more than anything. When he didn't respond except to cock his head to the side, I lay a hand on his chest and rubbed my fingers over his shirt. Right over his tight little nipple.

His eyes opened wide and his nostrils flared. "Right. Yes. Okay."

The woman from before came up, flicking her long hair and sticking her nose in the air. She looked like a horse in heat, and it wasn't attractive.

What's her problem?

"Are we going back to your apartment tonight, Alpha? You asked me to join you in your bed yesterday and we decided tonight would be best." She slid a nasty look my way, her eyes practically reduced to slits. Then she flicked her gaze back up to Angus and had the gall to bat her eyelashes.

The Alpha glanced between us, his worry obvious in the downward pull of his lips.

This wasn't my place to interfere. Especially if they'd already arranged something.

I took a step away. "I'll come back later, if that's okay? How long do you need? An hour?"

More? I had no idea. If it had been Sam I would have been right to interrupt after about five minutes.

"No." Angus's arm snaked out, grabbing me around the waist and pulling me into his hard form.

His gaze was on me, intense and lustful. I didn't want to look away. I only wanted to drown in how much he wanted me, and how much I returned that need.

I peeked over at the bitch in front of us who'd tried to take Angus off me. She'd transformed into an even more hideous beast. Her mouth was twisted up like a cat's ass and her hands sat on her hips in a striking pose of anger.

"What the fuck is this, Angus? You think I'm going to share you with some little gay boy? Not a chance."

Angus laughed, but it wasn't because he thought she was funny. The sound was dark and dangerous. It made me shiver against him and cling to the muscled torso that rumbled with disdain.

"No, Silky, you won't be sharing me with Clayton. He'll be in my bed every night from now on, so I suggest you find someone else to service you."

Ohhhh... Burn.

"Why you..." She hissed, her eyes narrowing and her nostrils flaring as she took a step forward. Then she stopped abruptly and I hid against the Alpha.

I didn't see the look Angus gave her in answer to her outburst. I didn't want to see how angry he was. I could feel it in the vibration of his skin. So, I buried my head into his shoulder instead, inhaling the salty scent of his testosterone.

I could imagine how scary he'd be when he grew angry and I was sure it would top anything I'd ever seen from any other shifter.

"You'll regret this," she threw at us as she stalked away.

I clung tighter and closed my eyes.

"You ready to go?" Angus asked gently, tugging at me to disengage me from his side. I let him push me away and I lifted my chin, aching for his lips on mine.

"Yes."

He grabbed my hand tightly and pulled me down the street, away from the bustle of people eating and into his pack's apartments. A place I had been staring at for five years and envying all the people who lived here. Now I was one of them.

I knew I should leave the female out of our conversations, it wasn't really my business. But then again, was she someone I had to worry about now that I had the man she wanted? "She's pretty angry." I couldn't help but say as Angus opened the door to his apartment and led me inside.

He shrugged as he locked the door behind us and put his arms around me, big and firm. "She'll get over it. She knew she wasn't my mate."

"And I am?" I managed to ask, though my throat tightened and my voice shook as I got the question out.

The big beautiful Alpha stared at me for along moment. My belly quivered with fear and need all at the same time. I wanted to be his mate, so badly.

"I don't know, but I think we should find out."

I liked the sound of that. "How do we do that?"

Angus chuckled, his blue eyes dancing with light. "We fuck."

My heart leapt in my chest and then began to pound against my ribs like a bongo drum. "Oh. Well...that sounds good."

Angus stared down at me, his eyebrows knitted together with apparent worry. "Are you able to? I mean, how are you feeling? Is there anything I should know about Sam, or anyone else? I don't want to set off some sort of PTSD reaction."

I stepped back and pulled off the oversized dirty tank top I still wore. I wanted out of these clothes and I needed to feel good.

"PTSD? What were you, a shrink back in the day?"

Angus mimicked my movements, stripping himself of his top, and then reaching for the zipper on his jeans as I pushed my own pants down to my ankles. When I stood back up, I knew my arousal was obvious. Angus couldn't stop staring at my cock.

"Ah... No. A fire fighter."

I laughed, unable to stop the reaction as happy hormones flooded my brain, making it impossible for me to concentrate.

I could see Angus in yellow overalls... A fireman's hat. Back in the day, I would have wanted my house to catch on fire just so he could throw me over his shoulder and save me.

"Oh fireman... Please... Rescue me," I cried playfully and Angus growled, the throaty rolling sound making the hairs on my back stand up.

"Definitely." He pushed his own jeans to the ground and walked forward, his heavy balls swinging against his thighs.

My knees weakened and thankfully Angus scooped me up, throwing me over his shoulder like in my fantasy. He didn't stop there. Angus kept moving like an unstoppable juggernaut, his hard body hot beneath my belly as we moved into the bedroom and he threw me down onto the bed. I laughed as the softness cushioned me, the elation I was feeling intoxicating.

Angus's face grew serious. "I want to begin this by saying I've never had a male lover before, so I may need a little guidance here and there."

Oh, now that's perfect.

"I would love to," I said as I slipped off the bed, fell to my knees, and took his heavenly cock into my mouth.

Angus's groan filled the room as his flesh filled my mouth. The slightly salty flavor and the heat of his skin had me begging for more.

"Oh God, you're good at that." He moaned as his hand slipped into my hair, holding me gently against him.

His tenderness tugged at my heart and I tried not to remember all the bad memories of the last few years. I forced myself to focus on the present and slid my hands over his thighs and around to his rock-hard ass. I gripped tight and moved my mouth up and down on him.

Yum...

I pulled one arm back and wrapped a hand around the base of his cock, my fingers encircling his massive girth barely. I sucked on the large bulbous head and risked a glance up at his face.

His eyes were closed and sweet ecstasy contorted his face. Inside my mouth and within my grasp his cock was getting bigger, and thicker by the moment.

I shifted focus again, deciding to explore more of his body. I fondled his heavy balls, enjoying the crinkly hair and the soft skin. Then I reached under him to tap a finger lightly against his asshole.

He flinched back, panting hard. "Go slow, yeah?"

I nodded, surprised to find myself, although ten years the junior, having more experience in this field than him. "Okay."

I moved to my feet and wrapped my arms around Angus's neck, going up onto my tiptoes to kiss him once again. He groaned and wrapped me up in his big arms. His tongue spearing my lips and devouring me. Angus thrust his pelvis against my belly in an impatient way, and his cock poked into me like a hot rod of steel.

I was more than ready for him. My body thrummed with arousal and need. I wanted to feel Angus's cock thrusting into my body. Feel him consume me and challenge that being inside of me that Sam said was toxic and dangerous.

I knew I wasn't really a bad person. I just needed an Alpha strong enough to take me.

I pushed against his chest so that he'd let me go, and he did with a confused look on his face.

"You gonna fuck me, Angus?" I asked, stepping back, turning around, and presenting to him by going down on my hands and knees on the bed.

He stepped closer and ran his roughened hands over my hips, making me quiver and shake. "How do we do this so I don't hurt you?"

No one else had ever asked me such a thing.

"Ah...we need some moisture. Lube is a thing of the past."

Or so I'd been taught by the men who I'd been with over the past few years.

"I have oil!" Angus exclaimed with excitement.

I turned around and looked over my shoulder at him. What sort of oil?

"Perfect." Or so I hoped.

He raced out of the room and I waited for him to come back. Also something I never did. Generally I was grabbed and used quickly. I never had time to think about what was happening. Sam had been hard and aggressive once we begun, and fast. It was over before I knew it, most of the time.

I pushed any thoughts of Sam away as Angus re-entered the room. "Here, hold out your hand."

I did as he asked, balancing my weight on my other three appendages. He poured some yellow oil into my hand. I didn't know what sort. Canola? Sunflower? Olive? I didn't care. If it was edible, then it was good to go.

"Stroke yourself, I want to feel you cum too," he said and my balls tightened with arousal.

Now that was hot.

I reached for my cock and he ran a hand down my back. I shivered at his light touch and wrapped my hand around the shaft, gasping as hot pleasure shot through me. Angus slipped his fingers between my ass cheeks and began touching me there.

Yes. There. Please...there.

I pushed my pelvis back, gasping as my own hand stroked faster. Forcing me closer to completion. The thick head of Angus's cock pressed against my ass and I bucked, needing him inside me. I rocked harder and he didn't move.

I wanted to know if we were mates. I needed to know if this could be different with him. Heat spread down my thighs and my balls were so tight I was afraid I'd spill on the sheets before he was even inside me.

I flexed my hips back against his cock, wanting the feeling of stretch and fulfilment he could surely give me. Hot pain spread through my lower body as he thrust into me. I rocked on his cock, moaning as my flesh burned. I couldn't stop.

"Ah..."

I met his thrust as he forged forward, holding my breath as the pain intensified.

When he was finally fully seated inside of me I began to sweat.

"Just...pause. Please." I panted, the pain now blinding inside my head. My cock had softened and I needed to breathe through it. If I could just have a moment to wait for it to go away, I was sure this would work fine.

And amazingly, when Angus did as I ask, it did. Slowly, but surely, the pain receded. The relief was massive. I worked my hand on my flesh once again. Faster and harder, needing the pleasure to overcome the pain.

"Fuck me, Alpha. Please." I was begging now and I didn't care.

Angus gripped my hips hard with his huge hands and began thrusting in and out of me. The pressure was intense. I could feel him so deep inside of me I didn't know how he fit there.

Angus groaned above me. "Damn.... Fuck, Clayton, you feel, like, heaven."

I closed my eyes and pumped my horny cock faster, ripples of pleasure flooding my nervous system. Wave upon wave of heat flowed over my skin as Angus moved harder.

His hands gripped my hips, and his moans filled my ears. My balls began to tighten and I thrust my hips back to meet his. Angus's gasps grew louder and I worked my length with furious strokes.

"I'm..." Angus gave me a moment's warning, and I grabbed his hand on my hip and held him to me.

He thrust to the hilt inside of me so deep I could have burst. Then he began to orgasm.

I wasn't ready to cum myself, but I loved being the one to bring Angus to his peak. I squeezed his hand tight and enjoyed the satisfaction flowing over me. Pulses of seed squirted inside me, and all of a sudden my body began to shake. My balls tightened up against my body and my own orgasm ripped through me like a brush fire. I screamed out as my eyes slammed shut and my cock pulsed with a pleasure I'd never known. Liquid fire filled my belly as my cum spread on the sheets beneath me and I collapsed forward, my muscles turned to jelly.

We fell down to the bed together, Angus's cock sliding out of me as we nestled into the covers, his arm wrapped around me.

"What was that?" I asked, panting hard as I struggled to open my eyes. I was nowhere near ready to orgasm when Angus had finished, so how had I come so easily? So quickly?

That had never happened for me, not during sex. Maybe when I was fifteen and had just started to touch myself, but that was a long time ago now.

"What do you mean?" Angus asked, groaning and rolling onto his back with a strong air of satisfaction about him. He stretched like a cat on a rug after a bowl of cream.

I twisted around to face him and dragged my eyelids up out of the soup of bliss that they swam in.

Focus!

"Didn't you feel that?" I asked, mystified that he hadn't experienced the same thing I had. Or was that what sex was like for a true Alpha?

Angus's eyelids were dropped to half-mast and his smile spoke of major satisfaction. "You're going to have to be more specific than that, because I can hardly hear you above the ringing in my ears."

I pushed up onto my elbow and stared down on him. "That's exactly what I mean. Sex has never been like that for me." I swallowed hard as doubt rose, clamping down on my throat. Was he being serious in that he didn't consider this a special event?

"That good you mean, I hope?" Angus asked, his grin spreading wide as he blinked so slowly I wasn't sure his eyes would re-open. But they did. Barely.

"Yeah, of course. But..." I was beginning to feel stupid now. How could I explain this to him if he didn't share it also?

Maybe Angus was used to sex being this good and I was just making up an importance that shouldn't be attached to it? That had to be it. What did I know about functional, healthy sexual relationships?

Anger and jealousy threaded through my veins, hot and poisonous. Was this what he'd experienced with Silky too? Did all Alpha's make their partners come like that?

My jaw tightened and my mouth twisted hard.

I bloody hope not.

"Lie down, Clayton, I can barely keep my eyes open." Angus's soft voice and searching hands made my doubts slide to the background of my mind. Asleep, but not forgotten.

"All right." I gave up the fight to make him see this as more. I slid down next to him, in his soft clean bed and he dragged me close, letting the heat of his body warm mine.

"I'm so glad you're with me, Clayton. Here. Now. I know this world is totally fucked up, but this is the first time I've been happy in a really long time."

I kissed his hairy chest, tasting the tang of his sweat and sighing as I laid my head back on his shoulder. "Me too."

And that had to be enough, for now. Any lingering feelings that there was so much more for us to experience would have to be silenced and pushed aside until the right time.

With vampires in the power seat and my old pack not speaking to me, danger was around every corner.

I closed my eyes and focused on the small peace I'd found. In the arms of an Alpha.

CHAPTER 5
ANGUS.

A week after I'd taken Clayton in to be my house mate, things had never been better. I looked forward to waking up in the morning, going to work with him by my side, then coming home again together. Clayton was sweet and cheeky and sexy as hell. Not to mention, a hard worker. An addictive combination.

I'd never imagined myself having a male mate, but with the attraction that roared between us I had to face facts. He was the only person I could see myself with.

When you added in the myths I'd heard about Omega's and Alpha's being the perfect partnership, I was beginning to believe that we were bound to be mates for life. But was Clayton ready for such a thing? For the strongest of all bonds? Mated to me, a man who seemed to incite the worst in our enemies. It was taking all of my strength and self-discipline to play along so that we didn't all end up in a fight with the vamps.

Did Clayton love me yet? Or was I simply a means to an end in this vicious world?

"Silky." I nodded at the female who'd once shared my bed as we walked back to the center of town after work. Surely, she'd gotten over her jealousy of Clayton by now?

"Fuck off," she flung back and walked further away from me. Something she wouldn't have dared to do if we were back in the old world. Disrespecting an Alpha in such a way would carry with it a major penalty. And she knew it.

Bitch.

Clayton's hand slipped into mine for a moment, drawing me back to the warmth of my present day and the loss of all the old ways. "Don't worry about her. Sour grapes, as my mother would say."

I nodded and tried to ignore the gripping coldness in my gut. Silky had always been a good companion, of a sort. A necessary means to an end when we were both lonely. She'd never shown any signs of being vindictive or nasty.

That had obviously changed. Since I'd chosen to take Clayton in, she'd become a person I didn't recognize anymore. The death stares I received from her rattled the Alpha inside me. The Alpha long buried and not allowed to surface, for fear of death. Not just for me, but for my pack. The people I still loved and protected, though our cohesiveness was not what it used to be.

My hands tightened into fists and I pushed the anger down, hard. I shouldn't be blaming Silky for how impotent I felt in this world ran by power hungry vampires. It wasn't her fault that I couldn't be the Alpha I wanted to be. The vampires were the main reason for that. Them, and this horrible new world. I was certain the crack-pot who devised the virus that killed off all the humans must have been a vampire. Their lust for power was insatiable.

The idiot hadn't thought about what they'd all feed on with the humans gone, but then again, who knew what the original plan was? And if it had gone down accordingly or not.

"Do you think the vampires will ever decide to just kill us all?" Clayton asked suddenly and I pulled him to the side, close to the entrance to our apartment block.

"What are you talking about?" My mother had always said that

Omega's had incredible instincts, and if Clayton was foretelling trouble, then I was listening.

Clayton shrugged, his gaze darting away as though uncomfortable. "I just always wondered, that's all. If they didn't need us for blood, what would they do with us?"

I shrugged, very quickly wanting to finish this conversation. I wanted to focus on the connection building between us. So, I let my hand run over Clayton's cheek and turned his face back to mine. I liked looking at him, much more than I wanted to admit to myself. Life in this world was a fleeting, precarious thing, and I didn't want to even think about what would happen to my sanity if something happened to Clayton now.

My pack needed me, but I wasn't sure I could handle the loss of my mate. One of the main reasons I wasn't rushing into a true mating just yet.

"I don't know, Clayton. But for now, we're safe."

"True."

My little Omega cuddled into me and my hunger for food moved sharply into a lust for his body against mine.

"How 'bout you go up to our apartment and I get us some dinner?" I suggested.

His eyes lit up and he turned to press his pelvis against my hip. "You'll bring it back to the apartment?"

I dropped my head and kissed his luscious lips, unable to stop myself. "I will. You go get yourself naked for me and I'll meet you in bed with our food."

Clayton's gorgeous face transformed into a beautiful smile as he absorbed my words and nodded happily.

I watched him walk away, loving the strength of his back, the muscles that were beginning to grow on his thin frame. Some food, decent sleep, and physical exercise every day and he was blossoming.

Once Clayton was safely inside my apartment building and heading for our home, I turned and made my way into the center of the city.

I did have to admit that the vampires did have everything running well. We had jobs, electricity, food, and water every day. But we were living under an oppressive dictator who wanted to rule us by sheer force. With threats to our lives and those of our children.

And I couldn't live with that.

I wandered to the street where the food vans and troughs were set up. I could smell a stale flour and meaty scent. I tried to imagine that it was an exotic Indian restaurant. With pappadams and curries for all.

I stepped up to the long line, watching as the different shifters moved around each other with caution. To my right sat another wolf pack, or what was left of one. They were devoid of children and men. Most of their elders had been killed in the fighting, and the children were soon picked off by the vampires afterwards. The women looked utterly worn down, and I didn't know why they didn't try to integrate with us.

To my left was a group of shifters that smelled feline, though I'd never seen them in animal form so I couldn't tell which big cat they were exactly.

The numbers were stacked in our favor in this city. There was ten times the shifters than there were vampires, even when you took into account their daylight protectors, the cougars. We outnumbered them dramatically.

I didn't know why we couldn't just get our shit together and as a group, work out a way of getting rid of the vampires. But if we succeeded, would that take us back to the times of fighting amongst ourselves? Would packs turn on one another and throw us into the dark ages once again?

I grabbed up two plates and offered them to the dirty women serving us.

"Thanks."

The women ducked their heads as I moved along the line, collecting more flavors and food. I grabbed some flat bread and slid it onto Clayton's plate. He needed more calories with the hours he was working now. I turned to head back to the man I would soon make my mate and was shoved from behind, hard. I fell forwards, dropping my food to the dirt.

"What the fuck?" I twisted around and clenched my fists, ready for the fight this person obviously wanted.

There were three men in front of me. All Betas. A foot shorter than me, they exuded a scent of fear and anger.

"You killed our Alpha," they claimed, an aggressive tilt to each of their jaws.

The front one had his teeth clenched and his chin jutted forward as though he wanted a fight.

I looked closer and recognized one of them from Clayton's old pack.

"Firstly, I didn't kill anyone. Sam broke the laws and the vamps followed through with their punishments. Secondly, he was no Alpha. So, don't go spouting some vengeance plan, because I gotta tell you, you guys deserve a better leader than that."

The three men looked between themselves, steam practically blowing out their ears as they snuffed and snorted.

I wasn't interested in this shit. I'd dropped Clayton's food, and they were going to pay for that. "Now, you are going to re-fill some plates for me, because I need to take some food home."

The man at the front of this merry band of Betas narrowed his beady eyes at me. "Get your own god-damn food."

I already did... I took a step closer to the Beta and stared down my nose at him. I didn't want a fight, but since they'd started it, I was certainly going to finish it. I grabbed him around the back of the neck, forced him forwards until he was almost kissing his own knees and growled at the other two, "Stay."

They did, and I dragged the Beta to the end of the food line.

"You are going to stand in line and get me my food. I didn't start this, but if you force me to defend myself, I am not accountable for the consequences."

The idiot began to laugh, which sounded like a strangled chortle from where I was standing.

"You're finding something funny?" I asked him, struggling to hold in my temper. This idiot was really pushing his luck. Didn't he know that I could crush his skull with my bare hands.

"Yeah. I do."

My gut began to twist and I suddenly knew something was wrong. This was a diversion. I wrenched him back up, grabbed his twisted and dirty ponytail, and held him tight. "What's funny?"

He flicked his gaze to me and I saw the devilish merriment dancing in his eyes. "You're here talking to me while the boys lay into your little slut. I hope he remembers how to take it like a good Omega."

Fuck! I ploughed my fist into the beta's gut and he doubled over. I didn't stop to check where the others were, I just started running.

No! Fuck… No! Not now.

My heart pounded like an anvil against my ribs and my throat tasted like the acid of my heaving stomach. I jumped over some stray children playing in the street and caught a whiff of open sewer that needed to be fixed up. Then kept running.

Silky was standing outside our building with a grin on her face, obviously keeping guard. Fucking bitch. I could hear groaning from inside the hallway.

Damn. Fuck. Shit.

I ran straight past her, pushing her roughly out of the way as I wrenched the door open and belted up the hallway. An angry cry met my ears as I raced into my apartment and saw two men laying into Clayton. He was bloody and on the ground. His clothes had been ripped from him, but he was fighting back.

These guys needed to die.

I kicked the door shut with my leg and released my hold on the animal inside me.

Fuck the consequences.

My black Alpha wolf ripped forward, shredding my clothes and pouncing straight over to the man who'd been hitting Clayton with a bat.

My muscles hurt like they were empty. Like they had no blood in them. My legs were awkward as I ran. It had been so many years since I'd shifted, this body felt foreign to me. But my mate needed me and I wasn't going to fail him again.

I sunk my teeth into his arm and ripped sideways, pulling his hand off in a spray of blood. Lightning pain shot through my face and jaw as I made my wolf body move against its will.

He screamed out and I bit into his thigh, sinking my teeth deep to the arteries.

Die, fucker!

The other guy ran for the door and I bounded after him, grabbing him by the calf and ripping the muscle off the bone. The man screamed out in terror and metallic blood slid down my throat and sprayed my face.

All I could see was red, and my beautiful Clayton still lying on the ground.

Hurt. Broken. Bleeding.

When I'd promised him I'd never let him be hurt like this again.

Anger shredded the last of my humanity and I ripped into the man before me, tearing at essential veins until he was bleeding out in a river of red.

"Angus! Come back! Angus!" Clayton was calling for me and I stared at him, not understanding why he'd be calling to me.

He was getting up off the ground, his head cut open, his face bruised and broken.

Those...fucking...dick heads...

"Angus, my beautiful Alpha, come back. Shift back."

He was trying to calm me down, and I didn't understand why. There was another man still alive and I wanted him dead.

"Angus, they'll come and see you shifted. Hurry."

My vision began to clear. The all-encompassing redness dissipated like a lifting fog. I let go of my wolf, the poor shifter body that I barely lived in anymore. Coming back to human was even more painful than the original shift, if that was possible. My arms and legs cried out in agony as the muscles twisted and shrank.

I closed my eyes and dropped back my head so I didn't cry out like a weakling.

Finally, the pain receded like the tide, taking with it my strength. I slumped against my table and grabbed hold of a chair for balance. *Fuck. I'd be useless if anyone wanted to fight me now.*

Clayton ran around behind me and locked the door. Beautiful boy. Worried about me. Then he came straight to me. "Angus, oh my God. Are you okay?"

He ran his hands over my sweating body and my heart squeezed tight in my chest.

"Me? Are you okay? How badly did they hurt you?"

His pants were on the ground where he'd left them and his shirt was ripped so bad it slithered off his shoulders the moment I touched it.

Completely naked now, covered in purple and red bruises, he shrugged. "I've been worse."

And that statement almost did me in.

"Alpha, please don't kill me." The pleading words came from the man on my floor.

I pushed myself to my feet, as straight as I could stand, and pulled Clayton behind me.

"Why shouldn't I?" I growled, glaring at him with all the strength I could manage.

The only thing keeping me from grabbing a knife from the kitchen and finishing the job was the fact that it didn't look like they'd raped Clayton. If that had been the case I would have dragged myself over on my hands and knees if I'd needed to, and got the job done.

The Beta was holding his severed arm to his body, blood still seeping down his chest.

If he'd been human, he'd be dead already.

"Because I can help you. Give you information on what's going on in your pack, my pack. I'll work for you." The Beta bartered for his life.

I narrowed my eyes at him. "My pack? Are you telling me that my own people are going up against me? Against Clayton?"

He nodded rapidly. "Yes. And if you spare me, I'll tell you everything."

Anger pooled in my gut and I struggled to breathe. My wolf was so very near the surface of my consciousness. He demanded to be set free.

Clayton's hands were suddenly on my back. They were stroking my spine in a reassuring way. He caught my attention and dragged my humanity back to the surface.

I managed to push back the wolf and keep my human tongue. "I'll spare you. I want to know what Judas I have in my camp." I turned my head to look at Clayton, whose eyes were swollen and cut from this man's ministrations. "Only if you agree too, Clayton. This is your attacker. If you want justice, I'll gladly deliver it."

The Omega shook his head, appearing to barely think about my question. "No. I want to know what's going on too."

A trickle of blood ran down Clayton's face and he wiped at it with an impatient hand.

"Why don't you wash your face, get some clean clothes on, and come back? I won't start without you."

I cupped his chin with my hand while I spoke and Clayton met my eyes as though assessing my honesty. Then he nodded and headed off to the bathroom to do what I asked him to.

I collapsed into the chair, struggling to get my breath.

"It hurts, doesn't it? Shifting after so long," my prisoner on the floor said as he pulled himself to a seated position, and now leaned back against my kitchen cupboards.

"How would you know?" I asked him, ignoring my need to crawl over and pummel his face until he could no longer speak.

How dare they come into my home and beat on my mate?

Settle, settle.

My heart was still pounding and the sweat on my face was only beginning to dry.

"We go outside the city sometimes. Shift, run, do our thing. Then come back."

How did I not know about this? "How do you have time to do that?"

He tilted his head to the side.

"We don't really have a job. The vamps never got 'round to giving us one."

I grunted. "More like, you should be joining us up at the power plant, and instead you guys are sitting on your asses doing nothing all day."

He nodded slowly, as though he didn't want to argue with me.

Clayton came back into the room, his hair wet and slicked back. His body now covered in warm, dry clothes. I could see his accelerated healing kicking in on his face already.

"What did I miss?" Clayton asked. He sat down beside me at the table, his hand reaching out along the table top as though searching for me.

I addressed Clayton. "The Beta was just telling me that they run and shift outside the city borders because they've got nothing else to do in the day."

Clayton grimaced. "I never knew where they went during the day, but I'm not surprised. Sam's pack are ridiculously lazy."

"Better than being a cunt like you," the Beta spat at Clayton from the ground.

I stood up on legs that weren't entirely solid, walked straight over to the bleeding Beta on the ground, drew back my arm, and punched him in the face. The crack of breaking bone sounded in the room. I took a few steps back and looked at him.

The Beta fell to his side once again, blood gushing out of his nose.

"Mind your fucking mouth," I said to him. "This is my mate, and the man that saved your life. You'd be dead now if I had my way."

The Beta pushed himself back up and glared at me. "He's a traitor to our pack."

Seriously? This guy obviously wanted to die.

I stood up and stared down at him. "You betrayed Clayton the moment you let Sam beat him up every day. What sort of pack members stand by and let that happen?"

Suddenly there was banging on the door. "What's happening in there? Everything okay? Angus?" It was Silky's voice and coldness crept into my gut.

She waited long enough.

The Beta's smile said it all.

Fuck. She's in on it.

"Yeah, all good in here," I called out to make her go away.

"You sure? We heard growling and banging."

Yeah, I bet you did.

"Go away, Silky. My mate and I are getting to know one another."

There was dead silence behind the door, then grumbles as they moved away.

Fucking bitch. I'll deal with you later.

I looked down at our captor and my arms began to feel stronger. I was standing fine now and knew that if needed, I could throw this rubbish out on his ear.

"You were saying?" I asked, sitting back down in my chair.

"Ah... I'll help you and I swear I won't tell anyone what happened here."

That was a point. I hadn't even thought about the consequences of my actions there. I turned to look at my beautiful Omega whose first move had been to lock the door after he'd gotten up off the ground.

"Why'd you coax me back to human rather than let me kill this one?" I asked him.

"Because I was scared someone would see you in wolf form. You know the punishment."

God, he's lovely.

I nodded and turned back to the man before me. "Tell me what I need to know."

The Beta wiped at the blood on his chin. "Well, my pack wants blood. We're owed a debt over what you did to Sam. And if we can't get anything from you, then we'll take it from Clayton."

"Touch him and die." I growled and my heart rate spiked again.

The Beta's mouth twisted. "Like I said, the debt needs to be paid. You know that Alpha."

I did. But how? "What do you need? Food, clothing, shelter?" I could get them almost anything, and if it meant keeping Clayton safe when I wasn't around, I could be generous.

"We could use some more women," he said without humor.

"What about the women from southern packs? They have no men, no children. They would join your pack in an instant."

"We've tried. They are impossible." He wiped at his dripping chin once again.

If they weren't amenable to the idea, I didn't have any leverage over them to coax them into it. And could I in good conscience encourage women to join that pack? I'd ask Clayton.

"I'll speak to them, but there needs to be some sort of vouch for safety. If the rest of your pack treats women the way Sam treated Clayton, I'd rather go to war than hand over defenseless women to you."

The Beta opened his mouth, an angry look slashed across his eyes, but Clayton interrupted.

"The rest of the pack are quite timid in comparison, Angus."

"You mean like the two who just tried to rape you?" I said, looking straight at the Beta and not at my Omega.

"They've always treated me differently, I don't know why. But I've rarely seen a woman treated badly."

I nodded, absorbing everything. An Omega was such a rare find, I hadn't thought any existed. I wasn't surprised that Sam had feared Clayton's power.

"I'll speak to them," I declared. If it was mutually beneficial for both groups, I didn't see why they couldn't be stronger together.

The Beta nodded in acceptance of my promise and relaxed against the cupboards. His bleeding seemed to have stopped, his shifter genes knitting his flesh together where I'd torn at him.

A man in my pack may as well be dead without a hand to help him work and feed his family, but obviously Sam's pack had got far too used to being lazy if this Beta begged for his life despite his torn limb.

"You were going to tell me who in my pack was against me," I reminded him.

The Beta looked at me as though I should know. "That chick that was knocking on the door. Silky is it? The dirty blonde with the big tits."

I nodded, my gut churning below my heart and making me sick. I knew what was coming next.

"It was her. She said she'd guard the door if we wanted free range on Clayton. I didn't really want to go after him, to be frank. Not my style. But Tony wanted revenge, so I came along for the ride."

I'd heard enough, and I wasn't sure I could control my temper much longer.

"Get out. And make sure you stick to your promise. Not a word about what happened here. Your hand was an accident at the mill, or whatever."

He struggled to his feet, slipping and sliding in a pool of his own blood.

"Yep, an accident at the mill it is. What are you going to do with Tony's body?" He nodded his head towards his fallen pack member.

I shrugged. My first thought had been that I might just move out of the apartment for a year and let him rot.

But I was comfortable here and had finally got the place clean and organized.

"Don't know. I'll work something out. You need him?"

The Beta shook his head. "Nope. He ran away as far as I know."

I watched the Beta as he left my apartment, opening, then carefully shutting the door behind him.

Clayton ran over to the door and locked it once again, going down on his knees to kneel beside the fallen Beta.

Perhaps they'd been lovers?

"I am so glad you're dead, Tony. You were a real asshole." Clayton's dry voice cut through any possible jealousies that had surfaced and a laugh bubbled up inside me. "What are we going to do with him?" Clayton asked, gesturing to the man who was still bleeding over my tiles.

"Maybe I should offer him to some of the hungry vamps that patrol," I suggested.

That would be a simple and easy way to get rid of the body. Mostly. They tended to leave a lot of flesh after draining the body of blood.

"Yeah, that might raise a lot of questions though."

And I didn't need any more attention than I'd already gotten, but hiding was not my style.

"True, but then again, a peace offering to Vincent may be the next move. I'm not sure how long I can stay here under the rule of the vamps anyhow."

Clayton stood up and moved to my side. "Do what you need to do, Angus. But if you're gonna offer him to the vamps, they like 'em fresh."

Good point. Better get on it.

"So true, and I think that's just decided it for me. Time to find Vincent."

CLAYTON.

Standing next to a dead body again was giving me the creeps. The hairs on the back of my neck were erect and my belly churned with memories of my family's deaths.

My friends. My lovers.

Everyone had died on me in the past ten years, and although I thought I'd grown pretty good at becoming numb to the trauma... I was wrong.

I looked down at the floor of Angus's apartment. There lay a man that had beaten me and tried to rape me today. Who had succeeded in the past.

He was now dead and for some horrible reason, that was very satisfying. And sickening to me.

Why was this world so cruel, and disgusting? Why were we always at war? Never safe?

I moved away from the dead Beta and curled up into a ball on the couch, in my clean clothes I'd been given by my Alpha. I loved these leggings, and was so glad Angus had kept three pairs, despite the fact they didn't fit him and no one in the pack wore them. I liked to think that he held out hope that I would come to him one day. I'd certainly had dreams of him.

I needed to cling to something like that, because there had to be a reason we'd both gone through so much shit before now. I only wished he'd found me five years ago. We'd be so much happier and stronger now if he had.

A nagging childhood memory swam up to meet me and for once I didn't fight it for fear of the trauma it would invoke. It was my mother telling me something about my mate. I closed my eyes and listened hard, the words swimming in circles around in my mind. I listened harder and heard it. What I'd been praying for, what I'd always known.

My eyes popped open and I jumped up. "I knew it!"

I'd always known there was something special about me! And it was this. My mother had once told me that an Omega, when properly mated, could give an Alpha twice the power. The strength. The healing capacity.

I was his steroids! And I could be forever—if we mated properly.

But a true mating was a meeting of hearts and souls, not just bodies. I was ready to connect, whole-heartedly to my amazing Alpha, but was he?

I bit my lip, unsure on the answer to that question.

The front door opened and I pushed the thoughts away for the moment. I'd tell Angus about my revelation when we had time, and preferably after I knew how he felt about me.

"Vincent wants him," Angus announced, scooping up the dead body on our floor and throwing him over his shoulder.

"You're going to just take him out there like that?" I squeaked.

That could spell death for Angus.

Damn it! We need to mate, like now! I wouldn't worry so much about him if I knew he was stronger.

"Yep. They were the terms. You stay here and clean up if you can, I'll be back."

Angus turned to walk away and I stuck to his heels.

"Not a chance. I'll clean the floors later."

The Alpha lingered by the door and I gave his shoulder a push. I wasn't being left behind.

"Let's go."

Angus grunted in a strange sound of acceptance and we both walked outside into the darkened night. The sun had gone down while we talked to Craig and now the vampires would be out and roaming.

We had some streetlights luckily, but it was still eerily dark out here in comparison to the inside of our apartment.

The vampires were waiting in the street, a large group. At least ten.

My heart clenched tight in worry, but I stuck close to Angus, not wanting anything to happen to him. The wolves filled in behind us. Most of them my old pack.

Following Tony's dead body.

Damn. This was bad.

The hairs on my arms rose and my ears tingled. We could both die. Right now.

"Here you go, Vincent. As promised."

There was a growl behind us as Angus dumped the carcass on the ground, still warm for the vamps.

"And this man was a traitor you said?" Vincent enquired, his leathery, creepy face making me cringe as he spoke.

He reminded me of some of the original Dracula movies I used to watch as a child. And he gave me the creeps.

"He broke pack law. They attacked my mate, and I punished him accordingly."

There was an aggressive titter behind us and Vincent's eyes lit up with the scent of a fight.

"Feed," he instructed his coven with a flick of his wrist.

The vamps opened their mouths like rapid bats, their fangs descending so that they could latch onto the flesh of my fallen pack member.

Vincent walked slowly towards us as his coven descended on the dead body. Angus met the vampire leader eye to eye and twisted us both so that I was behind him and we now faced my old pack.

"Does anyone have anything to say?" Vincent asked the mob.

"Yeah, Angus owes us!" one Beta yelled out.

"Double now! He's killed two of our men," another woman yelled out.

Vincent turned on Angus with a gleeful expression.

"Is this true Angus?"

My Alpha shook his head slowly.

"No. They blame me for Sam's death, but that wasn't my fault. He broke the law. You followed through. As for that sack of shit..." Angus indicated over his shoulder to where the vampires were draining the dead body. "He deserved to die for attacking my mate. No one tries to hurt Clayton and lives to tell the tale."

That wasn't entirely true, of course. But I was loving the stand Angus was making in my honor. Though, with ten Vampires at our backs and an angry pack in front of us, we may not live long enough to enjoy it.

"I make the laws Angus, not you," Vincent reminded my Alpha, with that sing song voice he had that somehow made him seem even more deadly.

The air around us went silent, crackling with nervous energy.

Where was Angus's pack when he needed back up?

"We may live under your laws, Vincent, but I'm still a wolf shifter and will discipline the wolves how I need to, to keep the peace."

I inhaled sharply as Angus took a stand I didn't expect him to.

"Really?" Vincent breathed, his eyes turning an eerie red. "I won't take a challenge to my position, Angus."

Angus crossed his arms over his chest. "And who will give you the electricity you need for the city if you kill me, Vincent? You know I'm the last of the Alpha wolves. You'd need every shifter in the city to work in the power plant to get done what my one pack does."

"Perhaps I'll just kill your little mate as punishment for your outburst then." Vincent snapped his fingers and my neck was pierced with sharp teeth.

I screamed out and lurched for Angus.

A feral growl ripped through the air and Angus's huge black wolf leapt at the two vamps holding me.

The sucking pressure and pain on my neck disappeared and I fell to the ground. I crawled forward, twisting onto my back so that I could see Angus taking out the two vamps, tearing them in two with feral clamps of his jaw. Then he sauntered back to me in wolf form.

On instinct I fell to my belly on the dirt and Angus walked over me, pausing when he had me completely beneath him. Protecting me. Engulfing me. Making everyone aware just how important I was to him.

He didn't move, but I could feel the vibration in his muscles, in his breath. The growl in his throat. The barely contained power and hostility.

Where was his pack? Where was his back up?

I lifted my head and saw Vincent step closer. Angus didn't move, despite the fact that a vampire's bite was deadly to him in wolf form.

"You can shift back, Angus," Vincent said, his voice sounding bored and relaxed.

I knew better than to trust his tones.

Slowly Angus began to change, his legs shrinking and his fur disappearing until he was crouching over me, naked and covered in blood.

"The punishment for shifting is death," Vincent declared, though no one moved to take Angus's life.

Then it came to me. The Omega power! I could give him so much more strength if he let me mate to him. He would be invincible.

"As is the punishment for touching my mate," Angus garbled between his still pointed teeth. "I have bowed down to you out of respect for the way you run this town, Vincent, but make no mistake, I am still an Alpha, and will die before you touch my mate again."

Angus stood on legs that I could see were still shaky. I jumped up and leaned against him to give him a crutch, wiping at the blood still pouring down my neck.

Angus pressed against me, wrapping an arm around my shoulders.

So much for wondering if he was ready to mate me or not.

From Angus's speech, and his actions, it seemed that the Alpha had already chosen me as his mate and the happiness that flowed through my chest made my knees weak.

"I cannot allow this," Vincent said, lifting his chin high in the air.

I empathized with the vampire. He needed Angus to keep working, and yet a punishment was needed for his "bad behavior".

"How 'bout we leave and never come back?" I suggested, finding my voice through sheer fear.

Angus straightened taller, though his muscles still trembled. Poor guy still wasn't used to shifting again. I couldn't imagine the pain he was in.

"Angus can't leave his pack, little one, don't you know how Alpha's work?" Vincent sniggered at me.

"Then we'll take the pack with us," I said and Vincent's gaze darkened.

He liked having powerful slaves like Angus and he wouldn't give them up in a hurry. "No." Vincent's word was absolute, and I began to panic.

What the hell could we do now?

The Omega power. Surely, I could help him?

"I have one more suggestion. You need a suitable punishment to be dished out, and yet Angus is not able to give you what you need. So, would a fight to the death be a suitable compromise? Angus against your biggest warrior?"

Angus stared down at me as though I'd lost my mind, but I had a plan of course, and didn't back down.

"Would that work, Vincent? As a way of settling the debt?"

Poor Angus wasn't saying anything, thankfully trusting me.

Vincent stuck his nose in the air. "The rule would have to be no shifting, and if Angus wins he would have to swear never to break that law again."

I bit my lip. I wasn't sure if the power I could give Angus would transfer into his human form, but if he was fighting a vampire, it would probably be safer to fight in human form anyway.

"That sounds fair, Angus? What do you think?"

He stared at me for a moment, and I put as much love into my gaze as I could. *Please trust me.*

"Alright. Tomorrow night," Angus agreed.

Perfect. We could do the mating tonight and tomorrow he could heal and be back better than ever.

Vincent raised his voice so everyone could hear. "Sun down in the town square, Angus. Don't be late. Remember, you can't protect your little mate every moment of the day."

Angus ground his teeth together hard enough to make a grinding noise like a truck putting on its brakes. Luckily though, he didn't say anything. And the old vampire swept away with his remaining coven.

Some of the other shifters fell away, seemingly content knowing that a huge fight was about to happen. I grabbed Angus around the waist to help him back to our apartment.

Two men stepped forward, whom I'd seen at the power plant but didn't know by names.

"Give him to us," one of them said and I looked up at Angus for permission. He nodded.

I lifted his arm off my shoulders and he fell forward onto the two men who practically carried him inside.

Silky was still standing by the door and I gave her the best death stare I could manage as I passed by. She looked away, and she was lucky she did. That bitch deserved a real slap down and if I didn't have Angus to look after, I'd be very excited to be the one to give it to her.

The two men placed Angus on the couch and he finally groaned loudly in pain, his breath hissing out between his teeth.

"Fuck that hurts. Twice in a few hours bloody almost killed me." He was panting now, finally showing how strained and tired he was.

"Alpha, we're so sorry we didn't know you were in here saving your new mate. Silky told us that you needed us back at the power station and we headed up there after dinner." The men's gazes dropped and their massive shoulders stooped.

Angus shuffled into a more erect seated position, his gaze hard. "She is to be banished from the pack. Alan. Tom. Make sure it's done. Give her to Clayton's old pack for all I care, but she is not to step foot inside this building again."

"Yes, Alpha."

They turned and left us alone.

Angus groaned. "This never would have happened ten years ago. My father's pack was strong, faithful. What we've got now is truly fucked up."

I knelt on the ground beside the couch and let him vent. The poor thing. I hated that this was the legacy Angus felt he was left with. "You deserve better than this, Angus. I'm so sorry."

He pulled himself up to look at me as though he'd forgotten I was there. "You'll have to explain to me why you offered me up for a fight that is surely going to get me killed."

His tone was rough and a part of me wanted to fall apart and apologize for being so stupid. But my mother didn't raise a weakling and I was no quitter.

"Okay, bear with me, because there's lots of steps to my crazy plan. First of all, I want to check that you don't want to just run away tonight? We can. I'll go with you, and I'm sure a few of the others would too."

Angus grunted. "Where would we go? I've thought about this so many times, and I don't know how I can keep my pack safer than they currently are. At least here we have housing, food, water. If I grab my pack, all the women and children, everyone, and run, what will happen when the vamps find us? They'd drain us all, and for what? So, I can be the Alpha I want to be? No. Fuck it, no!"

Wow, he really has thought about it.

"Okay, so running away is out of the question. Then the next step is..." I swallowed hard as anxiety gripped my throat. "Do you want to mate with me?"

Angus frowned. "I thought we already had...sort of."

I smiled up at his confused look. "I know. And I haven't asked if you want to be my mate because I thought we had time, and I was waiting for you to ask me. But the clock is ticking now and it needs to be done."

Angus began to smile brighter at me and dragged me up on the couch with him. "Of course, I want you to be my mate. I think me, and my rather possessive wolf made that pretty clear outside. I just wasn't sure you were ready, considering your history."

I grinned and cupped my beautiful Alpha's jaw, still covered with dry vamp blood. "I definitely want to be your mate, in every way possible. So, thank you for trusting me with this crazy plan. I know you were wondering what I was on, to suggest such a thing."

"Yeah, I was. I still am to be frank. Part of me assumed you were just giving us some time to work out a solution before tomorrow night."

That would have been a decent reason too, but I had one better. "Well, I have one already. That's not what I needed the time for." Excitement bubbled up inside of me and I pressed my lips to my Alpha's, gratitude flowing through me that such a beautiful man really wanted me.

"What was that for?" he asked, a soft smile on his face.

"Just happy... Anyway, I need to tell you something I only remembered a few hours ago. My mother once told me that as an Omega, I could give my mate more power than he'd ever dreamed of by mating with him. As an Alpha you can absorb my energy, and double your strength, you healing capacity, everything."

Angus's eyes widened. "Are you serious?"

"Yes. Not many people know about it. It was kind of a lost secret because so few Omegas are born. But if we mate tonight, by tomorrow you should be stronger than anyone in the city. You'll be able to beat Vincent's champion, hands down."

"Even in human form?" he asked and I had a moment of doubt.

"I believe so. My memory of the details is so foggy. We could find an elder to ask, but I'm not sure anyone would tell us the truth anyway. Even if we could find someone who knew more than me."

Angus struggled up so he was sitting properly, his feet now on the floor. "I do remember stories my mother told me of my great grandfather having an Omega mate after his first wife died. He was the greatest warrior our pack had ever known. Maybe his real mate was the reason."

"It's very possible," I said with a confidence I barely felt.

I knew this could work. It was my fear for Angus's safety that was beginning to make me feel sick. I grabbed my Alpha's hand and clung tight. "What if something happens to you, Angus? I'd die if they hurt you."

And I probably would now. Literally die. Without the protection of Angus, I'd be dead.

"Don't think about that. There's something we need to do tonight first." Angus grinned at me with lascivious intent. I slid onto his lap and wrapped my arms around his neck.

"And what is it that we need to do, Alpha?" I asked, widening my eyes in mock innocence.

Angus laughed, the sound as rich and perfect as a piece of chocolate from my childhood. He pulled me to him and stood up in a fluid, strong movement. I clung to the man that would be my mate, inhaling the scent of his hormones and loving the feeling of lust in my loins.

"Quick shower?" I suggested, my hands clinging to flesh covered in dry blood. *Yuck.*

He nodded, his chest rumbling in an earthy growl.

I couldn't help but laugh. I wasn't going to get many more words out of him tonight.

He put me down in the bathroom and flicked on the water.

Before I could assess the temperature, he jumped beneath the cold spray.

Brrrr....

He shook beneath the spray like a wild animal, flinging about his hair and rubbing at his skin until the water ran red and black.

I stopped to really take in the moment and let my gaze run over his amazing form. My stomach tightened as I couldn't help but stare at his aroused body. His cock jutted out like a rod. Pinkish water now ran down his hard, muscled body.

"You really are, the most beautiful man," I said, unable to keep my thoughts inside my own head.

He smiled and turned the water off, roughly towel drying his body and then taking my hand.

"I think you're the beautiful one," he managed to say, though the words were rough and tight.

"Thank you."

He pulled me tight against his damp body and I hissed out my breath with the sudden-ness of his cold flesh against my warmth. He pressed his lips to mine, his tongue flicking out to taste my tongue and I moaned with the heat flush he caused.

I fell back against the bed and pushed at my clothes. I wanted to be naked and our bodies pressed together. The black leggings fell away, then I pulled back to rip the T-shirt from my body.

Naked now, my skin began to burn for his touch.

"I need you... Please," I begged, lifting my arms to him.

"What do you need, Clayton?" Angus asked and my throat thickened with emotion.

"I need you to fuck me, claim me, love me." The words were flowing too freely now, I couldn't control them.

"Then I will," he declared, falling to his knees and lifting my legs so my knees pushed up closer to my shoulders.

He buried his head between my thighs, licking my ass. Probing deep, then moving higher. Suckling on my balls, then nibbling on the head of my cock which was already leaking profusely.

"Oh fuck!" I cried out. His mouth was wet, and hot, causing waves of ecstasy to roll over my skin. Building up into an incredible mountain of pleasure. I grabbed for his head and held on for the ride as he continued to devour me. His mouth made every part of me burn for him.

He lifted himself up, slicked his hard cock up with the oil he kept in the bedroom for us and hovered over me. Hands either side of my head now, he stared into my eyes like I was the only person in the world for him.

I needed us to be as close as humanly possible. As close as two people could possibly be. I lifted my legs up to place my ankles on his shoulders and grabbed for his cock with my hand.

"I love you," I said, wanting him to know how much I cared and how proud I was to be his.

Angus thrust his hips into my hands and I dragged him to the right position, setting his large arrow-shaped cock at my ass's entrance.

"I. Love. You." Angus ground out as he slid into me.

One inch at a time.

I opened, burned, and ached for him. I dragged on his hips, wanting him deeper. He forged inside me and my cock pulsed with longing.

When he was finally buried inside of me, his thighs were pressed against me and my balls were drawn up. Ready to come.

"Ah." I arched my back, waiting for him to start moving. There was some pain, but I was out of my head with need. I had to come, and soon.

Angus drew back slowly, until he was almost to the entrance, then shot forward in one big movement.

I cried out as tingles vibrated along the backs of my legs.

"You're mine. You're mine," Angus repeated over and over again as he rode me harder and faster.

I groaned and screamed as he drove me up and over that invisible mountain. My orgasm slammed into me like a semi-truck.

I squirted all over my belly. Hot, long streams as fireworks exploded inside my mind.

Angus gripped my hips hard and thrust once more, his seed flooding me and binding us together forever.

My body shuddered over and over again, milking up every drop of his seed until we collapsed into a heap of tangled limbs.

I was someone's true mate.

It was done.

And tomorrow, I may lose him.

And it would be all my fault.

CHAPTER 7

ANGUS.

The morning sun brought with it the beginning of the new day, and for me, it could be my last day on Earth, so I wasn't going to waste it working. I rolled onto my mate, who was covered in dried cum from a night full of fucking, and gave him a kiss to wake him up.

"Hmmmm, is it time to get up already?" Clayton asked, his hands moving up my chest and cupping my neck and face.

The beautiful Omega was so affectionate. I loved it. I could have his hands on me all day.

"I'm already up for you," I said, thrusting my pelvis at him and letting him feel my hardness.

"Again?" Clayton asked, his eyes going wide with surprise.

I laughed, loving the feeling of completeness rolling around in my blood stream.

I could sense on a cellular level, the difference mating with Clayton had made to my soul. I wasn't agitated, frustrated, or lonely. Everything was how it should be. I was at peace for the first time in my adult life.

"No. I'm sure you're probably too sore from last night. I just wanted you to know how desirable I think you are."

I swooped down and kissed him, needing his flavors in my mouth. He didn't disappoint me, he never did. He melted against me like ice in summer, pressing so close I could feel his need to be a part of me.

When he groaned, I pulled away, not wanting to push his body past its limits.

I thought I'd probably done that last night anyway.

"So, what are you going to do when you win the fight tonight, Angus?" he asked me, tousling my hair like he didn't have a care in the world.

I didn't expect to win this fight, despite what Clayton had told me about the extra strength I'd get from him. The vamps were going to attack in a pack, and I only had one hope to win, and that was to shift and rip them apart.

But one lethal bite of their fangs, and I was gone for.

"I don't know. What do you think I should do, mate?"

I had a mate. A beautiful mate. And I loved him.

"Well," Clayton began, chewing his lip in that way that I adored.

God, he's beautiful...

"I think you need to work out if you want to stay here or not. And if you want to leave San Fran and set up somewhere else, are we taking the pack with us?"

I narrowed my eyes at him. "Why wouldn't I take my pack with me?"

He looked away as though embarrassed, or intimidated. I didn't want him to be either.

"Come on, Clayton. Be honest with me."

"Well, they certainly didn't help you out by looking after me. Nor did they come to help when you came barreling in here last night."

I went to interrupt and he waved his hands at me. "Oh, please don't take offence to any of that. I know you're a good man, and a good Alpha, but your pack's loyalty could be better."

I sighed and relaxed into the pillows, pulling him against my chest. He was right.

"I know. The pack isn't what it used to be. We lost so many good men and women in the fighting, and all the work we have to do at the plant, and the vamps have really worn everyone down. You may be right…"

I'd never even considered just taking Clayton and leaving, and I wasn't entirely sure that was the safe, sensible, or right option.

I shook my head. "No. I could never leave my pack behind. And I don't think I want to stay here if I win the fight either. I want out of this city and away from the fighting. I'm sure we can find some other option."

Did we want to live without housing? Without food or clean water? With the possibility of running into other dangers and new enemies?

Clayton lifted himself up on my chest and turned around so he could look at me while we chatted. "I agree. Maybe we could stay in San Fran and simply move to the other side of the city? Stay where the houses and food are, but remove the danger of the other shifters and the vampires?"

I didn't think that was a good option either, but I couldn't see a better way just yet.

"I'm not sure that's possible, but there's only one way to see. And one step at a time." I had to win the fight yet.

Clayton rolled away from me and stretched out on his back. "Yes. One. Step. At. A. Time." He ran his right hand down his lithe body and reached his cock. He began stroking in a hypnotizing rhythm that I could not ignore.

I rolled on top of him and pushed his legs up. "So, you're up for more?" I asked, though the answer was pretty obvious.

Clayton reached for my cock and wrapped his hand around the shaft. My breath hissed through my teeth as renewed heat flushed up my spine.

"Always." He sighed and I joined our bodies once again for the dance of mates.

~

Hours later, we were awake once again after a post-coital nap and there was a loud banging at the door.

"Who is it?" I called out, not caring who it was when my mate was sitting in my lap.

A strange growl came through the door and my heart rate picked up. That was a shifters sound and there was only one animal in San Fran that was allowed to shift.

"The cougars," Clayton squeaked, his keen mind putting it all together faster than I could speak.

"Go to the bedroom and lock the door," I managed to get out, getting to my feet and pushing him towards safety.

My teeth were already shifting, I could feel the bubble of heat in my blood. My shifter coming to the forefront as danger loomed in sight. The vampires ruled this town with fear and threats. I would not live under those conditions any more

The door burst open, right off its hinges, and in stalked two large cougars, growling and baring their teeth in the most threatening mode possible. They stepped in opposite directions, intent on circling me.

"Shift back and explain yourselves, or I won't be liable for the consequences," I shouted.

Would any of my pack come to help me? Was there even a pack to fight for?

When the cougars ignored me and continued to prowl, I realized with a deafening thud, that most of my pack would be at the power plant. Working. Where I should be...

Fuck.

I let go of my humanity and shifted faster than I ever had. There was no pain, there was nothing. Nothing but fluid magic that made me want to howl to the moon in its beauty.

The cougars froze.

I whirled and bared my teeth, ready to attack. I wasn't sure I could beat them both in a fight to the death, but I was going to try.

Then I heard a calm, female voice that somehow penetrated the anger of my mind.

"Shift back. All of you," she commanded.

The cougars shifted back instantly, leaving two young men in their wake. They were barely twenty-one, pimples still adorning one of their faces.

Sick to my stomach that I'd been so close to killing such young men, I let go of my wolf and was soon also human, naked and standing in my living room.

Fucking fantastic.

"Who the hell are you?" I asked the woman now closing my door and moving into the living room.

She had long, silver hair and I hadn't seen her before. Which was incredible considering I knew almost everyone. It was hard to tell her age too. I could feel the strength of the shifter magic in her, but she was a woman. And she'd have to be sixty years old. At least.

"Angus, I am Tameethia. Alpha mate of the cougar pack that once dominated south San Francisco."

I nodded once. She wasn't making any moves that indicated that she would attack, but how did I know that?

A door opened and Clayton ran to me. I put an arm around him and he pressed close.

"You shouldn't have come out."

He ignored me and turned to face the woman in our home.

"So, you're what all the fuss has been about," she mused, her gaze roaming over Clayton's form.

"Yes," he answered simply.

Her gaze stayed on Clayton for an unusual amount of time, and then she shifted her focus to me. "Hmmm... Well, I'll get to the point of my visit young Alpha. I am here to offer you a deal."

"A deal?" I asked, unable to fathom what on Earth this woman could offer me.

"Yes. I know you are going up against the vampires tonight."

Everyone in the city would.

"Yes."

"You don't realize what they will do to you, or your pack, if you lose."

Oh yes I did, and I had the rest of the day to work out how I was going to minimize that effect.

"Angus won't lose," Clayton injected, and I squeezed him tightly.

"Let her speak," I said, not wanting to chastise him, but his blind faith in me was not correct.

The older woman smiled at Clayton. "You two have mated? Good, that makes the odds of the Alpha winning, even if he is bitten, considerably higher."

"Pardon me?" I asked. Had I just heard her correctly? Had Clayton been right about our mating making me stronger?

She smiled again. "You didn't know? Surely your parents have told you the stories? Or has all that been lost since this horrible world was created?" Her question seemed to be rhetorical, as she settled herself onto the couch and didn't look for an answer.

The two cougars moved to stand behind her in a protective, submissive way. Grandsons perhaps? Not that it mattered.

"The cougars and the wolves are very similar in our genetic makeup, and I have always been friends with members of your species. So much so that I have heard the tales of your Omega boys. They are the perfect mate to a strong Alpha, and his bond will protect you, Angus."

"Even against a vampire's bite?" Impossible, surely?

"Yes, even against a vampire's bite. I have not told Vincent, nor any of his brethren this, but you are by far the strongest man in this city. With Clayton by your side, you will be able to withstand their strongest attack."

Relief and pride flooded through me, but I focused on the woman in front of me. There would be time for celebrations later. "Then what do I need you for?" I asked.

The lines on her forehead deepened. "To protect your mate, of course."

My heart stopped.

Then as Clayton shifted against me, warmth filled me again and my brain went into hyperdrive. As did my heart rate.

"What the hell does that mean?"

She was still as calm as ever, which for some reason made my blood burn even more. Didn't she understand what was at stake?

"The vampires intend to put you in the ring, attack you as a group, and get the non-participating vampires to hunt down your mate as leverage. Even if you do win, how are you going to protect him against the vampires, and his old pack, who I'm pretty sure still want him dead. Do you have a pack of strong Betas to protect him?"

Her lips were quirking up now and she was really beginning to annoy me. Mostly of course, because she was right. I didn't have a strong, united pack who would fight to the death for my mate.

"Clayton, get me my clothes."

He ran off and I stood as straight as I could. Although nakedness was a normal part of being a shifter, having a life or death conversation with a clothed ancient Alpha mate was not fun while showing your cock to the room.

Clayton came back with my jeans and a tank top. I pulled the bottoms on, and then the tank, feeling more human now while clothed.

I rested my butt on the dining table, unable to sit while in the presence of these animals. "And just why would you protect Clayton for me?"

"Because I think San Fran needs a new leader, and you are the man for the job."

I smelled a rat. These cougars had made a deal with the devils for power, and I didn't think their integrity was very high.

"And why should I trust you when you have spent the past seven years protecting the vamps?"

Her mouth drew down on the sides as she looked at me. "Because I hate the vampires more than you can possibly imagine. They killed everyone in my pack, leaving only the oldest and youngest of us. These boys are my grandchildren. The vampires killed my sons, my nephews, everyone I loved, and then held the babies as hostages until we agreed to help them. We're as much a prisoner in this world as you are."

My belly tightened at the vivid picture she painted, and my own remembered pain of those first few years where there were so many deaths. "So, what do you want of me, Tameethia?" I asked.

"I want you to defeat them all. And then we can all sit down and discuss how we are going to turn San Fran back into a city of thriving occupants, rather than the sickening slum it has become."

I eyed her surreptitiously. She was of the old world too. Did she really want it to go back to the way it was?

"That sounds good in theory, but how are we going to change things? Tell me what you'd do tomorrow."

She nodded. "First, I would evenly distribute the jobs of running the town. The fact your pack alone does the power plant is ridiculous. There should be a rotating roster for all the wolf shifters to do that job, keep the feline shifters on water, and get the other lousy layabouts on their feet. We need more rules, more support, and better security. I would assemble a council, an Alpha from every pack to stand in and speak for their people. I believe in democracy, not what the vampires have made us become."

I couldn't help liking the old woman. She reminded me far too much of my own mother and grandmother. Fiercely strong women who believed in the strength of the pack and its people. And who believed in the goodness of all.

"Alright, Tameethia. I will agree to this with you. Where would you like to meet?"

"I will come and get your mate myself and hide him with my grandchildren. Put him in some clothes that cover his face, and I won't let anyone touch him."

"Done." What other choice did I have? "And if I die?" I had to ask, because I didn't think the odds were highly stacked in my success.

"Don't ask that," Clayton admonished, hitting me with an open palm across the arm.

The old woman got to her feet with regal grace. "As long as he behaves himself and is no bother, I will hide him for as long as necessary." She met my gaze with a powerful stare. "But Angus, I am counting on you to succeed tonight. The fates of all our people, and all the generations to come, depend of you being able to rid us of these tyrants."

I nodded to her and the two grandsons transformed back into the large cats that had, for so long, held San Fran captive.

Watching them go I finally saw the signs of their youth. The smaller legs, the darkness of their fur.

All the adult men had been killed...

I shivered at the idea of such a thing. We'd lost many men too, women and children also. But for the vamps to deliberately attack the strongest members of their packs must have left them extremely weak.

As Tameethia was passing through the door I called out, a nagging worry in the back of my mind asking for clarification. "Can I ask... With all the men gone for so many years, who were the cougars that roamed the streets through those early years?"

They had been huge. Powerful. Terrifying to any who would go up against the vampires.

The old woman turned back to me with a smile. "That was me, and the other women who had been left. Unlike you wolf shifters, our females shift also, and like you, our size is determined by our rank. I was always the largest cougar you would have seen."

My respect for the woman intensified as she gave me a final smile and left.

I sat down into a chair with a large thud and Clayton ran off to shut the door.

"They fucked up the hinges pretty good." He snarled at the door as it swung uncertainly, no longer able to lock or close.

"It's alright. It's not like we need to worry about security today."

Clayton turned back to me and stalked back over to the couch, the hairs on his arms standing on end in an obvious way.

"What's wrong?" I asked.

He couldn't possibly be scared by such a woman, could he?

"Nothing," he said, rubbing his arm viciously. "I just hated all that talk about you dying, because that is not going to happen." He practically spat that last bit of his sentence out and I wanted to laugh.

"I'm glad you're so confident." Because I wasn't.

"I am," he said huffily and began roaming around the kitchen. "Want me to make you something to eat?"

Probably a good idea.

"Yeah, please. There's some tuna on the top shelf I've been saving."

"Fish. Bleh," Clayton said, screwing up his face and sticking out his tongue.

"It's protein," I explained, and that was all that mattered. I needed as much strength as I could get for tonight.

Clayton opened two of the small tins and scooped them into a bowl for me, laying it down on the table in front of me and then sitting on the chair nearby.

"So, you really think it's worth sticking around for? This pack? San Fran?" Clayton said, his teeth sinking into his lower lip.

I picked up the fork and forced all the doubt from my mind. "Yes, I do. It's my home."

And my family's home. I wasn't abandoning it. And I wasn't

leaving my people either. The packs may be broken, and weak, but there was strength there still, I was sure of it.

And if there was nothing else to cling to other than Clayton, then I would stake my whole life on him and his survival. He was worth fighting for. Hell, he was worth dying for. But that wouldn't serve me, or him, to leave him in this fucked up world alone.

Yes... My lips lifted into a smile as strength filled my heart.

I would fight to win. For Clayton.

CHAPTER 8

CLAYTON.

To say I was shit scared would be the understatement of the century.

I'd spent the rest of the afternoon buried in Angus's lap. I didn't want to leave him. I was terrified to. Something told me that if I left his side something terrible was going to happen.

Even as his pack had filtered in around dusk to give him their best regards, I hadn't moved. I couldn't believe they'd gone to work, and just forgotten about him for the day. Some of them had even had a go at him for the lack of power they'd have tonight. Without Angus, they hadn't been able to move half the amount of metal around and therefore the city would suffer.

I'd snarled at that guy—stupid asshole—and told him they better get used to it. Because if Angus was killed by a vampire tonight, then no one was going to be there ever again to do their work for them.

Bloody use less cowards. They are no better than my old pack.

No, that was the fear talking. Angus's pack worked harder than any other group in San Fran, but I was just so bloody scared!

"Sit here, little one," the old lady cougar said to me, pointing to a seat on the ground next to the children.

I pulled the hoodie off my head, a precaution the old cougar had insisted on. "How long until the fight takes place?" I asked.

She shrugged. "A few hours perhaps. You'll need to stay here with the children because I'll have to go soon. The vampires will want their body guards close by." She rolled her eyes as though sick to death of the job she'd been given. Which, considering the deal she'd made with Angus, she was.

"You still shift?" I asked her, still confused by the fact that the females of their group shifted also.

She smiled. "I can, but rarely do. I oversee everything though, and Vincent likes having me at his side. Plus, I want to be close to the action tonight."

Her green eyes suddenly took on a vicious gleam and hope sparked inside me. If she was willing to fight also, my mate had more than just a chance of winning.

"So, do I. I'm not being left out," I told her.

There was no fucking way I was being left behind to wait and see if Angus came back alive or not.

"Yes, you are. You will stay here, or I will chain you up. You are my responsibility and I will not let you get hurt."

Panic rose in my chest like a hot, overwhelming tide. "Listen, Tameethia, please. I know you can understand how this feels. You were an Alpha mate too. He is stronger with me there. I know he is. And I cannot, I repeat, *cannot* wait around not knowing if he is alive or dead."

She glanced sideways, her resistance crumbling.

"Please, please! You have to know that the waiting is worse than anything. My heart will stop a thousand times tonight out of pure worry. Please don't leave me behind."

Tameethia rolled her eyes at me. "Stop being so dramatic. I understand. Of course I do."

She blew out a long breath and I struggled not to scream at her. Woman or no woman, she was still a powerful shifter and I wasn't sure I could out run her.

"Alright, little Alpha mate, I'll help you. But you will do as I say, got it?"

"Yes, ma'am."

I would do whatever she said. After all, she was a powerful shifter and I was only an Omega. My ability to protect myself was very limited. But that was only until I knew the outcome of Angus's fight. Then all deals were off.

"Put your hoodie back on. If I'm moving you through the town, then you need to be inconspicuous, alright?" she said.

I nodded blindly. "Yes." I grabbed for the black hoodie I'd thrown on the floor.

"Now, I will get you as close to the fight as I can, but you must remain hidden, and you must stay with my daughter. Mechelle. Because remember, the vampires main goal tonight is to destroy Angus and the resistance rising in the city. You are the key to his strength, so do not get caught."

A shiver coursed up my spine as her words embedded deeper into my mind. I wanted to be his biggest strength, but I could be his biggest weakness. I didn't want that.

Was I being selfish in wanting to be there? Because she was right. If I was caught, then all hope was lost.

"I'll be careful. I promise."

Despite the danger, I couldn't shake the feeling that I needed to be there for him.

"Okay. Follow me. Watch the footpath and do not look up, even if someone speaks to you."

"Okay."

I pulled the hoodie over my head and scruffed up my hair so it fell over my face. Being invisible used to be daily goal. Surely, I could manage it for a few more hours.

She sighed out in big, dramatic fashion and turned back to the door that we'd entered.

We stepped out into the city once again, and the melee of noises entered my mind like a buzzing beehive. People everywhere. I so wanted to look up, and around, but I kept my head down and stayed close to Tameethia.

She wove through the streets and when we finally stopped, I had no idea where we were.

"Mechelle, this is Clayton. Do not let anyone have him. I mean it. No one." Tameethia pulled my arm until I was tucked against the wall. "Stay here."

I nodded. "Thank you," I whispered to her, though the pounding of my heartbeat in my ears made it almost impossible to know how loud things truly were around me.

"Don't get killed, young one," Tameethia said, and disappeared.

I risked a look up, slanting my head so my face wouldn't be seen.

There was a woman there. Standing in front of me. Protecting me. Probably ten years or so older than me. She wasn't speaking to me. Instead, her full attention was on something in the distance.

"What are you looking at?" I asked, shifting closer to her.

She didn't need to tell me, the answer was in sight.

Fifty feet away lay an old boxing ring. It had been dragged into the center of town so that there was a proper show on tonight. Angus was nowhere to be seen, and as night had fallen, I could feel the unnatural movements of the vampires around us.

"I can't believe there's so many people here," I whispered to Mechelle and she stepped closer to me.

"Everyone knows what is going on tonight, and everyone wants to see the vampires fall. We're all sick of their way of running the city and your mate gives us a chance for a new beginning."

Hmm, yes, my mate.

"He's almost here. Can you see him?" I asked her, the hairs on the back of my neck standing on end. Angus was nearby. He had to be.

A shudder ran straight through me and I saw him in my mind, on his knees, blood gushing from an open wound in his throat.

"No." I gasped, pain striking me in the chest as I fell back against the stone wall.

"What is it?" she whispered, grabbing me by the arm.

"I saw..." I gulped, fear rising in me like a fire alarm, wiping out all of my senses in one clear swipe. "I saw him dying."

The cougar shifter growled. "We can't let that happen. How can we change that fate?"

"I don't know... I don't know..."

I reached inside for my intuition. There had to be some way for me to save him or prevent this from happening. Or maybe it was just my own fear aiming to bind me up so I couldn't move?

"I need to stay hidden, but can we get closer. Please?" I asked.

She looked around, her feline shifter eyes keen in the darkness. "Yes. But don't let go of me."

She grabbed my hand tightly, interlinking our fingers so I couldn't unlock them even if I wanted to.

We wove through the crowd of people on the street, my heart pumping like a steam engine. Adrenaline zinging through my blood stream.

The hand that held mine was sweaty, but I clung tighter as she pulled and pushed through the throngs of people who'd come to see the downfall of the vampires. I had an ally in this woman, Mechelle, and I was going to use her if I needed to.

I can't shift. I can't fight. What can I do to save him?

Tears stung my eyes, but I kept my head down and made my feet move when they would have stumbled from fear alone.

Mechelle pulled me to a light pole and pressed us both up against it.

"Stay with me," she said, and wrapped her arms around my waist like a girlfriend would.

Happy for the support she offered, I leaned against her and tucked my face into her abundant red hair.

I could feel him like he was right behind me.

"He's here," Mechelle said into my ear, her throat catching with excitement.

I nodded and turned around a little so I could squint with one eye at the spectacle.

My knees buckled and I grabbed for Mechelle. She held on tight and for the first time in my life, I was grateful for the cougar shifters.

"Don't lose your lunch. You need to focus."

God, he looks beautiful.

Angus had come in nothing more than a cut off pair of old jeans. Surely that was a choice for modesty, because nothing else was covered. His huge chest gleamed with good health and his abdominal muscles were as fit as any boxer. His arms were as big as tree trunks and the look on his face was one of gritty determination. He pumped his fists together and shifted his weight from bare foot to bare foot like an old boxer.

"He looks dangerous," Mechelle said, her tone full of admiration.

"He is. But so are the vampires."

There was a surge of lighting as the electricity in this area of San Fran got turned up.

Vincent stepped into the ring, followed by a large young male vampire.

The crowds around the ring began to quieten.

"Thank you all for coming tonight. It seems there needed to be a more public spectacle to reassure people that we are still very much in control of the city."

There was an angry murmur around the crowd and Angus rolled his eyes.

Yeah right. Reassure people.

A smile tugged up my lips and inside my belly the fear calmed.

"Angus will face off against my best fighter, in a bid to get back some of his freedom. Although the punishment for such disrespect is death, Angus is by far one of the most productive member of our city, and would be sorely missed if he was gone."

I held my breath, hoping for a reprieve in this madness.

"Therefore, I have decided to extend a pardon to the Alpha wolf, and will ask only for fifty years of service in replacement for his sentence."

Anger brewed in my belly, despite the fact I should have been feeling relief. Angus would be working in that power plant until the day he died anyway, so this was not a new offer. It was a way for Vincent to get out of this fight, and for him to keep his thumb down on the wolves, while maintaining power in the city.

There was quiet as the city held its breath.

Would Angus give in at the last minute and bow to the power of the vamps?

"No thank you, Vincent. I'd rather fight."

And die, were the unspoken words behind Angus's decree.

A cheer went up all around us and my belly trembled in fear once again.

"Very well. You know the rules. No shifting. One on one."

Vincent calmly stepped out of the ring and lifted his hand. "Begin."

The crowd surged forward as the vampire and Angus faced off against one another. The vampire snarled and sneered, his ugly face grotesque in its paleness.

Stupid blood suckers. I'd like to see them looking so smug when the sun comes up in the morning.

Angus and the vampire began to circle one another. The vampire had a crew of men and women behind him, hanging off the ropes and hollering to him.

Angus had men too, which I was glad to see. They looked grim and determined, though I doubted any of them would jump up if Angus needed them to.

The vampire lurched forward and I gasped, grabbing hold of Mechelle as Angus danced sideways and swung his arm in an arc, sending the vampire flying sideways into the ropes.

"Yes!" I yelled, excitement bubbling inside me.

The vampire snarled and bared his fangs, flying at Angus and trying to bite his neck.

Angus grabbed the vamp by the throat and slammed the huge guy into the mat. An almighty crash went through the center of the city as Angus lifted his fist and beat into the vampire's face over and over again. Angus's arms and shoulders bunched stronger and bigger until finally he stood up, grabbed the vampire's head, and ripped it from his shoulders.

A huge cry went up around us as I watched in disbelief. My mate had beaten the vampire's best warrior. As he should.

My mate, my alpha.

Cold dread curled up my spine and I yelled out before my eyes even saw anything. "Angus! Behind you!"

He must have heard me because he swung around just in time to have a hoard of vampires jump on his chest.

CHAPTER 9

ANGUS.

The pain that splintered through my chest and neck was like the very fire of hell. I screamed out and tried to pull them free, swinging my fist at the vampires crowding me.

My hand connected and one of the males went down, then the next was at me. Biting my arm, drawing blood. The pain was intense, but I could feel my rage increasing. I knew it was safer to stay human. A vampire's bite in my wolf was deadly...or so I'd thought before I'd met my mate and the cougar shifter who had explained it all so well.

Another vampire clamped down on my neck, their arms going around my shoulders to hold my body in place as they attempted to drain the core of me.

No choice now. I'd be dead soon enough if I stayed in this body.

I cried out and pulled the vamp off my back, letting go of my humanity and feeling the rise of the Alpha inside of me. The one who never should have been kept down. The shift came on me. My teeth were first.

I twisted around and sunk my newly pointed teeth into the male vampire in front of me, tearing at his shoulder and spitting out the flesh as the blood oozed between my teeth. A massive growl ripped through me as I saw a dozen more vampires jump into the ring.

The cougars were behind them, on the ground, unmoving.

My body dropped to the ground and transformed into that of my huge black wolf. I let the snarl rip through my teeth, flexed the strong muscles in my legs, and charged forward. The vampires stumbled and tripped to get away from me, but I pulled them back into the ring.

They were like rag dolls to my new and improved teeth. I dragged them back and ripped their limbs off.

Pain burned in my hind legs as two of the vampires bit me, their venom leeching into my bloodstream.

No!

I tried to ignore the panic rising in my mind. Generations of fear of vampire venom coming in to paralyze me. I twisted and turned, then two more wolves staggered into the ring and dragged the vampires off me.

My Betas. They came to help.

I leapt forward and tore at the necks of the vampires still around, black blood spewing everywhere as there were screams of panic around us. The whole city was running for their lives, and Vincent was at the center of them, standing still, as though he were the center of the world.

I'll get to you later.

The wolves increased in numbers as my Betas stepped up to fight my fight. Other shifters were standing up too. I could see some of the lions and cheetahs prowling around aimlessly.

I wasn't sure if they were going to be an ally or an enemy, but I'd deal with them all later.

The vampires fell in huge numbers now and as I leapt off the stage to confront Vincent, I let go of my wolf and transformed back to human.

There had been no pain with the shift, and I was confident that I would be able to shift back to my Alpha wolf quickly if needed.

"Well, it looks like you are the victor today, Angus," Vincent drawled, not moving an inch amongst the fray of running, screaming people.

I stepped forward, carefully. Time slowed down around me as the people cleared away and the animals moved closer.

"It's time for the vampires to leave, Vincent."

His eyes sparkled with anger and I knew then that I was going to have to kill him.

Suddenly, I was being dragged back and down. A new group of vampires had me by the throat. The waist. My legs. I tugged and pulled hard at my captors. Vincent's sickening smile hovered in my line of vision as vampire venom began racing through my muscles.

Out of nowhere, an almighty growl ripped through the air. A huge cougar came over the top of Vincent. His smug expression changed to one of shock as the big cat ripped at his throat.

Tameethia, who was still standing beside Vincent, fell away and transformed into the biggest cat I'd ever seen.

The wolves were on me, tearing away the vampires at my neck.

My vision was blurring. My blood was draining away.

I was on the ground, but I couldn't get up.

And I didn't know why.

There was more screaming as those that had attacked me were destroyed.

Vincent was laying on the ground in front of me, choking to death on his own blood.

There was a whole group of cougars now. Huge, lethal creatures.

And at the center of it all, was my mate.

I pushed myself up higher to see. I blinked rapidly. No, it couldn't be. They'd hidden Clayton away. Surely, he couldn't be here.

"Angus!" Clayton was now on top of me, patting his warm hands all over me.

He seemed upset, and I didn't know why. Tears were streaming down his face. "Don't die, Alpha. Don't die. You can't leave me."

I lifted my hand up to cup his beautiful face. The rest of the world had fallen away as my strength leeched from my muscles.

"It doesn't matter, my lovely mate. I don't matter. It's only you. I want you safe. They'll look after you now. The vampires are gone."

I lay down, not able to keep my head up any longer. I'd never thought how it would feel to die. I'd assumed, like living, it would be painful. But it wasn't. There was a coldness, but it was peaceful.

I closed my eyes, praying to the heavens that the cougars would take him in. Surely, they would. He was such a good man...an asset to any pack.

"No!" Clayton's voice came through my mind like a boom gate. "Help me, what do I do?" His hands were on me, and for some reason, I could feel pain in my legs now. Aching, burning pain.

Fuck. What are they doing?

And who was he talking to?

I cracked my eyes open and I could see Tameethia, and another woman crouching over me, talking furiously to Clayton. He nodded suddenly and bent to kiss me. His lips were warm, and so lovely. I lifted up to meet him. He dipped his head and sunk his teeth into my neck, sucking hard.

"Ah!" I cried out at the pain he was inflicting. "What are you doing?"

He grabbed my face and shook me.

I opened my eyes wider, getting annoyed at him now. Why was he trying to save me?

"You are not dying on me, Angus. I need you. I love you. And I am saving you."

I loved him too, but I'd been bitten a dozen times. I'd saved them from the vampires. That was all that was important. What did Clayton think he could do?

"Keep biting him. Suck out the venom if you can. You aren't a shifter, so it won't poison you," a woman I didn't recognize was saying to Clayton.

He shimmied down my body and set his sharp teeth into my leg.

"Ah," I cried out, grabbing for him to make him stop.

Two people came beside me, my Betas, holding a hand each and gripping hard.

"Fuck. You guys too?"

Terry smiled, his head cut open and blood dripping down his face. "Sorry Alpha. You aren't dying on us today. You've got a whole city to clean up now."

I groaned, images of a new world rolling through my mind as Clayton systematically went from one sore spot to the next burning hot spot.

"Ah. God. Clayton."

I wanted to scream at him, '*you're killing me,*' but I knew it was the opposite. He was saving me, and the road back to the living was so much more painful than the road down to death. My arms and legs began to tremble and I sat bolt upright. My stomach heaved and I spewed out a foul-tasting black vomit. I turned my head and threw up again, choking on the smell of death on my breath.

"He may need some of your blood to cleanse him, rebuild him. He's lost a lot of blood." That woman was speaking to Clayton again as she handed him a knife.

"Pour it in here," she said, pointing to a gaping hole on the side of my thigh.

Clayton nodded and wrapped a hand around the blade.

"Who are you?" I asked, staring at the woman with the intense eyes and air of leadership.

"My daughter," said Tameethia as she stepped up next to our group.

Clayton hissed in pain and I looked over to see him placing down the bloody knife, opening his hand and squeezing his palm until a steady stream of blood poured onto me.

"What are you..." I reached out to stop him, but my Betas grabbed my arms.

They didn't need to apply much pressure. My whole body had gone weak.

"More," the woman above me said, and Clayton moved his hand to another sore on my leg.

His blood soothed my wounds, making my muscles calm their trembling and my belly churn in hunger.

I stared at my young, small mate. My perfect other half. My Omega.

"You're healing me."

He looked up and smiled. "Of course. I told you I could."

I nodded and leaned back, letting myself sink back into the earth once again. Clayton has said that he would save me and he had.

A FEW HOURS LATER DAWN APPROACHED AND I WAS FINALLY able to stand up and move around once again.

People had formed in groups. Cautiously waiting for the call to action. To know what changes the death of the vampire reign would bring.

As I staggered to my feet, pulled on the jeans I was handed by my mate, and walked over the blood-smeared stage, a weird sense of purpose flowed over me. This was it. My moment in time when I was exactly where I was meant to be. At the exact place I should be. Doing the exact thing I was born for.

Clayton was one step behind me and as I reached a hand out, he clasped onto it.

Another piece of my shattered heart fell into place.

Clayton was my true mate. The one born for me. And no matter how we had met, or who we'd known before now, he would be my forever.

Tameethia stepped up on the floor beside me, her pack of cougars close by.

"Please, come closer." I gestured to the groups hiding in the alleyway, in abandoned shops, and openly on the streets. "I know you all have questions, but I would like to start by introducing myself and this woman beside me. I am Angus, Alpha of the Highland Wolves. This is Tameethia, Alpha mate of the South End Cougars."

There was a round of tittering remarks and scowls from some of the other packs.

"We need to get San Francisco back on its feet. A livable city for us all without the daily threat of our children being killed, or our lives being taken away. I liked the world before the humans died, and I would like to see us go back to that sort of life.

"Tameethia has suggested a city council. An alpha or leader from every group will need to step forth and we will band together and work out how best to make this city work for us. Those of you who are too lazy to work, will be asked to leave. This is a tough new world we all live in, and I know the only way forward is to help one another. As we used to."

I stepped back and gestured for Tameethia to step forward.

She began speaking about the tyranny of the vampires and how we could rise to become one of the strongest families on the planet. I turned my attention away from her and focused on my mate. His intense eyes, and his soft skin. "I never thought we'd get here, Clayton. To a time where peace and unity was possible."

Clayton smiled and pressed himself tighter against me. "I'm not sure it's going to be an easy ride, Angus. There is a lot of people in this city that are far too used to doing nothing." He scowled at the crowd and I ignored his fears.

"Clayton, you have empowered me to be the strongest man in this city. I am unbeatable, and from now on, my word will be law. We will get this city back to what it used to be, and life will be better for all of us. I promise."

I kissed his forehead and put my arm around his shoulders. I wasn't sure if we could ever get back to the sort of life we had before the humans were killed off, but damn it, we had to try.

"I know you will Angus. Because you are a true Alpha, and you will live and die for your family."

I squeezed my mate tightly to me and let the love I felt for him flow freely between our bond. "You're my everything, Clayton. And I want to build a world that you want to live in."

Clayton sighed and pressed closer.

It would be a long road back to health, and just as Clayton's blood had painfully pulled me back to the land of the living, it would be worth it in the long run.

THE END

Book 3 – The Alpha's Omega Mate is available: HERE
Or read on for a sneak peek into the book.

CHAPTER 10

ERIK

I glanced around my pack's homes and let a smile of contentment stretch across my face. My people were happy and more importantly, healthy. Their laughter and conversation filled the streets.

I was proud of what we'd accomplished here. All we'd managed to survive since the world had gone dark and all the humans had died.

"Time to go?" Timmy, one of my Betas, asked as he sidled up next to me. The energy bouncing off him was both excited and happy.

We hadn't been out hunting for a month, and as a wolf shifter who needed to shift and run, Timmy was as excited as I was to be getting outside today.

I lifted my chin and gestured towards the town. "Just waiting on Allen and Frank, then we can go."

Timmy nodded and joined me in leaning against the outer perimeter fence.

"I can't wait to stretch my legs again." I said, twisting my neck until it crackled and popped. "It's been too long."

Timmy nodded. "Yeah, I know. It's a pity we can't go out more often."

I grunted in acknowledgment, but didn't say anything. They all knew why we couldn't leave the safety of our homes too often, and I wasn't about to lecture the young Beta once again.

Despite the fact that we were powerful wolf shifters, there were feral, dangerous creatures outside these walls. A vampire bite was deadly to a shifter when in wolf form.

Luckily most of my pack had never even seen a vampire, much less gotten into a fight with one.

"Here they are."

I practically sighed with relief when Allen and Frank, another two of my Betas walked toward us. My wolf was anxiously pacing inside my mind, ready for the time when he was the one in control.

Frank pulled a cart along behind him that we could use to transport the bounty of our hunt.

"Great. Let's go."

I reached for the large handle and pulled on the strong levers that held tight our front gates.

The metal pulleys clanked and groaned as the huge metal door rolled open.

Freedom.

I took a deep inhalation of cool air, the beautiful expanse of countryside opening up before me.

"It's great to have that door open." Allen said as he stepped up next to me. He was a few inches shorter so his shoulder, when pressed against me, touched mid bicep.

"I know." I agreed, as my wolf growled inside of me.

We forged forward, using the old, worn path amongst the thick trees and overgrown shrubs.

The sun was shining on us, the warmth on my skin making me ache to be in wolf form.

The vampires were asleep and I couldn't sense any other shifters in the area. We'd need to split up if we had any hope of finding enough food for the entire pack.

"Let's set up at the base of the hill, shift, and run. We can hunt in pairs today."

I led my men down the path and eventually found the spot we always made our central point.

It had an old, rusted park bench and was cleared for ages all around. For safety, we could see in every direction, eliminating any chance of a surprise attack.

"Remember the last time we were here, and we had to deal with that bear?" Allen asked as he stripped off his clothes and rolled his shoulders in anticipation of the shift.

"Yeah, I still reckon we should have caught him and eaten him." I said, smiling at my Beta, who had been terrified by the wild animal.

It was so rare to find large animals to hunt now. The need for blood for the vampires, and meat for every other shifter, had decimated the supply.

But spreading out further for more meat was not worth dying for.

"All right. Allen and Frank, you head north, Timmy and I will go south. Stay together and kill anything you need to."

Allen and Frank nodded, a soft growl rolling through them as they both dropped to their knees and shifted into large, brown wolves.

They headed off and Timmy, the young one, turned to me.

"Alpha, why can't we go out further? I mean, wouldn't we have a better chance of catching more meat if we could travel more distance?"

I put a hand on Timmy's shoulder. "We probably would find more meat if we traveled further away from the pack, but that's not the question. The question is, what else would we find? Another pack of wolves? Cheetahs or lion shifters? You've never seen a vampire in hunting mode, have you Timmy?"

Timmy shook his head rapidly.

"Well, I have, and I can tell you, nothing's more terrifying than a ravenous vamp whose bite is lethal to a shifter in wolf form."

Timmy's gaze dropped and I reached for my own worn shirt.

"It's better than we have less food, but we're safe Timmy. Trust me."

I hated being the party pooper all the time, but my father had entrusted me with the safety of the pack. And that wasn't a responsibility that I took lightly.

His head popped up. "I do, Alpha. I didn't mean any disrespect."

I winked at him and dropped my blue jeans and shirt onto the park bench beside me.

"I know. Now, stick close by me and if I throw you some food, just carry it with you until I lead us back here, okay?"

Poor thing would probably gobble up the first rabbit I threw at him, and I wouldn't blame him. It had been weeks since I'd tasted any fresh protein, though the preserved jerky and vegetables we ate kept us strong.

"Okay." Timmy put his own clothes on the table next to mine.

He was a good kid, and his father had been a close friend of mine. But Timmy had a rebellious streak in him that reminded me far too much of myself at his age.

And that didn't bode well for his safety in this new world.

"Follow me."

I exhaled and dropped to the ground, letting the magic of my ancestors flow through me.

A loud rumble rolled through my chest and the howl in my mind grew in volume as my large, black wolf sprung forth.

Fur sprouted from my skin as my muscles and bones began to contort.

Pain shot through my spine as I extended my head and let out a howl as the transformation was completed.

It had been a month since my last shift, and it was always painful.

I panted, waiting for the tingles of fire to recede.

As shifters, we weren't meant to stay in our human forms for so long. But I couldn't open the gates more often that I already did.

Perhaps I should encourage everyone to shift inside the compound more often?

Food for thought later.

Timmy whimpered beside me, a small brown wolf staggering sideways as he became accustomed to his shifter body once again.

I tilted my head and began running through the woods. Trees dashed by my face, the cold earth firm beneath my paws.

So many amazing sights and smells. I'd really missed it.

There was a scatter and movement up ahead and I charged forward, sensing a small rabbit and diving into the bushes to grab it.

I sunk my teeth into its neck and tore sideways, killing it quickly.

The blood ran over my jaws and I licked it away.

We hadn't eaten meat in a week, and though my belly screamed for more, I threw it towards Timmy.

He picked it up by the ear in his mouth, a somewhat disgusted look on his wolf face.

If I could have laughed, I would have.

At least he wasn't tempted to eat it as I'd first expected.

I set off running again and this time sensed a larger animal. A deer, maybe.

Near the water.

I turned east and kept running, my blood pumping harder in my veins as we got closer. There were tingles all over my body and my cock ached with need.

What were these curious feelings of lust pulsing through me?

Strange.

I shook off my confusion and slowed my pace. I kept low, hiding behind some bushes and creeping up on my prey.

I stopped. Shock rippling through me.

There, by the water wasn't a deer as expected, but a young male, his dark hair cut short against his lean face.

He was alone, and disheveled. His clothes looked and smelled like he'd slept in them for a month.

The boy... the very beautiful boy, knelt by the river and cupped his hands, scooping some of the clear water up into his mouth.

His groan of relief made my cock pulse, and if I was surprised by my earlier lustful feelings, I wasn't anymore.

This was who I was attracted to, and my relief was keen.

At least I wasn't suddenly getting aroused by the hunt.

I let go of my wolf, though he clung tight to stay, howling at me to grab this young male and hold on forever.

I shook off the feeling of mateship, confused by my attraction to this young male. This stranger.

I generally preferred females for sexual activities, though my pack would accept any mate I chose. Male or female.

"Stay here." I whispered to Timmy, not sure if this stranger would be dangerous or not.

Yeah, keep telling yourself that. You just want this guy to yourself.

The young male's head came up and he jumped to his feet, looking around for whatever about me had spooked him.

What sort of creature are you?

"Don't be afraid." I said softly, stepping out of the bushes towards him. Had he heard me when I'd spoken to Timmy? His hearing must be heightened considerably.

Yet he looked human. But that was impossible.

The young man whirled and took one look at me, his bright gaze clashing with mine for a split second before he bolted away like a frightened rabbit.

My wolf leapt inside me, riveted by the chase. But I held him down and refused to shift, though I raced after the young boy in my human form.

He was too irresistible to resist.

He darted through the trees with great speed, and my heart pounded in excitement as I went after him.

He took a wrong step around a large tree, caught his foot on a swollen root and tumbled to the ground.

I grabbed hold of his thin arms and yanked him to his feet, his bright blue eyes catching my attention as he gasped and heaved in breath.

"I'm not going to hurt you. Please stop running."

I was struggling to breathe myself and as the boy in my arms began to relax, we both became aware of my erection, which now pushed against his belly.

These were the moments that shifting, and being naked, were quite inconvenient.

Heat rose in my cheeks as I tried to dismiss my reaction, which was very unusual for me. Being thirty-five this year meant my body usually was more restrained.

"Sorry about that. Now, I'm going to let go, but you can't run. My wolf will just force me to chase you again."

The young boy swallowed hard and I could see the fear in his eyes. He wanted to flee. But he didn't move as I released my hold on his thin shoulders.

"You're a wolf shifter?" He asked quietly, his voice a strange timbre I hadn't heard before. He had a slight southern accent too.

"Yes. And what are you?" I took a deep sniff of his scent, but couldn't detect anything distinct. "You can't possibly be a human, they've all died off."

"Um... I'm not a shifter..." The young boy stammered, then stopped and swallowed hard again.His delicate Adam's apple bobbing up and down in his throat.

I took a step back and looked him up and down, from his torn sneakers to his disheveled hair. "You're not a vampire, obviously," I gestured to the sun above our heads. "Then what are you?"

The boy's smile was beautiful when it arrived. It began as a little twitch of his lips, a slight twinkle in his blue eyes. Then it spread across his face, transforming him into one of the most beautiful creatures I'd ever seen.

I fell back a step, my gut hollowing out as though I'd been sucker-punched.

"It's so strange that you don't know what I am. You're an Alpha after all, aren't you?"

He gestured to my still erect body and I nodded. My height and general body size were generally a giveaway for my rank, but he seemed to be indicating more to my arousal.

Though what did that have to do with me being an Alpha, unless he was...

"You're an Omega." I breathed, letting my gaze roam over his body in a delicious way that made my balls throb.

He bit his lip and I wanted to sink my teeth into his mouth.

"Yes. So, you do know what I am."

"I do." And that was why my cock was behaving so badly.

As though he could read my mind, the Omega's gaze dropped to my groin, redness staining his face when he glanced back up at me.

"So, this is a pretty normal response then?" I asked, gesturing to my straining, thick cock.

He glanced away. "Ah, yeah. Kind of. For an Alpha, especially."

"Have you met many of us?" I asked, surprised. I didn't think there'd be many Alphas left, but then again, what would I know of the world as it was now?

I tried my best to keep my pack and town running smoothly, and kept out all the other crap.

"Ah yeah...a few..." The kid looked down again and this time I noticed the angry slash that pulled at his mouth.

There was a story there, but probably not the time to ask yet.

"Alright... well..."

I couldn't leave him here, but taking him back to the pack may put us in danger.

Or was it more dangerous to leave him out here where he may tell someone about us?

I let my gaze wander once again over his fine face and lean body and my decision-making abilities moved south.

"I think you need to come back to the pack with me. You need some food by the looks of you."

The kid's head came up and his eyes grew wide with fear.

"Where are you going to take me?"

I frowned at him. He sounded strangely terrified, and I certainly meant him no harm. Quite the opposite.

"Don't be scared. I have a pack, hidden in the hills. We've survived pretty well since the virus hit so you'll be safe and fed with us. Plus, I can't have you running off and telling anyone we're here, so I think you should come back with us."

His foot shifted so that the toe now pointed outwards, a clear sign he wanted to run.

I sighed. "Hey, look. I told you, don't run. Let's start at the beginning. I'm Erik." I held out my hand to him and waited. This was how people used to introduce themselves.

Hopefully this guy was old enough to remember that.

The Omega glanced at my fingers and down to my still-hard cock, then back up to my eyes.

"I'm Corey. And you're still naked."

A laugh bubbled in my throat. The first, for a very long time.

I let out a long breath. I had the strangest feeling of happiness flowing over me as I stood here in the woods with this beautiful young man.

"Okay, Corey, well, I'll introduce you to one of my Betas, and then we're all going to walk back to the meeting spot. You can't shift, can you?"

He shook his head rapidly, his fear a palpable cloud around him.

"Just hang tight, okay?"

I reluctantly glanced away from the Omega, half expecting him to run for the hills the moment my back was turned.

I raised my hand and waved to Timmy. "Come over."

Timmy's head popped up out of the bushes and I turned back to the Omega, strangely relieved to see him still standing there.

As Timmy walked over, Corey took a quick step closer to me and a part of my wolfie personality puffed up with pride.

Timmy was twenty-one and as I looked at them side by side, I realised the Omega was a little older than Timmy probably. Which was good. I didn't want to be lusting after some teenager.

"Timmy, meet Corey."

Timmy grinned at the Omega, his bubbly personality shining through in his smile. "How's it hangin'?" Then he burst into a round of giggles.

I rolled my eyes but when I looked at the Omega, he seemed to be more relaxed.

"Ah, I'm the only one clothed, so yeah—it's hanging fine, thanks." Corey replied.

"What are we doing then, Alpha?" Timmy asked me.

"We're taking Corey back with us. We can't leave him out here for some vampire to find."

"You shifting?" Timmy asked him and I gave Corey a smile.

Timmy couldn't tell what he was. As a Beta, the Omegas were a weird thing.

"No, Corey can't shift."

Timmy looked up at me with a confused, frowny face.

"He's an Omega."

THE ALPHA'S OMEGA MATE

NEW WORLD SHIFTERS BOOK 3

ERIK.

I glanced around my pack's homes and let a smile of contentment stretch across my face. My people were happy and more importantly, healthy. Their laughter and conversation filled the streets.

I was proud of what we'd accomplished here. All we'd managed to survive since the world had gone dark and all the humans had died.

"Time to go?" Timmy, one of my Betas, asked as he sidled up next to me. The energy bouncing off him was both excited and happy.

We hadn't been out hunting for a month, and as a wolf shifter who needed to shift and run, Timmy was as excited as I was to be getting outside today.

I lifted my chin and gestured towards the town. "Just waiting on Allen and Frank, then we can go."

Timmy nodded and joined me in leaning against the outer perimeter fence.

"I can't wait to stretch my legs again." I said, twisting my neck until it crackled and popped. "It's been too long."

Timmy nodded. "Yeah, I know. It's a pity we can't go out more often."

I grunted in acknowledgment, but didn't say anything. They all knew why we couldn't leave the safety of our homes too often, and I wasn't about to lecture the young Beta once again.

Despite the fact that we were powerful wolf shifters, there were feral, dangerous creatures outside these walls. A vampire bite was deadly to a shifter when in wolf form.

Luckily most of my pack had never even seen a vampire, much less gotten into a fight with one.

"Here they are."

I practically sighed with relief when Allen and Frank, another two of my Betas walked toward us. My wolf was anxiously pacing inside my mind, ready for the time when he was the one in control.

Frank pulled a cart along behind him that we could use to transport the bounty of our hunt.

"Great. Let's go."

I reached for the large handle and pulled on the strong levers that held tight our front gates.

The metal pulleys clanked and groaned as the huge metal door rolled open.

Freedom.

I took a deep inhalation of cool air, the beautiful expanse of countryside opening up before me.

"It's great to have that door open." Allen said as he stepped up next to me. He was a few inches shorter so his shoulder, when pressed against me, touched mid bicep.

"I know." I agreed, as my wolf growled inside of me.

We forged forward, using the old, worn path amongst the thick trees and overgrown shrubs.

The sun was shining on us, the warmth on my skin making me ache to be in wolf form.

The vampires were asleep and I couldn't sense any other shifters in the area. We'd need to split up if we had any hope of finding enough food for the entire pack.

"Let's set up at the base of the hill, shift, and run. We can hunt in pairs today."

I led my men down the path and eventually found the spot we always made our central point.

It had an old, rusted park bench and was cleared for ages all around. For safety, we could see in every direction, eliminating any chance of a surprise attack.

"Remember the last time we were here, and we had to deal with that bear?" Allen asked as he stripped off his clothes and rolled his shoulders in anticipation of the shift.

"Yeah, I still reckon we should have caught him and eaten him." I said, smiling at my Beta, who had been terrified by the wild animal.

It was so rare to find large animals to hunt now. The need for blood for the vampires, and meat for every other shifter, had decimated the supply.

But spreading out further for more meat was not worth dying for.

"All right. Allen and Frank, you head north, Timmy and I will go south. Stay together and kill anything you need to."

Allen and Frank nodded, a soft growl rolling through them as they both dropped to their knees and shifted into large, brown wolves.

They headed off and Timmy, the young one, turned to me.

"Alpha, why can't we go out further? I mean, wouldn't we have a better chance of catching more meat if we could travel more distance?"

I put a hand on Timmy's shoulder. "We probably would find more meat if we traveled further away from the pack, but that's not the question. The question is, what else would we find? Another pack of wolves? Cheetahs or lion shifters? You've never seen a vampire in hunting mode, have you Timmy?"

Timmy shook his head rapidly.

"Well, I have, and I can tell you, nothing's more terrifying than a ravenous vamp whose bite is lethal to a shifter in wolf form."

Timmy's gaze dropped and I reached for my own worn shirt.

"It's better than we have less food, but we're safe Timmy. Trust me."

I hated being the party pooper all the time, but my father had entrusted me with the safety of the pack. And that wasn't a responsibility that I took lightly.

His head popped up. "I do, Alpha. I didn't mean any disrespect."

I winked at him and dropped my blue jeans and shirt onto the park bench beside me.

"I know. Now, stick close by me and if I throw you some food, just carry it with you until I lead us back here, okay?"

Poor thing would probably gobble up the first rabbit I threw at him, and I wouldn't blame him. It had been weeks since I'd tasted any fresh protein, though the preserved jerky and vegetables we ate kept us strong.

"Okay." Timmy put his own clothes on the table next to mine.

He was a good kid, and his father had been a close friend of mine. But Timmy had a rebellious streak in him that reminded me far too much of myself at his age.

And that didn't bode well for his safety in this new world.

"Follow me."

I exhaled and dropped to the ground, letting the magic of my ancestors flow through me.

A loud rumble rolled through my chest and the howl in my mind grew in volume as my large, black wolf sprung forth.

Fur sprouted from my skin as my muscles and bones began to contort.

Pain shot through my spine as I extended my head and let out a howl as the transformation was completed.

It had been a month since my last shift, and it was always painful.

I panted, waiting for the tingles of fire to recede.

As shifters, we weren't meant to stay in our human forms for so long. But I couldn't open the gates more often that I already did.

Perhaps I should encourage everyone to shift inside the compound more often?

Food for thought later.

Timmy whimpered beside me, a small brown wolf staggering sideways as he became accustomed to his shifter body once again.

I tilted my head and began running through the woods. Trees dashed by my face, the cold earth firm beneath my paws.

So many amazing sights and smells. I'd really missed it.

There was a scatter and movement up ahead and I charged forward, sensing a small rabbit and diving into the bushes to grab it.

I sunk my teeth into its neck and tore sideways, killing it quickly.

The blood ran over my jaws and I licked it away.

We hadn't eaten meat in a week, and though my belly screamed for more, I threw it towards Timmy.

He picked it up by the ear in his mouth, a somewhat disgusted look on his wolf face.

If I could have laughed, I would have.

At least he wasn't tempted to eat it as I'd first expected.

I set off running again and this time sensed a larger animal. A deer, maybe.

Near the water.

I turned east and kept running, my blood pumping harder in my veins as we got closer. There were tingles all over my body and my cock ached with need.

What were these curious feelings of lust pulsing through me?

Strange.

I shook off my confusion and slowed my pace. I kept low, hiding behind some bushes and creeping up on my prey.

I stopped. Shock rippling through me.

There, by the water wasn't a deer as expected, but a young male, his dark hair cut short against his lean face.

He was alone, and disheveled. His clothes looked and smelled like he'd slept in them for a month.

The boy... the very beautiful boy, knelt by the river and cupped his hands, scooping some of the clear water up into his mouth.

His groan of relief made my cock pulse, and if I was surprised by my earlier lustful feelings, I wasn't anymore.

This was who I was attracted to, and my relief was keen.

At least I wasn't suddenly getting aroused by the hunt.

I let go of my wolf, though he clung tight to stay, howling at me to grab this young male and hold on forever.

I shook off the feeling of mateship, confused by my attraction to this young male. This stranger.

I generally preferred females for sexual activities, though my pack would accept any mate I chose. Male or female.

"Stay here." I whispered to Timmy, not sure if this stranger would be dangerous or not.

Yeah, keep telling yourself that. You just want this guy to yourself.

The young male's head came up and he jumped to his feet, looking around for whatever about me had spooked him.

What sort of creature are you?

"Don't be afraid." I said softly, stepping out of the bushes towards him. Had he heard me when I'd spoken to Timmy? His hearing must be heightened considerably.

Yet he looked human. But that was impossible.

The young man whirled and took one look at me, his bright gaze clashing with mine for a split second before he bolted away like a frightened rabbit.

My wolf leapt inside me, riveted by the chase. But I held him down and refused to shift, though I raced after the young boy in my human form.

He was too irresistible to resist.

He darted through the trees with great speed, and my heart pounded in excitement as I went after him.

He took a wrong step around a large tree, caught his foot on a swollen root and tumbled to the ground.

I grabbed hold of his thin arms and yanked him to his feet, his bright blue eyes catching my attention as he gasped and heaved in breath.

"I'm not going to hurt you. Please stop running."

I was struggling to breathe myself and as the boy in my arms began to relax, we both became aware of my erection, which now pushed against his belly.

These were the moments that shifting, and being naked, were quite inconvenient.

Heat rose in my cheeks as I tried to dismiss my reaction, which was very unusual for me. Being thirty-five this year meant my body usually was more restrained.

"Sorry about that. Now, I'm going to let go, but you can't run. My wolf will just force me to chase you again."

The young boy swallowed hard and I could see the fear in his eyes. He wanted to flee. But he didn't move as I released my hold on his thin shoulders.

"You're a wolf shifter?" He asked quietly, his voice a strange timbre I hadn't heard before. He had a slight southern accent too.

"Yes. And what are you?" I took a deep sniff of his scent, but couldn't detect anything distinct. "You can't possibly be a human, they've all died off."

"Um... I'm not a shifter..." The young boy stammered, then stopped and swallowed hard again.His delicate Adam's apple bobbing up and down in his throat.

I took a step back and looked him up and down, from his torn sneakers to his disheveled hair. "You're not a vampire, obviously," I gestured to the sun above our heads. "Then what are you?"

The boy's smile was beautiful when it arrived. It began as a little twitch of his lips, a slight twinkle in his blue eyes. Then it spread across his face, transforming him into one of the most beautiful creatures I'd ever seen.

I fell back a step, my gut hollowing out as though I'd been sucker-punched.

"It's so strange that you don't know what I am. You're an Alpha after all, aren't you?"

He gestured to my still erect body and I nodded. My height and general body size were generally a giveaway for my rank, but he seemed to be indicating more to my arousal.

Though what did that have to do with me being an Alpha, unless he was...

"You're an Omega." I breathed, letting my gaze roam over his body in a delicious way that made my balls throb.

He bit his lip and I wanted to sink my teeth into his mouth.

"Yes. So, you do know what I am."

"I do." And that was why my cock was behaving so badly.

As though he could read my mind, the Omega's gaze dropped to my groin, redness staining his face when he glanced back up at me.

"So, this is a pretty normal response then?" I asked, gesturing to my straining, thick cock.

He glanced away. "Ah, yeah. Kind of. For an Alpha, especially."

"Have you met many of us?" I asked, surprised. I didn't think there'd be many Alphas left, but then again, what would I know of the world as it was now?

I tried my best to keep my pack and town running smoothly, and kept out all the other crap.

"Ah yeah...a few..." The kid looked down again and this time I noticed the angry slash that pulled at his mouth.

There was a story there, but probably not the time to ask yet.

"Alright... well..."

I couldn't leave him here, but taking him back to the pack may put us in danger.

Or was it more dangerous to leave him out here where he may tell someone about us?

I let my gaze wander once again over his fine face and lean body and my decision-making abilities moved south.

"I think you need to come back to the pack with me. You need some food by the looks of you."

The kid's head came up and his eyes grew wide with fear.

"Where are you going to take me?"

I frowned at him. He sounded strangely terrified, and I certainly meant him no harm. Quite the opposite.

"Don't be scared. I have a pack, hidden in the hills. We've survived pretty well since the virus hit so you'll be safe and fed with us. Plus, I can't have you running off and telling anyone we're here, so I think you should come back with us."

His foot shifted so that the toe now pointed outwards, a clear sign he wanted to run.

I sighed. "Hey, look. I told you, don't run. Let's start at the beginning. I'm Erik." I held out my hand to him and waited. This was how people used to introduce themselves.

Hopefully this guy was old enough to remember that.

The Omega glanced at my fingers and down to my still-hard cock, then back up to my eyes.

"I'm Corey. And you're still naked."

A laugh bubbled in my throat. The first, for a very long time.

I let out a long breath. I had the strangest feeling of happiness flowing over me as I stood here in the woods with this beautiful young man.

"Okay, Corey, well, I'll introduce you to one of my Betas, and then we're all going to walk back to the meeting spot. You can't shift, can you?"

He shook his head rapidly, his fear a palpable cloud around him.

"Just hang tight, okay?"

I reluctantly glanced away from the Omega, half expecting him to run for the hills the moment my back was turned.

I raised my hand and waved to Timmy. "Come over."

Timmy's head popped up out of the bushes and I turned back to the Omega, strangely relieved to see him still standing there.

As Timmy walked over, Corey took a quick step closer to me and a part of my wolfie personality puffed up with pride.

Timmy was twenty-one and as I looked at them side by side, I realised the Omega was a little older than Timmy probably. Which was good. I didn't want to be lusting after some teenager.

"Timmy, meet Corey."

Timmy grinned at the Omega, his bubbly personality shining through in his smile. "How's it hangin'?" Then he burst into a round of giggles.

I rolled my eyes but when I looked at the Omega, he seemed to be more relaxed.

"Ah, I'm the only one clothed, so yeah—it's hanging fine, thanks." Corey replied.

"What are we doing then, Alpha?" Timmy asked me.

"We're taking Corey back with us. We can't leave him out here for some vampire to find."

"You shifting?" Timmy asked him and I gave Corey a smile.

Timmy couldn't tell what he was. As a Beta, the Omegas were a weird thing.

"No, Corey can't shift."

Timmy looked up at me with a confused, frowny face.

"He's an Omega."

CHAPTER 2

COREY.

"He's a what?" The Beta Timmy asked, and for once, I actually wanted to laugh at the dumbfounded expression on his face.

Why was my stupid, genetic mutation so bloody rare? The Alphas got hard just looking at me.

My gaze slid to the Alpha Erik's long, hard cock. Damn it looked delicious.

Case in point.

And all the other wolves didn't give me a second look, except maybe in disdain. I could neither hunt nor shift. And since the Alphas all wanted to fuck me, the jealousy amongst the other members of the pack, male and female, was quite high.

One of the many reasons I'd left my old pack.

"He's an Omega. Which means he can't shift." Erik tried to explain to the Beta again.

Timmy stared at me with a familiar expression of not under-standing.

"It's okay, I hate it too." I confided in him, taking a step towards him now. Away from the Alpha who felt as safe as the earth to me.

Timmy stepped a little closer to me, the flaccid state of his cock a clear sign he really didn't know what I was.

"Then what's the point, man? I mean, does that mean you're kinda like one of the girls?"

I couldn't help but smile at the Beta, who'd managed to deliver a classic insult in a way that was neither insulting nor degrading. It was obvious the young one was just trying to figure me out.

"If you're asking if I'm gay, then the answer's yes."

Timmy's eye brows went up and down a bit, and he stood straighter.

"Gay? You mean, you don't fuck girls?"

I shook my head.

This was like talking to a child rather than a grown man who'd weigh a good fifty pounds more than me.

"No, not at all."

Never had, and I didn't think I ever would. There was just no attraction to a pair of boobs and a pink clam.

"But, why?" Timmy asked again, his gaze shifting from Erik to me again. "I mean, I know guys are fun too, but never... ever girls?"

I looked between the men, surprised by their openness to my sexuality.

In some packs I'd have been punched or attacked in some way by now to make sure I knew how disgusting they thought I was. All the while they'd be feeling me up.

"Guys are fun?" I repeated. Not sure I'd heard correctly.

Timmy grinned. "Well, yeah. Most of the wolves like a bit of both, you know. Especially since they're so few females around. But I personally like a soft woman—big boobs, you know?"

I laughed, the sound as rusty as a tin can left in the sun for a decade.

"Ah, no... can't say I like big boobs."

Unless you're talking about massive pecs like Erik's, but that's a different story of course.

Erik cleared his throat loudly. "I think we better get back before the others start to worry we've been attacked. You all right to come with us, Corey?"

It wasn't really a question, but I appreciated the Alpha's insistence on manners.

"Yes, thank you."

I had so many questions about what he wanted from me when I got there. And what sort of state his pack was in.

Most wolf shifters I knew had disjointed packs, low numbers, no clothes or food. But Erik and Timmy both looked well fed and healthy, though I couldn't vouch for their clothing since they were both naked.

"So, what have you been doing since all the humans died?" Timmy asked as we walked through the bush that had hidden me well over the past weeks.

I stared at the young Beta for a minute, not sure where to even begin answering such an absurd question. "That's sounds so odd... when you put it that way. Most people consider it the end of civilisation. The beginning of Hell itself."

My pack had traveled quite a lot in the past decade and I'd met many different shifter packs along the way. All of them had been fighting for dominance, land and food, at one time or another.

There should have been an unending supply of it all since we now owned the whole world. And yet, as always, greed and power were everyone's main motivations.

"Hell? What are you talking about? There's not that much difference now, surely?" Timmy asked, his smile as infectious as the poison ivy I'd managed to pick up a few months ago.

"Ah... are you serious?" I looked towards the Alpha in front of us, but Erik didn't look around.

We kept twisting and turning through the forest until we were in a clearing I didn't recognise.

"Where are we?"

"Not far from our place." Timmy answered, throwing the bunny carcass that he'd been carrying into the wagon.

"We haven't got much, Alpha."

"I wouldn't say that," Erik murmured without looking at me.

A shiver coursed up my spine, making me shudder softly. The strange sensation combined fear and arousal all in one.

I wasn't really surprised by my instant attraction to the Alpha, of course. Erik was hot. But I'd run away from another sexy Alpha, and I had no way of knowing if this one was any better than the last.

Timmy and Erik began to pull their clothes back on and I was more than a little resentful of the tight fabric that wound itself around Erik's hot ass.

There was a rustle in the bushes and two more naked men walked into the clearing.

I jumped into Timmy and Erik pulled me into his side, soothing me instantly with a possessive hand gripping my hip.

"Hey, boys. You did very well." Erik greeted the men, who dumped several dead animals down onto the table.

"Who's he?" A blond guy asked, his face a mask of resentment as he stared at me.

I looked down and away. I was no match for a guy that size even if I could fight. Which I couldn't.

"Boys, this is Corey. Corey, this is Allen and Frank. You guys ready to head back?"

The Betas looked at the lack of meat from their Alpha and I could see the questions they wanted to ask lingering on their lips. Yet, they didn't say a thing.

The men who'd dumped the animals turned away and grabbed their clothes, pulling on the well-worn denim and shirts.

They were clean at least.

"Let's go." Erik said, grasping a gentle, but persistent hold on my elbow.

We walked up the hill, past the trees and the brush.

I couldn't see a thing and the hairs on the back of my neck began to sting and stand on end.

What did I know about these men? Nothing.

They could rape me, kill me and dump the body. No one would know the difference.

I swallowed the lump that rose in my throat, the rapid beat of my heart in my ears making me sick.

"Here we are." Erik said suddenly, and the men began to shift and move trees and brush.

Where?

Then suddenly the metal door appeared.

"Wow." I said, amazed at how well hidden the entrance was.

"Thanks." Erik grinned, then set about pulling open the door with his massive strength.

My mouth went dry as the muscles in his shoulders heaved and strained against the weight of the door.

Wow.

The door opened and revealed a bustling town. Well-kept houses along roads filled with people.

I stared, with my mouth hanging open.

It was like looking back in time, before blood filled the streets and there was a battle on every corner.

"Come on, Corey. Come meet the pack." Erik's insistent hand was on my shoulder and my feet moved automatically forward.

Through the door and onto different soil.

Toto, I don't think we're in Kansas anymore.

People bustled by. Children played in the streets.

The grind and pull of the door closing behind me made me jump, but Erik's hand was reassuring on my shoulder.

"I'll introduce you to my younger brother. He has a spare bed at his place. You may want to stay there while you're here."

I glanced towards the Alpha, surprised. He was handing me off to his brother? As what?

"You want me to fuck your brother?" I asked, confused. Sex had been my main use and bartering tool since my parents had died.

It was a dirty business, but I'd been lucky. Most of the men I'd been with liked my pretty face and rarely beat me.

Compared to some of the other Omegas and women I'd met over the years, I'd been well taken care of. Comparatively.

A deep growl cut through the air and I stumbled along the dirt road in my haste to escape the noise.

Erik grabbed me up when I would have fallen and pulled me back. He steadied me and I got my legs under me once again.

What was that noise for?

When I met his eyes, Erik's gaze was icy.

"Hell, no. Don't you dare."

I swallowed against the fear in my heart. I didn't want to cross this guy, but misunderstanding would be my downfall if I didn't ask the questions first.

"Then what do you want me to sleep at his house for?"

If I was honest about my sordid past, I'd been handed around to more men than I could count. Or easily remember.

But luckily my Omega blood, or scent, or whatever it was that I had, meant that I was destined to be mated to an Alpha.

All the Betas who'd tried to fuck me barely managed it most of the time. They couldn't seem to get it up for me.

Which frustrated the hell out of them, but at least they didn't take it out on me, generally. There were a few exceptions.

I took it personally for a while, thinking that my fucked-up, mutated genes meant that I was unfuckable. Unlovable.

But then those same douches that couldn't get it up to fuck me would lie to their friends about how well they'd done, and I realised that the problem wasn't me.

It was them.

It had saved my ass dozens of times, and I hadn't decided if it was a curse or a gift yet.

Erik glared down at me.

"I thought you'd like somewhere safe to sleep, because in case you can't tell, I'm dying to fuck your ass."

A moan rose through my throat and escaped my lips. It had been so long since anyone had touched me with anything other than disdain. I missed the affection of true connection.

I somehow knew that Erik wouldn't hurt me.

"Oh, fuck... don't do that. The moan thing..." Erik stepped away, breathing hard.

So, he wanted me, but he didn't want me? This wasn't making much sense.

"Are you mated already, Alpha?" I asked, assuming there had to be a reason for his abstinence. If he wanted me, why wouldn't he just have me?

What Alpha wolf held back on his base desires?

"No... but fuck. This is ridiculous. Let me introduce you to James, then we'll see where you want to stay."

I still wasn't understanding his logic, but I was quite happy to follow along, if it meant safety and food.

My stomach lurched and grumbled in hunger, and I put my hand to my gut to stop the obnoxious noise.

"Come this way for a minute." Erik tugged on my arm and I followed him towards what must have been the original strip of shops in town.

They were still all brightly colored and had people in every one.

"How are you still so self-sufficient? I don't understand."

"Hey, Millie. Can you grab me some bread, please?" Erik asked the older woman at the window of the bread shop.

The woman ran a shrewdly assessing glance over me, but did as she was asked and brought back a brown roll of something.

Erik thanked her and handed the food over to me.

"Here, eat this while we walk."

I opened my hands and brought the roll to my mouth, biting into the fresh dough and groaning in bliss. It was almost like the bread of old. Grainier and harder, but still amazing. Unlike anything I'd tasted in a decade.

"Come on, Alpha, how? Tell me how you've done all this."

They didn't seem to have been affected at all by the world turning on its head. If only they knew what the rest of the world looked like!

Erik chuckled. "We lived here before the virus spread, and we haven't changed anything. We've always been a very secluded pack. We weren't really interested in the cities."

"But how do you have..." I gestured around at the houses lit with electricity. "Everything. The food. Electricity. Don't tell me you have running water."

Erik shoved his hands into his pockets and looked down as though embarrassed.

No!

I must have died and gone to Heaven. Maybe I'd frozen to death in the forest? My version of eternal bliss would definitely be this. Time with the hottest guy on the planet, lots of food and warmth, above all else.

"Well, we had to re-jig a few things, but we already had our own water system rigged up, and most of our electricity came from a wind farm a few miles away. We've had to do repairs over time and we increased security against the vampires, of course, but that wasn't anything new."

I was dumbfounded.

"I don't know what to say."

And I didn't. The rest of the world was starving, and this pack had everything figured out.

"What's happening in the rest of the world, then? What about your pack? What happened to them?" he asked, obviously interested since I couldn't stop exclaiming how amazing his town was.

I wanted to lie about my past, but I didn't think I should.

But what would Erik think of the truth?

"I ran away from my old pack." I admitted, the pressure in my chest releasing the moment I opened up about that part. "The fighting amongst the vampires and shifters had gotten pretty bad, and I couldn't protect myself," I continued to explain, clinging to the vestiges of truth in my sentences.

"And your Alpha didn't protect you?" he asked, sounding disappointed.

"The Alpha of my pack died, and no one else was interested in taking me on." This part was a lie. There were plenty who wanted me, none of them Alphas.

"So, you were mated?" Erik asked, his voice a strange, deep timbre.

"Ah, no. He was mated to a woman."

Who hated my guts almost as much and she hated the fact her husband wanted to fuck me more than her.

Erik nodded and I could see that he wanted to ask additional questions, but more than enough had been shared for now.

"Here it is. James, you in?" Erik called out and I stood staring at the gorgeous little cottage before me.

I hadn't seen a house this well-preserved in all of my travels. It was like a magazine picture I'd found in a shop we'd ransacked.

The front door opened and a guy about my age with short-cropped blondish hair and a pair of jeans that hugged his slim legs popped out.

He was topless, like a lot of men around the town. Wolves had incredibly hot bodies, in both temperature and attractiveness.

"James, this is Corey. I found him in the forest today, and brought him back for some R and R. You okay with him sleeping in the spare bed?"

James's gaze slid my way and my legs went to jelly. This wasn't a nice man. There was violence in his blood, and I could feel it as strongly as if he had a knife to my throat.

James lifted his chin, "Yeah, sure. But why?"

James took a few steps in my direction, his dark gaze on me from hip to toe, and back again. I couldn't stop the panic from rising in my gut, nor the keening noise that built in the back of my throat.

He wasn't an Alpha, but he was close enough to one for him to realise what I was. And want me.

But I wouldn't be good for him, I knew I wouldn't be. And the memories of the past abuse I'd taken flooded back in like a summer storm.

I jumped at Erik, wrapping my arms around his neck and plastering my body to his.

"Please don't make me stay here, I want to be with you. Please, Alpha, please." I buried my head into his chest and took lots of short, sharp breaths, my whole body loving the scent of this man.

"No fucking way." I heard James say from behind me and I burrowed even closer.

James had just worked out what I was, and if he had half a brain—and the cruel ones always did—he'd be kicking himself for not grabbing me sooner.

Erik didn't say anything but I could hear his heart pounding against my ear like a bongo drum, reverberating through my sensitive skin.

I kept my eyes clamped shut and my fingers digging into Erik's shoulders.

Please, please, please, please...please!

There was silence for too long, and then finally Erik put me out of my misery.

"Okay, you can stay with me." Erik rumbled in my ear, pulling at my arms so that I would release his neck from my death grip.

James chuckled behind me. "He can stay here, Erik. Not a problem. I'm sure I can whip his ass into shape in no time."

James laughed but it sounded strained even to me.

Erik growled back and picked me up in his arms. I clung to his neck and buried my head into the safety of his neck as he carried me away from the Beta with the violent smile.

I'd found another pack, and they lived so much better than the last one I'd been a part of. But did that mean that I was any safer now than I was before?

Not with James around, that was for sure.

Only time would tell of course, but one thing was for certain.

Shifters were the same, everywhere you went. And as an Omega male, I wasn't really safe anywhere.

CHAPTER 3
ERIK.

orey was perfect in my arms. Like he'd been there always,
and always would be.

It was a fucking terrifying feeling and as soon as I got him back to my small house, I dumped him on the couch and retreated to the doorway, my chest heaving from breathing hard.

"Thank you. I couldn't stay with him." Corey shuddered, wrapping his arms around his legs and curling up into a ball on the couch.

Fuck, why did he have to look so adorable and helpless all the time?

"But you'll stay with me?"

Why?! Why! I can't NOT fuck you! Don't you understand? I wanted to scream at him.

I began to pace up and down the hallway. The heat of my anger and impotence annoyed the hell out of me.

The Omega got up off the couch and moved closer.

"Alpha, I really don't want to cause you any distress. If you'll just let me leave, you won't have to worry..."

I stopped my pacing and glared at him. "Don't even think about leaving."

I couldn't have that. Fuck, no! I could handle the sweet torture of him being here, in my home. But knowing he was out there, in that fucked up world? I couldn't handle that.

"But why?" The Omega blinked at me, his big eyes making me want to grab him and kiss the shit out of him.

I groaned in impatience and leaned against the door frame.

"Because I want you safe, okay? I don't want you out there starving, at the mercy of God knows what."

The Omega looked far too skinny, and if his stories about the world now being likened to a war zone were true, I couldn't send him back out there.

My wolf wouldn't allow it.

Corey began to shiver, running his hands up and down his arms.

"I haven't washed in weeks, I must smell so bad. Do you have anywhere I can clean myself for you?"

My throat ran dry as I imagined him beneath my shower head.

And on my cock.

"Ah, yeah. Come with me."

Clean himself for me? Why was he cleaning anything for me?

My imagination took over where my logical brain refused to go, and I was soon groaning in pain as my erection rose and throbbed against the inside of my jeans.

"The bathroom's in here."

I pushed open the door and Corey stumbled inside, his mouth wide open as his eyes darted around the clean room.

"Are you serious? You have an indoor bathroom? Don't tell me I can actually have a shower?"

He stared at me with incredulity etched into every line of his handsome, young face.

"Of course. What has the world come to out there?"

Corey began to laugh, tugging at his tattered t-shirt and his black joggers.

"You would seriously keel over if you saw how bad it was out there. When all the humans died we lost all power, running water, food production, the whole lot. Then everyone began to fight, shifters against shifters, the vampires against everyone."

He continued to tug at his clothes until he was completely naked, his clothes a mere dirty puddle around his ankles.

"Seriously Alpha, you have paradise here."

Corey turned away to flick on the water and I let my gaze run hungrily over his form.

He was skinny, far too skinny for my liking, but at least he didn't look too unhealthy.

The chefs would fatten him up. I'd make sure of it.

"How did you survive out there?" I managed to choke out, though my hands itched to grab his hips and pull him against me. I ached to feel the warmth of his skin on me.

"Oh, I know how to collect berries and wild fruit, and the like. I did a lot of camping as a kid, and when I ran away, I took some dried meat that kept me going for a while."

Corey stood beneath the water and moaned as the brown and red stains of the earth ran down his body.

"Oh my God, it's hot! How... Alpha... I must have seriously died and gone to Heaven. This is amazing!"

I cleared my throat as my nipples tightened and ached for his touch. He was arching his back to enjoy the water as he frantically rubbed at his skinny arms.

"Don't rush, by any means. But just so you know, we only allocate five minutes a day for each person, so you can't stay in there forever."

He twisted around to face me and put his head back under the water.

"Oh, sure! No problem, is there anything to wash with?"

I grabbed one of the soaps I had from under my sink and handed it to him.

"Some of the women make our bathing products. Go nuts."

There was a swirl of brown in the shower and his hair looked like it was matted together.

Despite all that, he was strikingly beautiful. He had thick, black eyelashes that framed his perfect blue eyes, and skin that should be worshipped.

"Amazing! Thank you!" he cried, practically dancing in the warm water.

I hadn't ever seen anyone so enthusiastic about a shower before. We really must be spoilt here.

Corey grabbed for the soap and used it to scrub his arms and legs quickly, taking time to wash over his flat stomach and even rubbed some soap through his hair.

"I think I'm going to need to chop all this off and start again." he said, referencing his dark brown hair, tugging on the thick strands.

"Maybe." I choked out. I needed to get out of there. If he didn't cover up soon, I was going to rip my jeans off and take him where he was standing.

"I better get back to work, so just take your time..."

"No!" Corey yelled, dropping the soap and charging forward.

He grabbed me by the arms and looked up into my eyes.

"Please let me suck you. I've been dying to do it all day."

Oh, for fucks sake... really? Have got to say no to *that?!*

"You don't have to..."

Corey dropped to his knees on the tiles and a growl rolled through my chest. I shouldn't just stand here. Surely I could rustle up the energy to stop him. Move away. Something.

He pulled at my jeans, finally getting the zipper open, releasing my swollen dick from its cage.

"Damn you're beautiful." Corey said as he wrapped a warm hand around the shaft and took the head into his mouth.

Sensation exploded up my spine and I twirled my fingers in his wet hair.

"Corey... you don't have to..."

Oh, fuck...

His mouth came off me and he looked up, his blue eyes filled with smoky lust.

"I want to. Well... I want you to fuck me actually, but if it's too soon for that..."

I reached down and pulled him up to his feet. He didn't need to ask me twice.

"Oh, I'll fuck you."

I kicked my jeans off to the side and lifted him into my arms. His legs went around my waist as naturally as breathing. I walked forward until he was pressed against the shower tiles, the hot water streaming over our bodies.

"Kiss me." I demanded, not caring how I sounded.

Corey's eyes went wide for a moment before he grabbed my head and pressed our lips together.

He was hesitant, I could tell. Due to past scars, or an aversion to kissing? I didn't know. I only cared that I needed to be close to him.

I sought a closer contact and speared my tongue between his lips and down into the wetness of his mouth.

Corey groaned and ground against me, his hard cock lying against his belly.

I grabbed at his arse, but needed better access to him.

I managed to flick off the water and walk out of the shower and into the bathroom. I lowered him down onto the bathroom vanity.

A perfect height.

"Lean back." I instructed him as I tugged at the drawers beneath the basin that contained lubes and oils for this very thing.

My fingers finally found the thin, round bottle I'd been looking for and I pulled it up to us.

"Hold out your hand." I ordered Corey, who was now leaning back against the wall with his legs still tight around my waist.

He held out his hand and I flicked the top off the lid and poured some of the sweet smelling oil into his palm.

He gave me a quizzical look and I grinned at him.

I'd only ever been with a couple of guys before, generally preferring the sexuality of a woman.

But I knew how I felt, and my need for Corey in this moment far surpassed anything I'd ever felt with anyone before.

"Play with your cock so I can watch you come." I snarled.

His mouth fell open for a moment, then his hand moved down to his beautiful, long cock and began stroking it.

"Good boy." I said as I poured some lube into my hand and applied it along my own dick.

I'd have thought with all the messing around it would have deflated somewhat, but it was still as hard as granite and pounding with blood.

I turned my hand around and began running my lubricated fingers over his ass.

Corey bucked and moaned against my fingers.

I slid my middle finger inside his tight, sweet ass and he cried out, pumping his fist along his cock even faster.

Damn, he's sexy.

A groan slid from my lips as my balls tightened beneath the shaft of my cock.

My eyes closed of their own volition as my wolf howled and jumped inside my mind.

This is my mate.

Oh, fuck.

This is my mate.

And I needed to calm down or I was going to shift mid-fuck, and I doubted that would be pleasurable for either of us.

I forced my eyes to open to slits and saw the most beautiful sight on Earth.

My mate, with his legs open, his cock hard, and his mouth open and panting with need.

I grabbed his calves and lifted them up so that his ankles were hooked over my shoulders.

"Yes. Please. Fuck me." Corey panted.

I lined the head of my cock up with the tight little star of his ass and slowly fed it into the heat of his body.

"Oh. My. God." Corey cried, arching his back and pumping his cock.

My head exploded in a shower of sensation and I couldn't hold onto my control a second longer.

I thrust forward, sinking balls deep into the perfection of Corey's body and my orgasm exploded, ripping through me like a virtual hurricane.

I grabbed hold of Corey's thighs and threw back my head, howling to the invisible moon and letting Corey drain me of my seed.

Heat splashed between us as Corey cried out.

I dropped my head to look at him, still spasming and writhing on the bench as my seed filled him. His mouth open in a wordless entreaty.

Corey's cock was limp against his belly now, white ropes of cum painting his body and mine.

Suddenly his eyes popped open and our gazes met.

The light in his eyes twinkled brighter than ever before and his lips smiled at me with never-ending enthusiasm.

"That was fucking incredible."

CHAPTER 4
COREY.

ncredible was right.

Holy fuck!

My mind buzzed around like an insect near a camp light. Totally brainless and wired at the same time.

Erik pulled me into the warm shower once again and washed the sex juices off our skin.

He'd said we were only supposed to have five minutes of warm water, but I was pretty sure we'd used up a week's worth.

Then he carried me to bed, and like the virtual fantasy that he was, he let me sleep.

I don't know how long I was out, because he woke me at some point and made me eat a beautiful soup that was so filling I barely finished it before I passed out once again.

I'd never slept so heavily before.

I could feel the heat of Erik's body next to mine all night, and my dreams were peaceful. I was safe.

The grey light of dawn reached my skin and as I began to stir, I stretched my body out as though I hadn't moved in months.

My muscles were tired and sore, despite their rest.Their first real rest in months.

I reached out my hand and bumped into a warm lump of muscle behind me.

My eyelids popped open and I blinked rapidly,

"Good morning, sleepy head." Erik's deep voice vibrated in my ear.

The memories of yesterday's bathroom fucking came rolling back in and heat flushed up my face.

"Good morning, Alpha."

Erik grabbed my hips and yanked them back against him.

His cock was hard. Like a lump of steel resting behind me, pressing insistently against my butt crack.

I moaned, despite myself, hungry for more.

"Call me Erik." The Alpha said.

I glanced over my shoulder at him as he hovered over me.

"What?"

"Don't call me Alpha. Only the young Betas do that, and I don't really like it anyway."

My lust forgotten for a moment, I rolled onto my back to look up at the big Alpha who was propped up on his elbow, staring down at me with beautiful brown eyes.

"What do you mean, you don't like being called Alpha? You are the pack's leader, aren't you?"

I couldn't have been wrong about such a thing? My Alpha-radar was always correct.

He chuckled. "Of course, I am. Have been since my father was killed ten years ago."

Right when the world changed...

"Then why can't I use your title?" I asked again.

This wasn't making sense. I'd never met an Alpha who didn't want his name practically engraved with it.

"Because I'm not just an Alpha. And I want you to call me Erik."

He repeated, the edge to his tone making it impossible for me to ignore him.

"All right." I agreed. I really had no choice in this one. If the Alpha wanted it... I swallowed hard. "Erik."

He looked like an Erik, too. Strong and super masculine. I'd always had a bit of a thing for the old Viking myths, and the men who looked like them.

He dipped his head and kissed me, his lips tasting of rain water and a sweetness I identified as being uniquely Erik.

I reached up for his hair, loving the feel of the short, manicured haircut beneath my finger-tips.

When he pulled away I lost my ability to cling to him. My body was utterly relaxed, and I stared up at him with fuzzy eye-sight.

"Can I ask you a question, Corey?"

"Anything." I replied.

"Why didn't you want to stay with my brother when I said you could live with him yesterday?"

I tried not to look away from Erik's intense stare, so I didn't look guilty, but I didn't want to tell the truth in this regard.

"I... ah..." I swallowed hard. What could I say to such a question that would be palatable to the Alpha?

Erik stared a little harder at me. "You don't need to lie to me. I won't be offended, or upset with you, no matter what your answer is."

What could I say to that?

"Well... I wanted to be with you."

"I know." Erik smiled, the tension in his body softening towards me. "But there was something about my brother you didn't like, wasn't there?"

How did he know?

"Well... he's not an Alpha, for one thing."

Erik's lips twisted up in an ironic smile. "Of course not. There's only one Alpha in a pack, and being the oldest of the brothers meant I was the natural one to take over."

I bit my lip, wanting to say so much more than I felt comfortable doing. My news would not be welcome, I was sure of it.

Erik lifted his hand and I flinched, expecting some sort of physical retribution for me withholding information. But he just ran his fingertips over my lips and stared down at me with lust in his dark eyes.

"I want to kiss you so badly when you bite your lip like that."

"Then why don't you?"

He groaned, a muscle flicking in his jaw as he clenched his teeth. "Because if I start, I'll want to continue, and I need to get up and get going today."

"What's on today that needs your attention?" I asked.

There were no jobs anymore, no bosses to answer to.

"We have to introduce you to the pack, and choose which job to give you until you find your place. I'm hoping after last night that you'll want to stay."

"Stay?" I asked, my voice raising into a squeak.

He wanted me to stay.

"Yes." He said, his eyebrows furrowing into a frown. "I assumed after last night you'd realise how much I wanted you to stay."

I searched my memory for anything that appeared unusual, or a show of intent.

Sure, the sex had been super-fast, intense, and mind-blowing, but I didn't think that alone would be enough reason to want me to stay.

"I want to stay. Very much." I answered quickly.

There was so much to tell him about my past, about my old pack. But now wasn't the time. We didn't know each other well enough yet, and I wasn't sure how he would react to the news that his pack may be in danger because of my presence.

"Great. Then let's go."

Erik stood up, his lengthy cock resting against his thighs.

My gut tightened with desire and as my gaze traveled upward, past his flat stomach and across his huge pecs. I met his eyes with what I hoped was a lustful expression.

"Please tell me I can talk you back into bed for another round."

Erik chuckled. "Come on, lazy bones. My men will already be wondering where I am."

I groaned and pushed myself to the edge of the mattress and stood up, my pulsing cock standing at attention, pointing directly at the man I wanted.

"You're going to leave me like this?" I asked him, gesturing down to my compass needle.

Erik groaned, stepping forward and wrapping a calloused hand around my staff.

"No. I'm not."

His mouth came down and he kissed me until I couldn't breathe. Until my toes tingled and my balls ached.

Then his hand squeezed and began to move. Up and down. Up and down.

Sparkles of pleasure spread along my skin.

I broke off from his lips and panted hard, digging my nails into his shoulders.

Erik bit down roughly on my lower lip and pulled me closer to his body so I could feel the swell of his erection. The insistent press of his hand against my arse while his fingers moved over me with fierce knowledge was glorious.

My balls tightened up under me and I began to gasp and moan.

Erik licked at my lips and tugged my cock harder.

He was going to make me come if he kept that up.

Flames moved over my back and up my spine until my shoulders were on fire.

The waves of heat surrounded and engulfed me until I couldn't stand it any longer and the pleasure shot out my cock in spasms of need.

"Fu...uck." I groaned, my energy draining away as my muscles turned to water.

Erik held me up, his intense eyes continuing to stare at me.

"You are so hot." Erik said, then bent his head and sucked on the skin of my neck.

His erection continued to persistently jab me in the hip and I couldn't summon the energy to raise my arms and grab it.

"Wanna take me back to bed?" I managed to ask, though only one of my eyes opened, partially.

Erik straightened to his full height and grinned down at me.

"I would love to, but we've got work to do. Shower time, for both of us, I think."

He pushed me back a little, bent over and lifted me up and over his shoulder.

I didn't bother putting up a fight as I draped down Erik's back like a sack of potatoes.

Bliss had descended like a cloud over me, zapping all my energy and bringing with it a beautiful sense of contentment.

Running water sounded and Erik slowly lowered me to my feet. Blood rushed to my head and I swayed.

Erik held me tightly, taking the shower head off the wall mount and turning the spray towards me.

I gasped at the shock of cold before the soothing flow of warm water started.

"So, what are we going to do today?" I asked him, as Erik rubbed me down with a bar of soap that smelled of flowers.

He groaned, this time in frustration and the noise skittered through me like an electrical wire.

I whimpered and stepped closer to him.

"I didn't mean it like that. I mean, what sort of jobs do you do? What will I do? How does your town function?" I plowed into the conversation, not wanting him to be upset with me.

He turned the water off and grabbed for a towel. "It sounds like you've never worked a day in your life."

I took the towel he offered and quickly dried myself, the flames in my cheeks burning hotly.

"I was thirteen when the humans all died, so yeah, I've never really worked a real job if that's what you mean."

Erik's shoulders relaxed a little. "So, you're twenty-three? Twenty-four?"

I shrugged. "Yeah, I suppose so. We don't really keep a tally of days that go by."

"We do, and I can tell you that it's been exactly ten years and eleven months since the virus was released."

"Wow."

That was a long time.

"Let's get some clothes on, and I'll show you how a self-sufficient town works."

I nodded and kept my mouth shut, not wanting to admit that I didn't know what he meant by that either.

I followed him back into the bedroom and he threw open his wardrobe.

I stared at the sight before me. It was like a department store. "Whoa. You have so many clothes!"

"They're not new, but yeah, we keep 'em in good condition." Erik casually pulled out a pair of jeans and a black short sleeved shirt and got dressed.

Just like a man from a movie.

Like he'd stepped back in time.

This was seriously the weirdest thing ever.

"O..kay." I reached for my dirty clothes laying on the floor.

The clothes I'd found years ago in a raid on an old shopping centre.

"Don't you have anything else to wear?" Erik asked, his tone confused.

"Ah... no." I answered.

"Well, don't put those back on. They're filthy. We'll head over to my sister's place today and get some things your size. She does most of the mending of the town's clothes."

"O...kay." I sounded like an idiot but none of this was making much sense. "So, do I go out wearing these? Or..."

I looked at Erik as he stared at me, then a flicker of amusement kicked up the ends of his lips.

"I'm deciding if is worth parading you around naked or not."

A full grin spread across his face now and I put a hand on my hip and flicked my hair out of my eyes with a flirtatious flourish.

"And what decision have you come to?" I asked as his gaze hungrily fed on my nakedness.

His eyebrows lowered and a wolfish growl rolled through his lips.

"You're mine. No one else gets to see you like this."

A quiver of excitement moved through my belly at the look of possession in his eyes.

"All right."

I reached for my worn, dirty jeans once again and Erik grabbed them from me.

"These are for the garbage. Let me see what I've got."

He threw my clothes into the corner of the room and stepped into his closet. He rummaged through, and finally pulled out a t-shirt and pair of shorts.

"These will be huge on you, but at least they're clean."

He tossed them to me and I brought them to my face, happily inhaling the clean fragrance and enjoying the softness of the fibres against my skin.

"Thank you."

I pulled on the shorts and tightened the tie as tight as I could.

The t-shirt looked more like a toga, so I grabbed one corner and tied it up.

Not too bad. They're so soft!

"Good. Now, let's go introduce you to Sienna, and then the rest of the pack." Erik turned and marched out the door without another word.

I scurried after the big Alpha, who seemed slightly disgruntled for some reason.

Nervous to show me to his pack perhaps?

I didn't really know what to expect, so with my stomach in my throat I ran after him, along the road and into a house with a large red door.

"Sienna!" Erik called out and within a moment, a tall red-headed woman stepped into the room.

"Yeah, Erik?" She answered, then her gaze swung to me. "Oh, it's true! Who is this?"

"What's true?" I asked, stepping closer to this woman who looked so much like Erik. Same nose... same beautiful skin...

"Everyone's been talking about the guy Erik found on the hunt and brought home. Is it true you're really an Omega?" She asked, stepping closer and reaching out a hand as though to touch me.

I went to her easily, instinctually trusting her.

I didn't really know why. Women had never liked me, but I wasn't a threat to her.

"Yeah, he's an Omega." Erik said as Sienna's hand gripped my arm, then pulled at my t-shirt.

"These clothes are terrible. Let me find something for you."

She pushed and twisted me around, gawking at me from all angles.

"Hang on."

She disappeared and then came back within a minute.

"Here. Black jeans. Blue and pink t-shirts. They should accentuate your eyes."

She put them down on the couch and then waited, as though she wanted me to change in front of her.

"Is there somewhere I can change?" I asked.

There was silence for a moment, then raucous laughter.

"You're kidding, right?" she asked. "Strip. Come on. I've seen every man in town naked. They're shifters, it's natural."

I conceded that my vanity was being ridiculous at this point.

And she was right. In the paranormal world, there was no shame in nudity.

I reached over my shoulder and pulled Erik's too big t-shirt off my back.

"Yeah. I know. But I'm not a shifter." I reminded her.

I pushed the shorts down my legs and grabbed for the black jeans she'd given me.

They fit like a glove and as I did up the buttons, I sighed at the softness of the denim.

"You have a real talent for guessing someone's size," I commended her.

"You have a nice body, but you're a bit thin. Is that normal?" She asked, and when I looked up I realised she wasn't asking me.

Erik shrugged. "He doesn't need to shift, so why does he need to be any bigger?"

I grabbed the pink t-shirt, my eye drawn to the candy color the same way I'd been drawn to my mother's dresses when I was a child.

I loved bright colors, but this world had not been kind to men like me and I'd taken to hiding any flamboyance I had.

"Wow." Sienna gushed as I pulled on the too tight t-shirt.

"I think it's a little small." I said, tugging at the hemline to bring it further down my body.

"No. It's perfect. Isn't it Erik?" Sienna asked.

I raised my gaze to Erik, who wasn't saying anything.

He nodded, a strange rumbling sound rolling through his chest. "Let's go."

He grabbed my hand and tugged me towards him.

Sienna's face broke into a smile so huge I could barely contain my answering grin.

"What was that about?" I asked as we walked along the road, in the sunshine once again.

Erik shook his head like an angry dog, grunting as he walked.

I waited, unsure of his reaction and where it had come from. Did he hate the clothes? Was he jealous of his sister taking a liking to me? Had I done something wrong? I didn't understand.

Several people stopped in the street when we walked past, gaping at us with their mouths hanging open.

Erik roughly grabbed my arm and corralled me into a small house at the end of the strip.

"Get in here." His words came out garbled but I did as he said, staggering into the small, dark house, my heart thundering in my chest like I was being chased by a bunch of wild dogs.

When I finally raised my head to look up at him, his teeth were pointed like a wolf, and his eyes glowed with an unnatural light.

"Did I do something wrong? I'm so sorry if I did..." My voice sounded weak and frightened, which I hated, but I didn't know what had just happened. Nor was I sure of what was about to happen.

Erik stalked forward and I backed up until I was pressed hard against the wall. I hadn't thought there was violence in Erik, but my instincts could have been wrong.

The room he'd pushed me into was cold and damp, and reminded me of the many abandoned homes I'd lived in since the dark times.

"You're mine. Do you understand? Mine."

He was trembling with a rage I didn't understand.

Or perhaps I did... somewhere, below the terror making my muscles quake came an understanding.

I moved my hand across to his groin, seeking and finding him hard and aching.

Erik groaned as I worked to free him from his jeans.

"Yes. I need you," he seemed to say through the moans as I freed his cock.

He pushed on my shoulders and I dropped to my knees, submitting to his need and my own instincts.

I took him into my mouth, working his long shaft with my lips and tongue.

He tasted salty and sweet, his flesh as hard as iron, and his skin as soft as silk.

His fingers slid into my hair, holding me to him.

I moaned as my own body responded to his desire, the tangy

scent of high testosterone rising in the air.

I fondled Erik's huge balls, letting my other hand slide down to my own cock, which was rapidly filling with blood.

Erik gasped and grunted, then pushed me off him with a suddenness that surprised me.

"Strip. Now."

I jumped up and peeled my new, black jeans from my hips.

Then he was lifting me, high on the wall, pushing my legs up and rubbing his cock head against my arse.

He was so wet with his own pre-come his cock slipped inside me with little resistance.

Erik thrust straight into me.

I cried out against the pressure and the jagged pain while I gripped tight to his shoulders so he wouldn't leave me.

Erik bit into my neck while he pounded me into the wall, over and over until I was screaming his name.

It was too much. The heat. The explosion of pleasure. The burning pain of a huge cock in my body.

Erik's cry of completion hit my ears just as the waves of ecstasy lit me up from the inside out.

My own orgasm caught up with me as my cock pulsed between us. Hot, sticky cum squirted over my belly as Erik filled my ass with his.

As the storm began to pass and the only sounds in the room were the quiet rise and fall of our breaths, the Alpha in my arms began to shake. I gripped him tightly. Was he crying?

"Shhh... it's okay..." I said, not sure what was happening to him.

Erik withdrew and I moaned at the pain of his loss.

He stood up straighter, holding tightly to me as he staggered across the room and fell onto something soft, probably a couch.

I couldn't open my eyes long enough to look.

My whole body felt like it had been turned inside out. My head was singing a chorus of angelic hymns and I couldn't have lifted my head from his shoulder if he'd paid me.

CHAPTER 5
ERIK.

What have I done?

I'd taken Corey like a wild animal. Totally unable to control myself.

I rocked him in my arms, running my fingers along his spine, into his hair and over his beautiful skin.

Tears prickled my eyes that I'd long since thought extinct. I hadn't cried since my best friend had been killed almost fifteen years ago.

"I'm so sorry." I said, the words choking off my throat.

Such a blow to my pride, I could barely get the words out. What sort of Alpha was I? To abuse an underling in such a way?

And not just any pack member, but the man I was sure was meant to be my mate.

I wasn't fit to be Alpha.

Corey pulled himself up, pushing on my chest to look up at me.

I dropped my hands away from his body, deeply stung. He was trying to get away from me, it was obvious. I shouldn't still be touching him like this, I knew that.

Corey frowned at me in the darkness.

My eyes had adjusted a little, but I still couldn't make out his facial expressions properly.

"Can we turn a light on, or something?" he asked.

"Ah, sure."

I didn't know where any of the lights were, but I could pull back a curtain.

I gently shifted him off my lap and onto the couch next to me.

I jerked up my pants and quickly did them back up while I searched for the edge of the curtain.

My stomach was in knots, my guilt at an all-time high. What should I do to make it up to him?

I couldn't force him to sleep away from me and the safety my rank entailed, but maybe Sienna would allow him to stay in her home. She had room, and she was the next best thing to me.

And the most important thing of course would be, he'd be safe, away from me.

I yanked back the curtains, the assaulting light of day charging into the room.

I whirled away from the light, blinking madly as my vision adjusted.

"Now, what's going on, Erik?" Corey asked, sitting up straighter on the couch, his eyebrows furrowed in worry.

"I... need to apologise for what I just did. And I'll make it up to you, if I can... I have some ideas..."

"Yeah... I know how you can make it up to me." Corey interjected, his voice strong and authoritative.

"Yes?" I asked, waiting for the payment instructions.

"You can do that more often. It was fucking hot."

I stared at him for a while, not sure I'd heard him correctly.

But then he stretched back on the couch, his lips curved up into a languid smile of satisfaction.

"Seriously. When you pushed me down to suck your cock, I almost blew on the spot."

I walked back to the sofa and slid down next to him, surprised when he threw a leg over me and straddled me once again.

"Ah... you liked it?" I asked, not sure I'd heard him correctly.

"Of course, I did." He sighed, then cuddled into my chest with his head in the crook of my shoulder.

I slowly lifted my arms back up to encircle his back.

"So..."

"Hmmm?" Corey sighed again and I stopped talking when I heard his breathing change into the steady rhythm of sleep.

There was no reason to say anything now.

This man was definitely my mate. What other man, or woman for that matter, could handle me at my worst? At my most dominant.

None of the women certainly could. If anything, I'd always held back with my previous lovers, innately understanding that they had no interest in experiencing the real me.

I'd never met anyone yet who could really accept that side of me, and my wolf had always known that.

Had always worked hard to keep my lovers feeling safe, and happy.

But I didn't need to do that anymore.

I could be as passionate, or demanding, or as aggressive as I wanted to be, without fear of hurting my mate, or the emotional repercussions that would follow.

The relief that came with that revelation was like a blow to my energy store. If I hadn't been sitting down, I would have fallen over.

Wow. This is going to be fun.

We lay there for too long, but I couldn't bring myself to wake him as he slept on my chest.

Totally vulnerable and trusting. Like a child, but so much better.

Eventually, my stomach growled loud enough to wake him. Corey lifted his head, his eyes filled with sleep and his mouth curled into a smile.

"Did I fall asleep again?"

"Yes, you did."

Corey stretched his arms above his head and leaned back.

"Hey, you didn't tell me why you went all weirdly hot on me just then. Do you hate the clothes I'm wearing or something?"

I glanced down at the skin-tight pink top and could have laughed at how ridiculous my jealousy seemed now.

My reactions to Corey were off the charts, and I was hoping my wolf would calm down once I finally claimed him properly.

"I... ah, got a bit jealous that other people were going to see you looking so hot, but it seems stupid now."

I should be proud of how sexy Corey was, not worried someone else was going to take him away.

A problem most certainly remedied by a proper mating, but I'd need to speak to some of the elders about that first.

Corey grinned. "Oh, yeah... definitely stupid. Because the only person in this pack that I want is you. I'm made for you."

Corey's eyes went wide and he swallowed hard, his Adam's apple bobbing up and down. "I mean... someone like you. A true Alpha."

I struggled not to smile insanely as Corey attempted to cover up the fact he'd just declared his intent, too.

He needn't have bothered, because his feelings for me were coveted.

But it was the word "true" that caught my attention.

"Were there other un-true Alphas in the past?" I asked, interested in his clarification.

Corey slid off my lap to face me from a further distance. "Um, well, there have been so many wars... fights over land and stuff, since all the humans died. A lot of the true Alphas died, and in their place rose a generation of Betas who wanted to be Alphas. But they're not the same."

"Of course not, there's only ever one Alpha at a time in a pack. And it must be the Alpha born to lead. He cannot be chosen."

I could hear my father's voice in my own words as I recited the laws I'd been taught since I was a child.

Corey bit his lip. "I know that—of course. An Omega is born as the perfect mate for a true Alpha. To increase his power and make him the greatest leader he can be." Corey said, again with the confidence and strength of voice as someone who was reciting a well-known verse.

"What do you mean, to increase his power?"

Corey's gaze dropped. "That's why Omegas are such a rare occurrence, and one easily killed or misused, but also very valued. Did you know that was why people crave us so much?"

I shook my head. Unfortunately, I knew very little about the Omegas. "We've never had an Omega born in our pack, not for at least three generations."

Not unless there was another non-shifting male I hadn't been told about, but I doubted it.

"Well, that's why so many men crave us, because of the power we bring to an Alpha. But there's a catch, of course. We only bring strength to a true Alpha like you. If a Beta grabs us, or tries to mate with us, the union fails. And instead of being a positive, we become a negative."

"In what way?"

Corey shrugged. "Different ways. Loss of sex drive, more aggression, lack of sleep, everything, really. The last three supposed 'Alphas' who tried to mate with me were not impressed with my 'supposed' Omega skills."

Hot lava poured through my gut at the idea that there were other men Corey had given himself to, or had taken what they needed and dumped him.

Either way, the acidic taste in my mouth somewhat softened the blinding red fury I saw inside my head.

"Ah... is that why you left your old pack?"

I knew there was a story behind why I'd found Corey alone in the forest, but hadn't pushed for full disclosure yet.

"Partly. I don't really want to talk about it." Corey's face was flaming red and a part of me knew I didn't want to know what he was going to tell me.

Because it would involve his ex-lovers, and other men who'd used him. And I didn't want to think of my mate like that.

"Okay, well let's get out of this place, then." I pulled at my clothes to right them as much as possible.

The men would be having a fit about where I was, I was sure.

"What is this place, exactly?" Corey asked as we walked back outside, the scent of my sperm still permeating the air.

And Corey.

"Just a house that isn't used anymore."

There was no way to hide the fact that I'd claimed the Omega as my own.

"Come this way."

We headed down to the main meeting hall where my brother and his friends stood around chatting.

"What are you doing?" I asked, expecting there to be some obvious reason why they weren't at their designated jobs.

My brother turned around with a strange leer on his face that I hadn't seen before.

"We're waiting for you to get your dick out of his arse, and answer a few Alpha-type questions for us."

My wolf, who had been sleeping soundly and contentedly inside of me, rose to the surface and took over my logical brain.

I reached out for my asshole of a brother and wrapped my right hand around his throat.

"Speak to me like that again, James, and I'll pull you up in front of the council for insubordination."

My teeth were shifting. I could feel them cutting into my lips.

James' eyes bulged as he grabbed for my arm, his feet scuffing in the dirt where I held him in the air, well above where he could naturally control his weight.

Corey's hand on my arm released the grip the anger had on me and I let go of my brother's neck.

He fell to the ground like the sack of shit he was.

I'd been blind to his crap for far too long. But no more.

I stared at Corey for a moment, the knowledge in his young eyes hard to compete with.

"This was what you were talking about, wasn't it?" I asked him.

Corey nodded infinitesimally, his gaze sliding sideways as though to warn me.

I looked back towards my brother, who was angrily getting to his feet, rubbing his neck.

"What the fuck is the matter with you? I'm your brother!" James yelled, as he had for all of our lives. My parents forced me to accept his tantrums and bad behaviour on the excuse of our blood bond, but it ended here, now.

"I'm your Alpha, and you will show me the respect necessary for my rank. Get back to your jobs."

"You're the one who's been fucking around all morning!"

A deadly growl slid through my teeth and I didn't even attempt to stop it.

"James, this is your last warning. Stop wasting all of our time because you're so fucking jealous you can't see straight. Go. Now."

I glared at him until he grabbed one of the other Betas who was standing next to him with his mouth agape, and they rushed off toward the crops they were supposed to be tending.

I blew out a breath as hard and fast as I could, willing the anger away.

I needed to shift and run, howl at the moon.

With Corey around, my wolf was so much stronger. His needed to be out, and free. He was far more powerful now.

"You okay?" Corey asked me, and I shook off the feelings of anger towards my brother.

"Yeah, I'm fine. Just fucking furious that my brother thinks he can control me."

Corey nodded. "Yeah, he does. But that's not what's dangerous about him."

"Oh, really? What's more dangerous about him than that?" I

asked, trying not to get pissed off at the fact that the Omega saw things so much more clearly than me.

Corey stepped closer, "It's the fact that he wants to be Alpha. He'll stab you in the back and climb right over your body, into your position, if he can."

"I'd like to see him try." I growled, wanting to grab Corey and run for some reason.

That instinctual reaction got my attention.

"Is that why he wants you too?"

Corey shrugged. "Probably. An Omega mate is a status symbol for any wolf, and because we're only meant to mate with an Alpha, the Betas always want to get their hands on me."

"He won't ever touch you, Corey." I said, pulling him towards me and pressing a kiss to his beautiful lips.

He slid his hands up around my neck and clung tight.

"I know."

I kissed him. Right there in the street in front of the whole town. For the whole world to see, because I'd found my mate. At last.

CHAPTER 6
COREY.

Erik showed me around the town and introduced me to so many people. Lovely people, whose smiling faces caught my heart. Who showed no sign of the decay the rest of the world was feeling.

The only relatives who seemed to be directly linked to Erik were his brother and sister, their parents having died years ago.

Everyone in the pack had a job, a concept I'd believed had died off with the humans. Whether it was maintaining the land they farmed, or the houses they lived in, or the clothes they wore, all contributed in some way. Even minding the children who were thriving, or cooking the meals for the whole pack.

They all had a purpose, and they all did it well. Or seemed to.

The way the pack functioned as a tight unit made me cling to Erik even more. I wanted to stay here and be a part of this world. I wanted to forget the decade of hunger. Of fighting. Of death.

But every moment I felt safe in the presence of the big Alpha in this town that time forgot, a tingle of fear would still course up my spine.

Would my old world find me and destroy all my new dreams?

I was sure of it.

I'd been given a job with Sienna, Erik's sister, who I loved. She was a beautiful woman, who treated me well, and loved her brother fiercely. Being around her was like basking in the sun's rays on a perfect day.

"I'm finished with these alterations, Corey. If you could take them over to Mrs Phelps for me?" Sienna said one morning as she handed me a pile of clothes. They all appeared to be long dresses and skirts.

I searched my memory. *Mrs. Phelps... Mrs. Phelps...*

"Yeah. Sure. Ah, she's the old lady with the red hair in the house near the hall?"

Sienna laughed. "Yeah, that's her. I'm glad you're getting to know everyone in the pack. Most of them are extremely nice. Anyone given you any trouble?"

I shuffled to the front door and managed to juggle the bundled clothing in my arms and turn the handle.

"No, everyone's been great so far."

Except your brother. James is an absolute prick.

"See you in a minute, Sienna."

I waved at the Alpha's sister and made my way outside, the sun on my face and the smell of freshly baked bread in the air.

What a life I had now. If I had died and this was my Heaven, then I was grateful.

I made my way through town, taking careful steps to protect my responsibility.

"Hi, Corey!" One of the young children called out, waving frantically at me as he hung from an open window.

"Hi!" I called back, loving the feeling of community and warmth in the town I'd stumbled upon.

Erik had been so supportive and patient with me over the past few weeks. My learning curve in this new environment was steep. He was so attentive, so eager to please. Especially with food.

Erik was off hunting again today. The whole town thought it was because of me. Sienna said that Erik had rarely let the men hunt more than once a month in the past, due to the threats from vampires and other packs.

But since I'd arrived, he'd gone out every week. Often coming back with huge kills, like deer, and even a bear once.

I worried for him when he was gone, but I knew that he was the strongest of all the men in town so I pushed those feelings aside and let logical thinking take its place.

"Hey, Corey!" Jordan, one of the teenage boys I'd come to befriend, sidled up next to me as I walked. "Whatcha doing?"

"Just taking some clothes back to their rightful owner. What are you doing, slacker?" I joked, elbowing the young man in the side.

Jordan laughed with the gusto of youth and began walking backwards so he could easily look at me while we talked.

I could tell the kid had a little crush on me, but he was a young Beta, destined for another Beta wolf, I was sure.

I was made for Erik.

"Talkin' to you." Jordan replied with a grin.

The elders of the town gave the children and youths of the pack a lot of freedom, and not many chores. It was a law that I liked. Everyone eventually grew up, and they should enjoy their childhood while they could.

"When do they finally give you a proper job? I asked him.

Jordan shrugged. "When I turn sixteen, they said. But I'm not too sure when that'll be. Winter, maybe?"

"Oh, to be young again." I smiled with Jordan, then grimaced as flashes of my own youth sprung to mind.

My parent's death. The scrounging around for food. Finding another pack, who enjoyed my body far more that I wanted them to.

I'd been lucky in some ways...compared to many others. But I wouldn't wish my life on the kid in front of me, ever.

"I want to be part of the hunting party next time." Jordan said, his excitement obvious in his joyful tone.

"You've got your shifting under control?"

He shrugged again, but this time his lips tugged down into a frown. "Ah, sort of. I can't shift at will yet, and I think that's what the Alpha is waiting for."

"Probably. You need to be able to defend yourself if someone attacks you, that's the biggest threat out in the forest."

Jordan's eyes lit up. "What's out there? I mean... apart from deer and squirrel? You've been far away from here, haven't you, Corey?"

"Yeah, I have... give me a minute?" We'd arrived at Mrs. Phelps' home.

I knocked on the door and the older woman promptly answered.

"Oh, thank you, young Alpha Mate. How are you settling in?" She took the clothes and looked up at me, appearing to wait for a reply to her question.

"Um... good, thank you. What do you mean, Alpha Mate?"

That was an expression I hadn't heard since I was a child.

"You two have mated, have you not?" she asked, her eyebrows drawing down into a question.

"Well..." *We've had lots of sex, if that's what you're asking.* "I don't know. What would it entail?"

She smiled gently, her eyes lighting up with amusement. "I think you need to speak to Erik about that."

She nodded her head and shut the door in my face again.

"That was strange." I muttered to myself.

Erik and I got along well, and we fucked a lot, too. I knew that had something to do with a true mating, but there had to more, surely? Or practically every couple would mate in their first sexual encounter.

My parents hadn't taught me the details before they died, and afterwards, no one wanted to mate me in the true sense of a relationship and partnership, anyway.

"What was that about?" Jordan asked.

I shrugged. I didn't really know.

"She thinks Erik and I mated, or something like it. I have no idea what she's talking about."

Jordan laughed. "Yeah, everyone's talking about how obsessed the Alpha is with you. My mom said she's never seen him so smitten. Whatever that is."

Heat crept up my neck and spread across my face. I slid my hand through my hair and looked away, trying to hide my uncontrollable response.

Smitten. What an unusual word to use.

"Really? How come? What's so different about him now?" I asked, interested in what other people saw, that I didn't.

To me, Erik was as he'd always been.

"Well, the hunting is a big thing. Going out so often just so you have plenty of meat to eat." Jordan replied.

I liked the compliment implied in that, but there was something more to the hunting, I was sure.

"I don't think it's just that." I confided in the youth.

Jordan stepped closer as we stopped outside Sienna's house. "What is it, then?"

"I probably shouldn't comment about such things, as I'm not a shifter, but I've been feeling Erik's wolf rise to the surface a lot lately. And I think the reason he's going out so much, is because he needs to shift more. Does that make sense? I don't know."

It sounded strange now that I was saying it out loud, but it was how I felt. It made sense to me that a man designed to be a strong, wild animal, should stretch his legs a lot more often than once a month.

"That makes perfect sense." Jordan agreed with me. "My dad's been saying how much better and stronger he feels when he gets to shift more."

"Well, don't tell anyone I said anything, but thanks for the chat. I better get back to work."

I waved at Jordan as I stepped back into Sienna's home.

It was more than that, for Erik, I thought. His Alpha wolf was always around when I was near. He growled and rumbled in Erik's chest so often I was concerned he'd shift halfway through sex sometimes.

"You making friends with Jordan?" Sienna asked me as I stepped into her sewing room.

"Yeah. He's a good kid." I said, sitting on the couch.

Sienna looked over at me, her keen eyes taking in my expression.

"Whatcha thinking about?"

This woman didn't miss a thing, and of all the people to talk to in this town, I trusted her the most.

"Um... mating. Like, a marriage mating. Does it still exist in this new world, do you think?"

Sienna laughed. "In our pack it does, I'm not sure about the rest of the world, but we haven't changed those laws."

"There are laws about mating?"

Seriously?

She smiled. "Well, not laws exactly, more like tradition. A mating can be conducted like a marriage. We have a party, a commitment speech, the Alpha to preside over it all."

I wanted to hold my tongue, but I couldn't. I needed to ask. "And the Alpha? How does he mate?"

Her lips twisted up as she glanced down at the shirt she was mending, and then back up to me.

"Well, it depends what you're really asking, Corey. Are you asking me if Erik is going to mate with you in front of the pack, or if he's already done it in secret?"

"What do you mean, in secret? Wouldn't I know about it, if he had?"

My chest tightened in anxiety. I hated knowing so little about shifter ways.

"You would, because a true mating requires both people to accept the other, and to commit to each other for life. If you haven't done that, then no, you aren't truly mated."

I chewed on my lip, my stomach in knots.

Erik and I hadn't talked about our relationship in such a way, nor about the future, either.

The relief I expected to feel didn't come. Instead there was a strange sense of urgency that told me I should be doing more to cement my relationship with him.

"Well, no, there's been nothing like that." I admitted.

Sienna nodded, her keen gaze on me.

"Then you don't have anything to worry about." She returned to her mending.

Yeah sure... nothing to worry about.

"They're back!" a female voice yelled from outside Sienna's house and I jumped to my feet.

"Do you mind?" I asked her as I took sideways steps to the door. I wanted to be the first one to greet Erik when he walked through the front gates.

"Of course not. Go." Sienna said, making shooing motions with her hands.

I grinned at her, yanked open the door and bolted to the front gate, which was opening slowly.

My heart pounded in my chest as the metal ground slowly along the tracks.

I bounced on my toes, then felt the familiar heat that flushed through me when I laid eyes on my Alpha.

"Erik." I whispered as he met my gaze and smiled broadly at me.

He sauntered forward, pulling behind him several large carcasses.

"I've gotta take these to the main kitchens." He told me as he walked forward with a huge load on his back.

I took the few dead birds he had strewn across his shoulders.

"Let me help you."

We walked side by side through the town, delivering the meat to the women who would prepare and cook the bounty for us.

"You guys had a great hunt." I said, glancing across at all the food the other men had brought home with them.

Erik dumped the carcasses of the deer at the door of the main kitchen and turned back to me. "Yeah, we went further south this time, and I couldn't believe the amount of game there was for the taking. There mustn't be any packs in the area for there to be so much food."

A shiver of unease coursed up my spine, the hairs on the nape of my neck prickling.

"Ah, south?" I repeated.

My old pack lived in that direction, and they were the last people I wanted Erik to meet.

"Yeah, a bit of distance from where we found you. Why?"

I shook my head. "No reason."

Erik and I kept back walking toward the entrance to the town.

"Where are you from, Corey?" he asked.

"All over, really. I was born in Ohio, then my parents moved us to Kentucky. Not long after that, the world changed, the pack wars started, and I got shuffled around for a bit." I swallowed as saliva pooled in my mouth, but tried not to let my unease become obvious.

"So, the pack you ran away from...?" he asked, leading off for me to answer.

"Isn't far from here." I rushed in to say. "But please, please, if you find them don't bring them back here. You can't trust them, any of them."

My heart was banging like a bongo in my chest. God, if those creeps found a way into Erik's town, they would cause absolute havoc.

Erik slung an arm around my shoulders.

"I have no intention of bringing anyone home. You were a once-off, weak moment..." I glared at him and he laughed loudly. "That I have not regretted, not for a single second."

I twisted in his arms and hugged him tight.

"Thank you."

Erik chuckled and held me, just as he always did when I needed him.

My life was perfect, and I was just waiting to see when the bubble would burst.

CHAPTER 7

ERIK.

I awoke to the strangest sound of grinding metal, and clanking gears. Were they seriously opening the front gate without me?

We had laws against that.

"I'll be right back." I whispered to the beautiful man in my bed, grabbed a pair of jeans and hurriedly pulled them on as I hopped to the front door.

Who could be leaving the compound without my permission?

Had there been a hunt organized today and I'd missed the memo?

I wrenched open the door, zipped up my jeans and ran for the gate.

It was wide open.

No way.

I bolted through the gate and pushed past the thick trees and dense shrubbery to find a bundle of clothes slung over the park bench we used as a meeting point.

And not hide nor hair of anyone to be seen.

"Fuck."

I could smell my brother's distinctive scent in the air.

He'd taken a group of our men on a hunting party without consulting me. It was more than wrong, it was downright illegal.

I trudged back up the hill, trying to get my temper back under my control. I'd go and see one of the pack's elders and make sure I wasn't flying off the handle for no reason.

I may have missed something—it wasn't out of the question. I'd been more distracted lately, with Corey in my life now. Perhaps the men had received permission from someone else to open the gates?

I stepped through the door once again, and pulled the gate tightly shut.

Everyone else was still asleep and as I glanced up at the pinkly lit sky, I realized that it must be just after sun up.

I shook my head as I walked through the streets.

My brother must have been desperate to lead his own hunting party, to go around me like this.

James had kept his head down since our run in a few weeks ago, but I didn't trust him.

Not with my pack, and certainly not with the man I wanted to make my mate.

The smell of freshly brewed coffee hit my nostrils and I inhaled deeply.

"Good morning, Fred." I called through the window of one of our elders.

"Ha! Erik! Come in." The older man who had been a good friend of my father's pushed open the door to his home and I walked inside.

"Would you like a cup?" he asked.

We had very little coffee left from the stores, but it wouldn't surprise me if Fred had hoarded some of the beloved beverage for himself.

"No. Not at all. Just came here to ask a question or two."

Fred poured himself a cup of java and sat down on a chair with it cradled lovingly in his hand.

"Shoot."

"Well, first, I just heard a hunting party leave the pack. Do you know if James had permission to take anyone out with him today?"

Fred frowned. "Ah, not that I know of, but he could have asked any of the others."

There were ten elders in total, and Fred was right, James could have asked any one of them if he may go out today.

I couldn't imagine many of them saying no to him.

"True."

Fred sat back further in his chair and stared at me with a half-smile on his weathered face.

"When are you going to mate the Omega?"

"Oh... well..." I found myself stumbling over my words all of a sudden.

Such a forthright, yet abrupt question. I hadn't been expecting it.

"Well, I'm not too sure, actually."

"You're not sure whether or not to mate him?" Fred asked, his eyebrows drawing up as though he was surprised by my answer.

"Oh, hell no. I'm sure about that." I swallowed hard, astonished by the sheer strength of my voice when I answered him.

"Then what's the problem?"

"There's no problem, so to speak. It's just that I'm not sure how to go about setting up a mating. Who's going to officiate the service? Is a public mating necessary?"

I hadn't been able to talk to anyone about this yet, though it had been weighing on my mind from the moment I brought Corey home.

I found the tightness around my chest easing as I spoke to Fred about it.

Fred took a sip of coffee and shook his head. "A public mating isn't necessary, but it would be nice, I think. We haven't had an Alpha mating since your parents, and that was almost forty years ago."

Fred smiled in remembered happiness.

"Yes. And you think me choosing an Omega will be... all right for the pack?" I asked, voicing one of my main concerns. "We won't have children. No new Alpha for the pack from my bloodline."

Fred waved his hand in a dismissive way. "Don't concern yourself with worrying about that. You need to choose the one who is your perfect balance, and that individual will be the perfect fit for our pack. Plus, there's the added bonus of your strength increasing once you mate."

"You've heard of that too?"

Why did everyone know more about this than me?

"Of course. And as far as children are concerned, the pack will adapt. Perhaps an Alpha will be born through one of the other bloodlines, or you will choose a woman to carry your babe in the future. Who knows?"

I nodded and let all the new thoughts fly around my mind. I could impregnate a woman if Corey allowed it, I suppose. If we wanted a child.

Fred was right, however. Fate had a strange way of making sure everything worked out, and I was sure that Corey was the one meant for me.

"Thanks, Fred. I think I'll go back to my bed for an hour or so before work."

Fred chuckled. "You do that."

I bid the elder goodbye and wandered back to my home.

Corey was still fast asleep, and as I climbed back into my bed and curled around him, a perfect contentment fell over me.

Corey moaned softly and moved his ass back into me, pressing closer as he always did.

My safe place. My home.

I closed my eyes and fell into a warm sleep, waking hours later to a ruckus at the front gate.

"Alpha! Alpha! Come quick."

I jumped out of bed, my heart pounding in my chest with adrenaline from the abrupt ruckus.

"What's happening?" Corey asked, jumping out of bed also.

I grabbed at my clothes as Corey picked up his.

"I don't know, but it doesn't sound good."

I ran out the door, towards the front gate where a huge crowd gathered.

What had happened?

My gaze darted around the town. There was no blood, no fighting. No more screams.

My wolf sensed danger, but wasn't jumping up to take over my body just yet, and I saw that as a good sign.

Corey was on my heels.

"What's going on?" I called out to the assembled group, my nose picking up the scent of strangers.

Strong. Male. Strangers.

"Oh, no." Corey whispered behind me, his gasp of shock vibrating through me and calling to my wolf to step up.

I stepped in front of Corey as he shrunk away and the townspeople moved back, making way for me to walk through the middle of the pack.

James stood with a group of three large men. All of whom were topless and shoeless, only wearing ripped and dirty jeans.

"Hey, brother. Look what I found in the woods." James indicated to the three men with a cocky grin that I wanted to smack right off him.

He'd brought these strangers into our home.

Into the safety of our hidden pack.

Without thought to anyone's safety or feelings, except for his own.

You'll never be a true Alpha. You care for no one except yourself.

I crossed my arms over my chest and focused on the man in the middle. He was the size of an Alpha, but the smile on his face hinted at an evil core.

"Gentlemen. I'd like to say welcome, but you're not. We don't allow strangers into our pack, and I don't know why my brother brought you here."

The man in the middle took a step forward, palms out and up, his body language completely open.

"We are in search of my mate, who got lost on a recent move between towns. I'm most concerned about his well-being, and James was kind enough to inform me that Corey was here."

The bottom fell out of my world in that one moment.

I couldn't move as everyone turned to stare at the space behind me, where I knew Corey had been.

My gaze slid from the friendly smile on the other Alpha's face over to the gloating grin on my brother's.

Oh, how I wanted to punch him.

"Ah... sorry? I didn't realise Corey was already mated. And you are yet to introduce yourself."

"Oh, my apologies. I am Roy, Alpha of the south forest pack. These are my Betas, Stump and Turkey."

I cringed at the friendly nicknames and the smile this guy seemed to have plastered permanently on his face.

If he thought he was taking Corey away from me, then he had another think coming.

I squared my stance and looked the other Alpha directly in the eye.

"I am Erik. Alpha of this pack, and also mate of Corey, so I think we need to sort something out. Don't you?"

Roy, or whoever this fucker was, let his smile drop. Anger rose in his eyes, and his mouth took the shape of an ugly sneer.

"Corey was mine first, and marriage laws state that whomever mates first, is the real owner."

"Owner?" I scoffed. "You're talking about Corey as though he were a piece of property."

Roy smiled once again, his stained teeth marring the slick, salesmen appearance his grin would have otherwise had.

"He is my property, and I've come to collect."

Roy actually took a few steps forward and a growl ripped through my throat.

I put one hand out in front of me, palm out. If he didn't heed my warning, he'd regret it.

"Listen, buddy. You need to stop. Right there. Possession is nine tenths of the law, and I am in current possession of the Omega. So, I suggest you get the hell off my property, and take my brother with you."

Roy fell back a few paces, exchanging looks with James. Both men seemed surprised by my words, their jaws falling open in simultaneous clown-like fashion.

James looked at me then, his expression hurt, if I could believe it.

"This isn't like you, Erik. Just let the little fag go. You can get a proper mate after he leaves."

I laughed. How could I not?

My brother had never cared for my happiness, nor the well-being of the pack. But he wanted me to get rid of the one person who completed me, and would make me stronger than any other Alpha once we mated?

Not a chance.

"I'll give you one more chance to leave. Timmy. Allen. Frank." I called my Betas and they flew to my side, flanking me with a strength I hadn't anticipated.

My wolf reached up and took hold of me.

I wanted the other man to shift because it would be the only way I'd know if he was a true Alpha or not.

My teeth began to shift and my skin burned with the change.

"Okay. Okay. We're leaving." Roy grabbed the other men and backed away.

My wolf howled inside my head, but retreated.

My body relaxed and my eyes uncrossed to now see in vivid color again.

My brother staggered after them and the sadness I felt surprised me.

"Go. And never return." I growled after him, and he didn't look back.

As soon as they'd tripped over the gate getting out, I stormed forward and wrenched shut the doors that kept us hidden from the outside world.

Or had, before James had exposed us to another pack.

Fuck.

Things were about to get messy.

COREY.

I couldn't stop trembling.

Even when I wrapped my arms around my body and clamped my teeth shut so tightly my jaw screamed in pain, I couldn't stop.

"Corey. Baby. You okay?"

I heard Erik's voice move closer and I uncurled myself from the ball I'd drawn myself into. Near our house, as far away as I dared go.

"Is he gone?" I asked as I lifted my head, seeking the reassurance I was sure wouldn't come.

Erik wouldn't have sent him away. Surely, I must have imagined such a thing.

No one ever went up against Roy and won.

"Yes, he's gone. It's okay. Come here." Erik reached down and picked me up, something he did so often now.

I should be embarrassed to be treated like a child, but instead it made me feel safe. Cherished. Loved, even.

"He looks like he's in shock, Erik. You better get him warm, and in bed. I'll bring him some food." Sienna's voice sounded over my head, and then she disappeared and Erik carried me into our bedroom.

The only place I'd ever felt truly wanted.

"Jump in here, and we'll get you sorted out." Erik urged me, pulling back the covers and placing me in bed.

I choked on a laugh and shuffled over to him, clinging to his side while he sat on the bed with me.

"You didn't hand me over to him."

Erik chuckled, running a reassuring hand over my back.

"Of course, I didn't, why would I?"

Because anyone else would have.

I didn't know of anyone who'd survived after saying "No" to Roy.

Then it hit me with the weight of a thousand cannon balls.

I shot up in bed and rolled onto the floor, my shaky legs barely keeping me standing as I hobbled around to Erik's side of the bed.

"I need to get out of here. You don't understand. He's going to come back and destroy your beautiful little town. Please! Erik. Send me out. I'll walk back and meet them. I'll stop him. You can't be hurt because of me."

Terror was creeping up my veins like an insipid disease. Erik... Sienna... all the lovely people of this quiet town. They wouldn't survive against the savagery of Roy's pack.

What have I done?

"Calm down. It's all okay." Erik took my hand and pulled me down onto the bed with him.

I sniffed as heat had begun to pour down my face. From my eyes. My nose. My throat had clogged up.

"It's not okay. I am so selfish. I didn't even think about what would happen to everyone if they found me. I honestly never thought they would. I'm so sorry."

I burst into tears this time, and hated myself for being so weak. Such a pathetic man.

I slapped myself in the face, roughly pushing away the tears as they fell. Relishing the sting and the pain that I deserved so whole-heartedly.

"You're not making sense. Stop. Breathe. Explain."

Erik's hands were still on me, patting me. His voice was so calm and understanding. I didn't deserve his kindness.

I got up, moving away from his warmth. I couldn't stay here. I'd find a way out and then I'd run back to Roy. He'd take me back and forget about Erik's pack. Surely, he would? I'd figure out a way to make him.

My bottom lip trembled and I bit into it, hard. Until I tasted blood.

I paced the room, the answer in front of me crystal clear. Unfortunately, I now knew that getting away from Erik was going to be difficult.

But for his own good, I was going to need to escape.

A calm descended over me and I turned to face him.

"Erik. Thank you for your hospitality, but I think it's time I left."

"Left?" Erik repeated, jumping to his feet, his huge body towering over me.

"Yes. I'll go back to my pack, and hopefully they will leave you alone."

Erik's eyebrows furrowed. "That's not how to deal with a bully, Corey."

"It's the best way I know how."

It was Erik's time to pace now. "You aren't going to go back to him, Corey. There's no way on earth I'm letting you do that."

"I can't think of any other way around it."

Erik stopped moving about and looked at me, his eyes intense and flashing.

"I can. You can mate with me."

"What?"

A smile spread over Erik's face. "You told me that if you mate with a true Alpha you could increase my strength. That would keep you safe, and the pack as well. Unless... Roy was telling the truth and you've already mated with him?"

Pfft. Hardly.

"No. Never. Sienna said a true mating is between two who love and respect each other. Roy treated me like a possession. Never a person."

A muscle flicked in Erik's jaw as he grinded his teeth.

"I'm probably going to regret asking this, but why did you run away from Roy's pack?"

I looked down and away.

It was time to tell the truth.

"Because he killed my best friend."

I could still see Perry's blood on my hands, splattered across the earth in front of me. My beautiful friend, who'd tried so hard to be my protector.

"You're going to have to elaborate, I'm sorry. I don't understand."

I sniffed back the tears that were threatening to fall once again.

"It's a long story, but the simplified version is... Roy is a possessive and aggressive Alpha. Unfortunately, he's a real one, so he spotted me immediately." I heaved out a sigh, and continued. "Luckily for me, he saw me as a prize, so he didn't inflict many injuries. But there was no real feeling or relationship between us."

"So why did he kill your friend?"

"Because we were close. Super close. Perry was my best friend, and I went to him for comfort, support, friendship... Roy was jealous as hell. One night, Roy smacked me around a bit for... God knows why. And Perry tried to defend me. He was a Beta, but a small one. Roy ripped him apart in a few minutes and he died in my arms."

The fight had gone out of me, as had the desire to run back to Roy. I may as well kill myself now. It would be faster than what Roy would have planned for me.

"Then you can't go back to him." Erik said softly.

"I don't want to, trust me. But James has shown him where your pack lives. You can't leave. And they'll come in droves."

Erik sat up straighter and pulled me closer to him. "Then we'll fight them. I'm not letting you go, and I'm not giving you up because my brother is an asshole."

I nodded, wiping away the rogue tears that were still falling from my eyelids.

"Yeah, he is an asshole."

Erik rubbed my back, and the motion reminded me of the Alpha's solution to our problem.

"So, you really want to mate with me?" I asked him, unable to believe that Erik wanted to commit to me so wholeheartedly.

"Of course, I do."

I had to ask it now or it would haunt me for all my days. "Because it will make you stronger and you can save the town?"

Erik laughed softly and shook his head. "Hardly. I've wanted to claim you since the first moment I laid eyes on you. This is just a good excuse."

"Really?"

Erik kissed me gently on the lips, then drew back. "Yes, really. I went to one of the elders this morning to talk about it, actually. Before Roy arrived. And sorted some of the details. So, really, his timing is perfect."

I laughed and pushed myself to a stand once again.

"Okay, then how do we do this? Because Roy and his pack will be back within a day, maybe two."

Could be faster if they really wanted to get back and get on with revenge.

"We go to Sienna, get ourselves some nice clothes, make a spectacle of ourselves in front of the whole pack, then consummate our pact as many times as possible."

My head was dizzy with the swift change of plans. But I liked the direction everything was going.

"Okay.... So, Sienna first?"

Erik took my hand and led me outside.

"I'll drop you at Sienna's first, because I need to see the elders, but I'll come back shortly, all right?"

I nodded and kissed him at Sienna's doorstep. "See you soon."

Erik headed off and I pushed open the front door to go in search of my soon-to-be sister-in-law.

"Sienna!"

"Are you okay?" she asked as she rushed forward, her face a contorted mask of concern. "I have some soup and bread for you."

"No, I'm fine. More than fine, actually. Erik wants me to mate with him so he can gain extra strength."

To stop the pack that's going to attack because of me.

Seemed so counter intuitive.

"Really?" Sienna asked, her eyebrows rising high on her forehead. "I know he wants to mate with you, but I don't think it's so he can get something out of you."

"I didn't mean it like that..." It did sound terrible the way I'd put it. I knew Erik wanted me for more than what I could bring to him. "I mean... I have so little to offer Erik in any other way. And with the possibility of my old pack seeking revenge, mating would make everyone stronger, safer."

It was sounding more stupid now, I should have just told her we were getting mated.

Her face contorted in a way that told me she wished I'd just made it simple too. "Okay, well I'm very happy for you both. Are you here for clothes?"

I nodded. "Yes, Erik said to come here for something special to wear. I'm not quite sure why, since most of the mating will include not wearing anything at all."

Sienna grinned at me. "Well, for an Alpha especially, the public part is important as well. So, let's see what I have for you."

Ten minutes later I was dressed in a black suit, white shirt and even a black tie.

"How do you still have clothes like this?" I asked, admiring the sleek look of the suit in the mirror.

I had distant memories of my dad and grandfather wearing

clothes like this, to weddings and social events. But that was so long ago.

"We kept everything, and I must say, we haven't had a huge need for these styles the last few years."

She smiled at me with a warmth I hadn't seen for too many years to count. "I can't believe my brother is finally getting married. I wasn't sure he'd ever choose anyone."

I laughed. "Not sure it was so much of a choice..."

She slapped a hand at me. "Of course, it was. Fate sent him the perfect mate, and you need to believe that if you're going to be the partner he deserves."

I swallowed the lump that had risen in my throat.

"Yeah... I suppose so."

"Now, you need to hide for a bit while I get my brother dressed. No seeing each other before the ceremony."

I laughed at her. "Are you serious?"

We were getting mated in approximately an hour... why bother with any of the other traditions?

"Most certainly. By now Erik would have organized everything, and the town will be getting ready. You need to hide in my room for a bit. Okay?"

It wasn't really a question as Sienna pulled me into a room and shut the door.

I sat down on her bed with a thump and a laugh.

What a ridiculous day we'd had so far.

I'd been so terrified when I'd seen Roy in town today.

So certain my life was over because I knew he'd punish me so badly for running away.

But then the whole world had spun on its axis.

Erik had fought for me to stay with him.

And now he was mating with me for life, so we could stay together.

I didn't know what was more miraculous. My love for him.

Or his love for me.

CHAPTER 9

ERIK.

The town was prepared, the elders were in place, and I was dressed in some too-tight monkey suit that my sister had made me wear.

When I'd asked for something appropriate, I'd hoped for slacks and a shirt, not a tux! Why would she have even kept such a suit in my size?

I shook my head, a soft growl rolling through my vocal chords as I glanced around the area the Betas had set up.

They'd done a good job. Everyone was here, and the whole town was dressed in their finest too.

Suddenly there was a silence descending over the whole "congregation" and my gaze was drawn to the two people walking up the makeshift aisle between my pack members.

Sienna, arm in arm with my beautiful Corey. Walking slowly up the aisle, his hair slicked down. His beautiful body clad in a classic black suit. So simple and stylish.

Theresa, one of our elders and my mother's best friend, officiated the ceremony.

I'd told her to keep it simple. We had pressing matters to attend to straight after.

Sienna released Corey's hand and he moved toward me, his cheeks aflame.

I reached out and drew him to me. Standing with him, holding both of his hands before the whole community.

My pack.

My heart swelled with pride.

Theresa stepped up and faced us, a huge smile on her weathered face.

"It is my utmost pleasure to officiate this mating ceremony between our Alpha, Erik Romkey, and his chosen mate, Omega, Corey Wentworth."

I smiled down at my soon-to-be-mate, the official use of our surnames making this seem so much more serious.

"Erik, do you take Corey to be your mate? To love him, protect him, and be committed to him, until death do you part?"

I nodded. "I do... and far beyond death, if necessary."

My beautiful Omega flushed an even brighter red as he returned my smile. I loved how intensely he felt all his emotions. How honestly.

I hoped he never lost that.

Theresa turned to Corey.

"Corey. Do you take Erik to be your mate? Do you promise to love him, and look after him, as only an Omega mate can?"

Corey nodded. "Yes. Till death, and beyond."

Theresa broke out into a huge smile.

"I can't tell you how happy it makes me to say, you are officially mated. Your pack loves you, Erik, and we want what is best for you, because we know that you only do what is right for us. Please, go. Seal your bond. And then tonight we will meet and discuss the coming days."

I nodded in thanks to Theresa, knowing that she fully understood the storm coming for us. We'd hidden from this war long enough, and tomorrow it would find us. In all its ravaging glory.

There was an eruption of applause from our audience as the pack members jumped to their feet and cheered.

Corey snuggled into my side and I drew him in tighter.

Now came the fun part.

"Let's go." I whispered into his ear.

He nodded and I swept him up into my arms and carried him away.

A wolf whistle broke through the air and cheers from the crowd crescendo as we walked away. I'd told the kitchen staff to throw together whatever banquet food they had.

Everyone would eat well today, while my new mate and I luxuriated in each other's bodies while we could.

Part of me was afraid that the choice I'd just made, of mating with Corey, would see the deaths of my people. Of our way of life.

But as I clung to him and looked around at the determined faces of my Betas in the crowd, I knew I'd made the only choice I could.

Bullies only responded to strength, and I was ready to be very strong, for my pack and my mate.

I took off at a run, Corey laughing in my arms as he clung to my neck.

I kicked open the door to our house and walked us into the bedroom, deliberately carrying him over the threshold like one of those old movies Corey talked about.

I'd considered taking him somewhere different, in honor of our "honeymoon." But loving him and his body would be just as sacred here.

"Let's get out of these monkey suits." I said as I put Corey on his feet and pulled down the curtains to give us the illusion of night time.

I didn't know how long it would take Roy's pack to come back to challenge us, so I wasn't waiting until nightfall to complete the mating.

I didn't even know exactly what to expect of this melding of an

Alpha and Omega pairing. Would I need to rest afterwards? How intense was this going to be?

"I think you look hot." Corey whispered as he stripped his jacket, shirt and trousers off.

I stood and watched while he got naked, loving the quiet strength and beauty that Corey encapsulated.

"Aren't you taking your clothes off too?" He asked me, stepping forward and reaching for my jacket.

"Yes. Strip me." I commanded, holding my arms out on either side.

Corey grinned as he walked around behind me and slid my jacket off my shoulders.

I instantly rolled my arms and stretched my neck.

Much better.

Corey came back around and set his hands to my pants. He slid the zip down over my aching cock and looked up at me through his thick eyelashes, desire evident in his eyes.

The atmosphere in the room intensified as Corey took me in his hands, fondling my balls and feathering his fingertips along my length.

I grabbed at my shirt and pulled it over my head, pushing away my shoes and pants so that I could take my mate in my arms.

"I love you." Corey whispered up at me. His warm hands slid up my arms and across my shoulders.

My heart expanded and grew, pumping harder for my mate who was so beautiful. And vulnerable.

"I love you too, Corey. More than I ever thought I'd love anyone."

And it was true. I'd long since given up on the idea of finding my fated mate. With no one in town fitting that description, and us so isolated from the rest of the world, I'd come to terms with the idea I'd need to breed with a local woman.

But I didn't need to, now. I could love the person I was meant to.

"Let me show you how much." I lifted him up, loving his hot

weight in my arms, before lying him down and turning him over onto his belly.

I ran my hand down the long line of his spine, the softness of his skin a stark contrast to the roughness of my fingers.

"Rise up on your hands and knees." I urged him and he did as I asked, kneeling on the bed for me.

I knelt behind him and kissed a trail down his back. Corey moaned and pushed back against me.

I grabbed his ass cheeks and softly pressed them apart, admiring the tight little star before leaning forward and licking it.

Corey jumped forward and I grabbed him, pulling him back onto my mouth.

"What are you doing?" Corey squealed, panting and trembling where he knelt.

"Loving you."

I pulled him back and kept a tight hold on his thigh as I extended my tongue and licked him, thrusting my tongue faster and faster, loving the taste of him. I wanted to take the time to prepare him in a way I hadn't done before.

Corey was moaning and gasping, pushing back against me with enthusiasm now.

I moved my hand from his thigh to between his legs, slicking it up with the lube I'd already put next to the bed and reaching for his half-hard cock.

I wrapped my palm around him and pulled him back towards me, stroking his flesh while Corey bucked beneath me.

"Erik! Please. Fuck me. I need you."

I flipped Corey onto his back and stood up, rubbing my cock with the lube on my already slick fingers.

"Don't worry, my beautiful mate. I won't leave you hanging. I want you just as much as you want me."

Corey got back on his knees and moved to the edge of the bed.

He put his head on the mattress and wriggled his ass, presenting for me in a beautiful way.

"You want me to fuck you, do you?" I taunted, stroking my cock slowly as I watched him dance for me.

So gorgeous in all his wantonness.

"Yes!" Corey cried, thrusting his hips higher into the air.

A deep growl grew inside me, my balls pulsing with heat and lust.

I grabbed his hips and lined my cock up with his ass, sliding it along his crack. Up and down.

Loving the feel of his hot skin against mine.

His body beneath my hands.

His desperate need for me shown in his moans, and groans, and gasps.

"Please. Erik!"

I pulled back, the head of my cock finding Corey's entrance.

Heat engulfed my spine as the need to mate called to me.

I grabbed hold of his hips and slid home.

Corey's body engulfed me and he cried out, pressing back. Accepting me. Wanting me. Needing me as much as I needed him.

I began to ride him.

Hard and fast.

I couldn't have stopped even if he'd begged me.

But luckily, I didn't have to. Corey was with me all the way. Reaching back, squeezing my hand where it gripped his hip.

Groaning and moaning and screaming my name.

My orgasm whipped through me with the strength of a tidal wave. I called out to him, and Corey answered with his own call.

Vibrations of light and sensation pulsed through me, taking me away. Changing me for something better.

Something whole.

I could *feel* Corey now. His heart beating with mine.

And then I began to fall, rolling to the side not to hurt my smaller mate.

And then the world went dark.

CHAPTER 10
COREY.

I woke up to someone painfully tugging on my arms.

I could barely lift my eyelids to open them to see who was annoying me while I was sleeping off my post-coital bliss.

"Quick!" A man hissed and my eyes flew open.

I knew that voice.

"What the..."

Pain splintered inside my head as James punched me in the face.

Two others from Roy's pack pulled me through the house, bouncing me off the couch and through the front door.

They were so loud I couldn't believe the whole town didn't hear them.

Where the hell were they taking me? And where was Erik?

The rocks cut my heels and feet as the men dragged me through the town, making a break for the front gate.

"Help." I tried to cry out, but my throat was tight and my eyes were swollen shut.

Then suddenly, there was an almighty growl from behind us and I knew my Alpha had awoken.

We'd both passed out immediately after our mating. I hadn't thought about the healing or energy it would require to get through it.

What fucking bad timing.

"Come on!" James yelled at we stormed through the gates and the men dragged me bodily down the hill.

Pain cut through me as tree after tree sliced through my flesh. I was so groggy, I could barely stand up.

My feet caught on a rock and I allowed myself to fall to the ground. I hit hard, and cried out against the pain shooting through my arms and legs.

James grabbed me by the hair and began pulling me along behind him.

Pain shot through my head and I grabbed for his hands.

"Let go!" I screamed at him as the noise of the cavalry got closer.

Growls and cries of Erik's pack thundered down the hill. They were coming.

Roy suddenly appeared, picking me up and throwing me over his shoulder.

The odor of him in my nose made me gag, and I kicked out at him.

He thumped me in the hamstring for that and I muffled my scream of pain the best I could.

Fuck, this guy was an asshole.

We were suddenly on solid ground once again and I was being pulled to a stand, completely naked, in front of the whole pack.

Great.

There were dirty, scruffy men everywhere. All Roy's pack. Dozens of them, as I'd suspected.

A huge, black wolf leapt into the clearing and Roy pulled me into his body, placing the cool blade of a knife at my throat.

The wolf, Erik, stopped, his body trembling visibly with rage.

"Shift back. We've got your little mate." Roy said calmly, pressing the blade closer into my neck.

It nicked the skin and blood trickled onto my chest. But I didn't make a sound.

Don't do it, Erik.

The black wolf shrunk down, until Erik re-emerged in his human form, his magnificent, naked body there for all to see. Clean, gorgeous and beautifully hung.

Then several brown wolves broke into the clearing, snapping their jaws and growling at us.

Erik's pack had followed him.

"We thought it best to have a chat outside the walls of your town. Wouldn't want to get all those nice, clean houses dirty, would we?" Roy sneered.

I turned my head and coughed to hide the fact I was gagging now.

His stench was horrible. How had I not noticed it before?

"No, we wouldn't want that." Erik managed to say, though his chest heaved as he struggled to breathe.

What was wrong with him?

Had I done something strange to him?

He didn't look the same.

"You should be thanking me. We could have come in and started killing people, but we're much more civilized than that. Aren't we, boys?" Roy laughed.

Thank God for small mercies.

The men around us agreed and Erik just stared back.

I closed my eyes as the horror of realization rolled in. Roy and his men could have killed any of the women and children while we'd been asleep.

Or done any number of foul things.

None of us had assumed they'd return so quickly, and how wrong we'd been.

"Roy, I'll go back with you. You really don't have to do this." I said as calmly as I could.

I sent a silent message to Erik, hoping he'd hear.

I'll find a way to escape. I'll come back to you.

"Not a chance in hell." Erik muttered.

"Oh, now you want to come back, do you? You filthy, little slut." Roy pulled my head back by my hair, inhaling deeply around me.

I could smell Erik's seed on me, and I was sure Roy could too.

"Just don't hurt anyone." I begged. All those children... "Just leave their pack alone. They have nothing to do with you."

Roy's laugh was cruel as he turned the knife over and ran it down my chest, slicing and nicking me ever so softly. Just enough to make me jump. Yelp. Want to cry for the shame of it all.

And with my mate watching, too.

No matter what he did to me, I wouldn't react anymore. I refused to.

When his knife reached the level of my cock he paused. "I think this should come off, don't you? After all, you don't need it. You're a fucked-up version of a woman anyway, isn't that right, Erik?" Roy taunted.

I didn't react. I held perfectly still, though fear slithered through me like a snake.

"What. Do. You. Want?" Erik ground out between his teeth.

I could feel his hurt. His anger. His shame.

It made me burn with my own.

I was an embarrassment to him. We should never have mated. I'd brought him nothing but stress since the moment we met.

"Roy, I'm going to ask you again. What do you want?" Erik spoke as he walked closer.

Roy turned the knife over and stuck the end of it into my side.

I gasped with pain and tried to pull away, yet Roy held me tightly by the hair.

"Stop right there, or the Omega dies."

Tears slid down the sides of my face, but I held perfectly still as I waited for Erik's response.

When it came, his voice was deadly quiet.

"Roy, if you kill Corey, I promise you, you will regret it. I will kill you and your Betas. I will track your foul scent home, and then I will kill everyone who knows you, or has ever heard of you. You will be dead, and more importantly, you will be forgotten. Gone. Forever."

Roy growled. "You're dreaming if you think you could defeat me in a fight, boy."

Erik laughed. "Of course I could, and you know I probably will. Why else would you be hiding behind an Omega and a knife like a pathetic woman? A fight to the death would be so much more appropriate between us. Two Alphas, after all. Should be a good fight."

I could feel the rage in Roy as he pulled the knife out of my side and flung me away.

Someone caught me and pushed me to the ground.

I hit hard and rolled along the grass, moving as close to Erik's pack as I could.

When I stopped rolling, I put my hand over the gaping wound in my side and looked back to see James' excited face as he watched he exchange between the two Alphas.

This is exactly what this dickhead wanted. To watch his brother die, so he could step in and take his place.

Fucker.

I pulled myself along the ground slowly, aiming for where Timmy stood gesturing to me.

"If I win, you leave and never come back." Erik was saying.

Yeah... you better kill them to ensure that.

I dragged myself another inch, and then another.

Timmy moved towards me, then he was running, pulling me to my feet and dragging me back to Erik's pack.

"No! Get him!" Roy was yelling, but it was too late. I was safely in Timmy's arms and within touching distance of Erik once again.

Relief wound through my chest like a cold breeze.

Thank God no one else in Roy's pack cared enough to watch me. Even James' hatred for me didn't outweigh his need to watch his own brother go down.

Erik looked at me, his smile one of sheer happiness, then he looked back at his nemesis.

"Normally, once I'd gotten back what I needed, I'd let the trouble go. But I have the feeling that if I let you go, you'll be a thorn in my side for the rest of my days."

Roy's snarl was vicious. "I'll be more than that. My men will beat down your doors, steal your wives and children. Your homes. You live far too comfortably up there, and I think my men and I need some of that."

The Betas around Roy sneered and laughed.

Yeah, they would love to live in Erik's town for a week. But they didn't know how to work, and they'd soon destroy everything Erik and his pack had fought so hard to protect.

Kill them all.

Erik turned around and looked at me, his stare intense as though he'd heard what I said.

In case he had, I sent him another message.

They'll destroy everything. The houses, the crops, the people. You need to kill them all.

Erik nodded once and then turned back to Roy.

"For the first time in a long time, it looks like I can't keep my promise, Roy."

"How's that?" Roy asked, his face an expression of confusion against Erik's too calm words.

"You see, you touched my mate, you invaded our homes and you've threatened all of us."

Suddenly the moods of the wolves around Erik shifted.

Timmy grabbed my arm and threw it over his shoulder as though he were about to make a run for it with me.

"No." I whispered to him. "I want to stay."

I wanted to watch Erik destroy him.

There was an almighty growl that ripped through the air as Erik once again transformed into a massive black wolf, so much bigger than the first time I'd seen him shift.

And it looked like Roy agreed with me. Erik was larger than any Alpha I'd ever seen.

Roy dropped to the ground, as did James, and together they shifted into two small, black wolves.

Hmmmm, wouldn't have picked an Alpha color for James.

The rest of the pack began to shift, brown wolves springing up on both sides.

"I'm getting you outta here." Timmy said, and he began to run up the hill.

I clung to my bleeding side.

"No. Take me back. I need to see this."

The forest exploded with the sounds of battle.

Growls and yelps. Screams of pain and torment. Huge thumping and shaking of the ground as the two packs fought to the death... for me.

For their pack's survival.

For land.

The fight went out of me and I let Timmy drag me up the hill. The war had finally hit Erik's pack and I was the bringer of the storm.

The thought made me sick to my stomach.

"Quick. Let's get you to the doctor."

The sun was setting now and as the darkness settled across the land, the cacophony of the pack war below sounded more ominous.

Timmy dragged me into a house I hadn't been in before. He laid me down on a medical table and an older woman came forward with a first aid kit and examined me.

"You need stitches." She left again and I turned to Timmy.

"You shouldn't have pulled me away. We could have stayed and helped."

Timmy shook his head. "No. The Alpha made it clear that if any one of us got the chance to grab you and run, then that was the only objective. To get you back."

My stomach lurched. "But I'm the reason these terrible people are threatening your pack. You shouldn't be protecting me."

Timmy laughed. "You're kidding, right? Number one, you're our Alpha's mate. The most protected person in the pack, and no one and nothing is going to change any of that. And number two, it wasn't you who brought those guys here, it was fucking James. They never would have found us without him."

I let my head fall back onto the pillow as the female doctor came back into the room with a needle and thread.

"Yeah, you're probably right."

She poured a hot liquid over my cut and I hissed in pain, squeezing my eyes shut so that I didn't cry out.

"I'm going to put some stitches in to stop the bleeding, okay?" she asked, though I knew I didn't have a choice.

I nodded and looked away.

Timmy sat on the chair next to the table I lay upon and grabbed my hand, offering support.

The needle went in to my flesh and I squeezed Timmy's hand, holding my breath.

"Um... you want something for the pain?" Timmy asked me.

"Whatcha got?"

The kid smiled dopily at me. "Um, I suppose I could knock you out."

That didn't sound like too bad an idea to me.

"Just keep breathing, I'm almost done." The doctor said, pinching and moving my skin as she worked.

"Okay." I said, focusing on Timmy's face rather than on the needle work. "How do you think it's going down there?"

Timmy looked out the door a minute, then back at me.

"I can't hear much of anything anymore. Hopefully that means it's all done, and we can bury the bodies in the forest."

"I just hope we won."

Timmy laughed at me. "Of course, we won! Did you see the size of Erik today?"

"Ah, yeah... I did, actually."

So, it hadn't been my imagination that he was significantly bigger than last time I saw him in wolf form.

"Dad said Erik would change once you and he mated, but I didn't expect it to be such a massive difference." Timmy said, squeezing my hand strongly while the doctor tied everything off and began washing away the blood on my thighs.

"Yeah... I had no idea what to expect." I admitted, my eyelids beginning to drop down of their own accord.

I couldn't stop them. And I was suddenly so very tired.

"You can sleep. It's okay." The doctor said, pulling a thick blanket up to my chin.

Timmy let go of my hand and tucked my arm under the blanket.

"Okay. But please send Erik in when he gets back, yeah?"

"Of course."

I really wanted to hear what had happened, and make sure Erik was all right.

But the shock of the night and the blood loss finally caught up with me and I passed out before I could think of anything else to say.

The twelve bodies of the Betas were easy to bury in the forest. We lost one of our own too, so we carried him home to bury him in our own graveyard.

The bodies of Roy and my brother were left to rot in the elements.

Fucking black Alpha wolves, my ass!

There was nothing Alpha in either of them. An Alpha did what was right for his pack. He was selfless, and often chose what was right, over what made him popular.

Something my brother never understood.

We were careful to cover our tracks when we trekked back up the hill, closed the gate firmly, and covered the door with debris.

We would need to set up a security system and a constant guard for our gates. We couldn't let what had happened tonight ever happen again.

"Alpha! You're back." Timmy said as he ran up to me.

"Where's Corey?"

"He's with the doctor. Is everything okay?" Timmy asked, his brows furrowed with worry.

I clapped him on the back. "Everything's all right now. We lost O'Malley in the fight, but everyone else is okay."

Timmy nodded and turned to head off in the other direction.

I reached out and grabbed his arm.

"Timmy, thank you for saving Corey. I don't know how I can repay you for that."

The kid had been so lightning fast in getting Corey, I barely saw him move. Then to run with him the moment the fight had started, had been perfect. Timmy's instincts were spot on, and in future stressful situations, I would remember that.

"Oh, no sweat. I was sorry I couldn't stay and help you guys fight, but I figured you'd fight better knowing Corey was safe."

I gripped the youth's arm tightly and nodded.

Yep, great instincts. He'll be a fantastic protector for Corey.

I let Timmy go and headed over to the doctor's house.

She was waiting for me outside, which I didn't see as a good sign.

"Does anyone need me?" she asked.

"There are a few injuries, but nothing too serious." I explained. "We lost O'Malley."

Her old face crinkled up even more. "Oh, his poor mother. I'd better go see how she is."

Before she left I asked, "How's my mate?"

"He'll be fine. Lost a fair amount of blood, but was still lucid before falling asleep. He's strong, Erik. A good match for you."

I knew that of course. But it was still nice hearing it coming from her.

I thanked the doctor and she left to console Mrs O'Malley.

A good match for me was the understatement of the century. He was brave, and honest, and sexy as hell. Not to mention the fact that he'd given me the greatest gift anyone had ever bestowed upon me. The ability to defend our pack and the people I loved.

Including my mate.

If he could forgive me for sleeping through his kidnapping.

I still couldn't believe they'd been able to take him, right out of our bed.

Fucking ridiculous.

Then I'd been so slow in chasing them down, my stupid legs hadn't been able to work right.

I'd explain it all to him, and then ask for forgiveness.

I took a deep breath, gathered my courage and headed into the small room.

Corey was asleep on the table in front of me and my breath caught in my throat when I looked at how beautiful he was. He'd nearly died tonight, and it had almost been right in front of my eyes.

I don't think I would have survived that. And that terrified me.

I'd always put the pack's safety first, above all else. But now that I had Corey, he came first.

Corey stirred and I went to sit beside him.

His eyelids fluttered open and when he focused on me, he sat right up.

He moaned in pain, but he still reached for me.

"You're back! You're okay..."

"Yes, sweetheart, I'm okay. I am so sorry you had to go through all of that."

Corey grabbed my hands tightly.

"I'm the one who needs to apologize. I'm the reason Roy and those other horrible guys were here. And If I'd been a normal wolf, I would have been able to fight them off. Instead you had to come rescue me, like I'm some fucking damsel in distress."

I had to laugh. My beautiful boy was blaming himself, as always.

"I didn't protect you, and that's on me, Corey. Not you. I failed you."

Corey made a dismissive gesture with his hand.

"No, you didn't. The mating probably just knocked you out too soundly. I could barely walk when they woke me up. If it wasn't for that, we would never have been taken by surprise."

"But without the mating I wouldn't have so completely obliterated them." I said, more smugly than I meant to.

"So, the mating did help you as we thought it would?"

"So much more than I thought it would, Corey. It is an amazing gift you've given me. And I thank you, from the depths of my heart for making me a better Alpha, a better protector for my people."

"Then you're glad we mated today? Because I don't want you to ever regret that choice."

I began to laugh. Obviously, the insecurities flowed on both sides.

"Corey, you are my mate, and I love you. I think I would die without you now. My heart beats with yours, and if yours stopped, mine would too."

THE END.